Praise for I

"Yu is the writer Girl wishes to be – remaking, in her own image, the young female protagonist, the Künstlerroman, the postcolonial novel, and the art of writing itself."
—*Guardian*

"*But the Girl* is a vivid novel of consciousness with a delightful sense of play. Jessica Zhan Mei Yu writes with striking originality that combines the irreverent and the philosophical about the ambiguities and ambivalences of contemporary life. A wonderful new novel for a metamodern world."
—**Brandon Taylor**, author of *The Late Americans*

"A unique and meaningful novel: refreshingly unsentimental, written with a directness that is both self-effacing and wry. The voice sometimes recalls Lucia Berlin, J. D. Salinger or Lorrie Moore but it's entirely her own."
—**Sharlene Teo**, author of *Ponti*

"A fiercely intelligent re-examination of literature through the lens of colonization, full of fire."
—**Alice Pung**, author of *One Hundred Days*

"With *But the Girl*, Yu offers a challenging and invigorating work of many faces."
—*Australian Book Review*

"Yu writes about the legacy of being a second-generation immigrant, racism, intergenerational trauma, the reclamation of English as a subject of colonization, and the pitfalls of academia with a biting incisiveness and gallows humour."
—*Books + Publishing*

"*But the Girl* is a debut that heralds a skilled and singular new talent."
—*The List*

Best Book of 2023 in *Marie Claire UK*

Best Book of August in *Guardian*

Best Book of August in *The Age*

Best Australian Fiction Book of the Year by *Readings*

Shortlisted for the Victorian Premier's Literary Award for Fiction 2024

AN UNNAMED PRESS BOOK

Copyright © 2023 by Jessica Zhan Mei Yu
First published in Australia by Penguin Random House and
in the United Kingdom by Jonathan Cape.

Published in North America by the Unnamed Press.

www.unnamedpress.com

Unnamed Press, and the colophon, are registered trademarks of
Unnamed Media LLC.

Paperback ISBN: 978-1-951213-98-5
EBook ISBN: 978-1-951213-99-2

LCCN: 2023947187

Cover Artwork by Zack Rosebrugh

Cover design and Typeset by Jaya Nicely

Manufactured in the United States of America by Sheridan.

Distributed by Publishers Group West

First U.S. Edition

But the Girl

the

Girl

a novel

Jessica Zhan Mei Yu

un

THE UNNAMED PRESS
LOS ANGELES, CA

But the Girl

One

It was an undecided and hazy spring, the spring that MAS370 disappeared, and I didn't know what I was doing in London.

Everyone kept asking me what had happened to the plane. I had become an unintentional figurehead for Malaysia Airlines. I was Australian (at least that's what it said on my blue passport) but my parents were Malaysian (red passport). And I looked like I knew something about it.

I wished I did. All I knew was that I was lost and probably wasting my time here.

I had been against Australia remaining a Commonwealth country and opposed to the British monarchy until I received a Commonwealth scholarship from a philanthropic organisation that had been set up in 1926 by King George V. The scholarship invited me to travel to London for a week to be 'enriched by culture' and then to Arbroath in Scotland for a month-long artist residency. Then I was going back to London to present my work at a postcolonial literature conference. Now I liked the Commonwealth and I decided that the idea of the monarchy was a mysterious and seductive one like religion or a beautiful stranger on a bus.

A man named Leon had been the one to email me telling me I'd been awarded the scholarship. I hadn't applied for it and I wasn't used to things appearing out of nowhere so at first I thought it was a scam. But then he had called me on the landline at home and he seemed real. He told me he was the arts manager at a philanthropic society in England that had been set up to lend Commonwealth countries a helping hand. He said that they had read some of my writing in magazines and such and liked it and that usually these scholarships were for visual artists but there was some interest in gradually introducing writers into the programme and did I have any projects I was working on just now? I told him I was enrolled in an English PhD programme here but I had always wanted to write a novel, a postcolonial novel, I added, to make it sound more legitimate.

Leon said I could choose the flight and he would book it. I took full advantage and chose a good airline at a cost I wouldn't have been able to pay myself. He told me it needed to be cheaper. So I chose a budget flight but he told me he couldn't be liable for what might happen on a Smart Wings transfer flight. In the end, the only flight that fit his criteria was a Malaysia Airlines flight, which was a proper airline but heavily discounted because no one wanted to disappear.

The transit flight to Kuala Lumpur was completely empty. I spread out across three seats and lay down to sleep. When I got to KL airport, I bought a copy of the *Star* which didn't mention anything about MAS370. It was as if it had never happened. Ikanyu had told me he thought the gomen knew more than they would ever let on. Of course, before this everyone had thought that planes couldn't disappear. But now that it had happened, it felt like if it was to disappear from anywhere it would be Malaysia. I supposed this was why Ma and Ikanyu and Ah Ma had immigrated in the first place. I knew that Ma had been heavily pregnant with me when she got on the flight. She said she'd held on tight to her pelvic muscles to keep me in until they got to Australia. I was born the day after they arrived. Her extreme willpower meant that I got the passport but I'd never quite got away from Malaysia, and I didn't know whether I wanted to or not.

The plane to London began to toss and turn like an insomniac and our food trays slid back and forth. Our chairs rattled like we were on a rollercoaster and a redundant turbulence announcement came on. The old man next to me yelped while the boy on my other side held onto his armrests. I could tell they were worried we would disappear. As always when something went wrong, I sat very still and did nothing. I thought about disappearing. It sounded quite pleasant to me.

'You're fine there, are you?' the man said.

'Yep,' I said.

'It's the Australian in you. Tough outback stuff.'

I'd never been called Australian before. It was nice. The last time I had really thought of myself as Australian had been in grade one. It was play lunch. There were these older girls sitting in the crotch of the big tree. We called it the Paper Tree because of its soft, tearable bark. Ugly sunburnt skin on the outside, but when you peeled it off, it showed a secret peach colour. They told me to come play with them. Their faces were smooth as stones. They asked me what I was. When I told them I was Australian, they told me no. Then they sang a strange song that I had never heard before: ching chong ching chong. They dragged the skin at their eyes back, till their eyes were cuts. They asked me to drag the skin of my eyes back and I did it. They laughed and I laughed because it was funny and we were all good friends now. The weather was warm and the sun was gold and I. I was happy.

Much later on Ma told me that when I was young, I thought I was white. I didn't *want* to be white or anything like that that. I just thought that was what I was because I knew I was real. I knew I was real and not made up because sometimes I tested it. Sometimes I bit my lip till blood came out and when the saltine pain came, I knew that I was non-fiction.

I took the tube from Heathrow to Green Park station. Green Park had deckchairs laid out and people were sunning themselves even though it was twelve degrees and looking like rain. I had only seen London in movies and I was pleased to see it looked and felt the exact same in person as it did on screen: grim and beautiful. This probably meant that I wasn't looking hard enough, but I was so tired of being clever. I was born clever because Ma was very sharp and shrewd and Ikanyu was very thoughtful and deliberate and they had passed these qualities on to me. And like immigrants everywhere they played without sheet music or instruments; every song they sang was improvised from start to finish. So, I had that too, a certain kind of freedom. It was the only real resource I had been born with and I exploited it fully. But I was starting to get sick of grinding my bones back into the dust to win scholarships and prizes and money and an existence. I was ready to enjoy the newborn pleasure of knowing nothing.

The philanthropic society's clubhouse looked right onto Green Park. I knew from the pamphlet Leon had sent me before I arrived that it was a Georgian building with yellow bricks. Rusticated quoins darted up and down the sides. I loved that new word: *quoin*. There was a *cartouche* that showed two angels holding up a globe with a ship sailing across it and, as if that wasn't enough, it had a *festoon* made of fruit and foliage dripping off of it. I walked up what I would have called the front steps but I now knew was a *portico* and peered at the Ionic columns with their scrolling, acanthus leaves. According to the guide, they meant eternal life, as well as sin and pain and punishment. That seemed to me like a lot of symbolic pressure for a thorny leaf.

I was directed to my room and discovered it contained crystallised ginger biscuits on a plate with scalloped edges and a teapot and a pen and a white dressing gown and letter-writing paper embossed with the crest I had seen on the cartouche. That made me happy. The long trip had caused a long and mysterious problem with my back to play up again. It was stiff and sore from sitting on the plane and I massaged the places that burned bright with pain. Then I fell asleep.

When I woke up, I had an email from Leon asking me to meet him in the clubhouse's foyer. He arrived in rolled-up shirtsleeves and the kind of linen shirt that is very nice when initially put on but gets so creased it becomes three dimensional in places after a day's wear.

'How was the flight?'

'It was great.' I tried to smile. Scholarships beget scholarships so this wasn't the first time I'd been given something. One thing I knew about being a scholarship girl is that it is important to simulate delight at everything you'd received. This is the exchange you make: your facial expressions for their funding.

'Very good. Blessing can't make it yet; he's still stuck in Johannesburg. He'll join you in Arbroath. Jack had a terrible time, by the sounds of it. He got sick and vomited for all twenty-four hours of his flight from Wellington. We'll see him tomorrow hopefully. Here is your per diem,' he said, handing me an envelope of notes.

I knew he had to give these to me at some point and it wasn't as if it was his money. But the timing (my gratitude contrasted with Jack's illness) obliquely confirmed to me what I had thought all along: that gratitude made me a good scholarship girl.

'Anyway, I can show you round tomorrow afternoon. I thought we'd go to the Tate Modern. Same spot at two?'

'Great.'

I woke up the next morning and went downstairs for breakfast. It was explained to me that cold breakfast items as well as toast and tea were free. But I would have to pay for anything hot. Apart from breakfast, I could go up to the Princess Maud room and have one meal with one drink a day on their tab. I had never ordered a drink at a restaurant before. My parents had only ever wanted to pay for solids and because of that I was the same. I took a tablespoon of every kind of cereal and muesli they had out and put it in a bowl with some milk and yoghurt. Then I ordered some toast and tea. The toast came with a rack of ten tiny jams in ten tiny jars which I stole after I was done. And then I put some fruit and rolls into my bag for lunch. After this, I had to decide what I wanted to do with my morning.

The clubhouse had a library and I was supposed to be sitting in it writing a postcolonial novel (at least that was what me and

Leon had agreed I would do while I was here) or maybe keep going on my dissertation. I had ostensibly taken a year's leave of absence from my English PhD programme to write my novel. But no one who takes time off their PhD actually forgets about it – they keep working on their research secretly while pretending they are flittering around being on leave. That was what I was doing.

And because I was always so full of guilt, in addition to the novel and the thesis, I was also writing a paper to present at a postcolonial conference that happened to run in London at the end of my time here. I felt guilt all the time in those days. I felt guilt when I worked on my PhD because I had been brought over to work on my novel. And I felt guilt when I worked on my novel because what was a pointless thing like a novel compared to a doctorate thesis? I felt guilt because whatever I worked on, I was taking the easy way out. Therapists were always saying guilt was not a useful emotion but I found it to be an extremely helpful one – guilt was the sticky, sweet, heavily carbonated energy drink that helped me power through each task, to keep going. I kept working and working – to what end, I didn't know.

At least that was what it usually did for me. I moved my body from my bedroom to the library but once I got there my body swerved towards a staircase and ran downstairs of its own accord. It kept moving and moving until I ended up on Oxford Street. I spent all of the time and per diem they gave me there shopping for clothes. I loved clothes and London had a lot of them. I was a lot more frivolous than people realised and I frequently made the mistake of thinking changing my clothes could change my life.

I had wanted very much to be a model when I was a teenager. I wanted to be discovered while I window shopped in my school uniform like Naomi Campbell or in an airport like Kate Moss. I had starved myself sometimes but it was no use. I was too short, and I had the wrong face anyway.

I only spent the money I'd been given, though. I was born to immigrant parents who had me at the hospital the second they were in Australia, which is another way of saying I was born financially anxious. It's impossible to explain this to someone who wasn't. This was always what had been so hard about being with my friends at university who never seemed to worry about money at all. They thought talking about money was crass because they had never had to think about it. I could never afford their respectability.

Perhaps this was why I felt so guilty about the shopping. That whole week, I would buy clothes on Oxford Street and feel beautiful for a moment and then I would hate myself for my lack of self-control and shove them under my hotel bed like a bad feeling. Every night I hid my new clothes under the bed so I could sleep. And every day when I returned to my room someone would have come into my room and the clothes and also the towels and bathrobe and sheets would be folded perfectly and hung, and the teapot and cups cleaned and replaced. No matter what shape I'd left the room in. It was the magic of hotels. Even the embarrassment of being cleaned up after, the kind of thing Ah Ma would do conspicuously in front of me, so I knew how disgusting and lazy I was, even this happened invisibly while you were gone at a hotel. So you could avoid both the drudgery of cleaning up after yourself and the shame of someone else cleaning up after you, and calling it love.

My Ah Ma told me all the time that she loved me. Though I don't know if you would call 'love' what she called 'love'. 'Love' is such a promiscuous, easy word in English. The 'love' in *I love tomatoes* is the same 'love' in *to love and to cherish, until we are parted by death*. It's strange and unnatural to say that unsayable word in Chinese unless you are a crying actress in a soap opera or a pop star with a new single to promote. Love is expressed in Chinese the way a poet writes about flowers – slantwise, in riddles, in rhymes, coyly. You have to read between the lines, be an intelligent interpreter of literature, to really understand it. Sometimes you have to read against the grain of the author's intention and sometimes you think you're crazy for imagining that love is even there. So, it's hard to explain what I mean when I say she loved me – or as she said when she was especially angry at me – she sayang me.

I remember feeling the empty 'oh' of loss and recognition when a teacher in primary school asked us to describe our grandmothers. This was the kind of masak masak that my parents said happened in Australian schools. Sitting around talking about grandmothers when there was real work to be done. Taylor, a girl who was more freckle than skin, said that her grandmother made the best apple crumble. And then a boy I don't remember much more of said something about lemon drizzle cake. And another girl mentioned honey joys. Foods with childish but lovely names that sounded like a person was eating the sun. And I wondered why my grandmother had never so much as opened the oven in our house. She certainly hadn't made anything with a silly, careless name like drizzle or crumble or joy.

When Ah Ma really cooked it was a long and bloody affair. For New Year's Eve, she bought a live duck, and killed and drained it in the backyard. The next day she sat on the cement steps of our backyard plucking the feathers off one by one. Her day-to-day cooking was inevitably fried over a huge greasy pan on the gas stove in the backyard that blew out an ugly smog that choked you. As she cooked, she opened her fist and gave me Spam sliced up and fried as a snack. Campbell's Chicken Soup boiled over the big fire with chopped-up frankfurters floating along inside it. Fried ikan billis with peanuts and sambal so spicy that just the smell made me cry.

Ah Ma was not the benign, cotton-wool-haired grandmothers of the other kids. She didn't knit scarves or bake cookies or whatever other aesthetically pleasing and completely unnecessary housework they did. She pulled weeds out of the ground with her hands, the wrinkles in her palms caked with black dirt; swept up the flame-like petals of the magnolia tree as they decorated the grass and threw their beauty into the red bin; knelt down onto the wooden floors and washed them with a rag cloth; ironed shirts with mathematical precision; burned rubbish; pulled clean clothes out of my cupboard to wash them; gossiped about my mother on the phone to whoever would listen; watched TV covertly when she was sure that my parents were out for a while; basically did everything a live-in maid from the middle of Malaysia would do, which is what she had been for most of her adult life. Ma told me that she had tried to tell Ah Ma that she no longer had to earn her bowl of rice, but she didn't believe her. She told me and anyone who would listen that my mother oppressed her, used her as free labour and held her housework to impossible and irrational standards, essentially she thought that my mother had made her life hell. She believed that she was still a kind of servant; of the house but not in it, essential to our lives but peripheral to them. She still didn't really know how much she meant to me even now – a second mother, a third parent, a thorn in my flesh that I would never remove.

She was a hard, brown-skinned woman with a bad temper. Her stamina for anger made me think of Eliud Kipchoge. Her focus and motivation made the mental and physical discipline of bitterness feel like an athletic feat. She would get so angry with me sometimes that she would scream at me for hours. But she never stopped the housework for me – she would rant and rave while washing the dishes I had dirtied, hanging the clothes I had worn and pulling the weeds from the grass that I played on. If I ran inside the house to avoid her, quietly sliding the glass door behind me, she would scream louder so that I would still be able to hear her, and the neighbours too. Sometimes she wasn't angry with me – it was Ma or, occasionally, Ikanyu that she was scream-ing about. But she still wanted me to hear her.

Sometimes I made her laugh. I was a kid, after all. But she felt that showing me her smile was like going out naked. As the laugh faded from her face she told me that she would punch me in the face and then *I would know.* This knowledge she was always trying to thrust onto me – what was it? An understanding of how the world's hard face wouldn't soften for me or something like it perhaps. She would laugh and laugh and then she would threaten to hit me and I would know that I was her favourite thing in all the world.

Being old and having worked too much, she was always in some kind of pain. She had gout which swelled her feet and legs, so they glowed with a raw shiny hurt. She had arthritis in her hands which made the housework she did everyday a ritualised torture. She had a heart condition which made her clutch her chest when we walked to the supermarket. She had slipped and fallen once while washing the driveway with soap and water and blood had unspooled from her brain. She applied pain to her pain like a balm as she scrubbed her hands raw with a thick brush and soap to get the brown colour off. She took a kitchen knife to the balls of her feat to remove the hard grey skin. I would walk into her bedroom after dinner and find her cutting at her feet, bleeding in her bedsheets, and watching *Burke's Backyard*. She grimaced but she never said anything because she was afraid of hospitals and doctors and death. She was kiasi.

The orchids were the only thing she really loved. But they almost never had the chance to bloom because she pruned them every day, lovingly cutting them back to nothing. Twenty-six black plastic pots that only sprouted long, green leaves all year around. If I played outside, she would hover around me, telling me not to go near them. They were a kind of dangerous magic, the orchids. Anything could happen around them.

There was only one year that I remember them blooming. I was six in Australian years. Seven in Chinese years, as Ah Ma would say. A single string of white orchids with a streak of dried blood in the middle. I wanted them so badly, but I left them alone like she said to. I lay outside on the grass instead, watching the sky while she hung clothes on the line, but she told me I would get my clothes and hair all dirty and then *who would be the one to get in trouble with Ma? Who would be the one to have to wash them? Har? Har?* I tried to help with putting the washing on the line but she told me I didn't know how to do it right. She rearranged the clothes I had put up so that the underwear and bras were better hidden by the bigger items – shirts and pants and towels. I ran inside and began pulling tissues out of the box on the coffee table, ripping them up and shaping them to make them into airy, white, tiny sets of clothing – day dresses and slips and gowns. They were beautiful. I loved clothes from such a young age and the beautiful women in the magazines who wore them. I saw them as a portal to another world that I would enter when I was grown.

Ah Ma came back in the house with an empty basket. She looked for me and found me sitting on the floor by the coffee table with my 'clothes'. I looked up at her and that's when I saw the mess I had made. Tissue-paper fragments had fallen everywhere like new snow, and I knew I wouldn't get away with it. She came over and ripped up the clothes I had made, screaming about how she had turned away for only a second and already I had made the house look like kiam chye and *who would pay for it? Her.* I was crying because she was always ruining everything. And then she began cleaning up the mess I had made ostentatiously as if to show me how much my very existence oppressed her. That was it. I ran to the garden and there were the white orchids looking at me. I took them into my hands and ripped them up into tiny pieces except one which I saved and wore in my hair like a woman from a shampoo advertisement. I looked into the mirror of the glass sliding door, admiring myself, when my reflection darkened and disappeared. Ah Ma snatched the door open and in her hand was her skinniest and longest bamboo ti nah. Skinny for speed and long for reaching my body as I ran. I ran and ran and ran all over the garden while she chased me and then I was backed up against the gate. I opened the gate to the front yard and ran onto the street and then the road. She was screaming my name and her brown skin had turned grey. A car skimmed past me and then another was honking at me – a sonic 'no' that terrified me. I ran back into the backyard and Ah Ma locked the gate while I cried. And then, as tired out as we both were, she still found it in her heart to beat me. *I sayang you*, she was saying as she did. *You might think I hate you when I hit you. No.* I *sayang you.*

Two

Leon was waiting in the foyer for me with a funeral face on.

'I have some bad news. Blessing won't be able to make it. His visa application was denied.'

'Why?'

'I'm not sure. Perhaps, he made it too late.'

The unsteadiness of Leon's 'perhaps' made the blame for Blessing's visa being denied slide back and forth between Blessing and his circumstances. Back and forth. Later I looked up what colour a South African passport was (green). I wanted to ask more about it but I knew I should drop it.

'Jack is here but he's in bed sick. Do you still want to see the Tate?'

'Okay.'

'Where did you go this morning?'

'Oxford Street.'

'Why?' He seemed genuinely confused.

'For lunch,' I lied.

'What did you have?'

'Pret.' This was the only place selling food I could remember in that moment.

'Pret.' He laughed. 'What did you have?'

'A sandwich.'

'Okay.'

'Yeah. It was really good.'

'London has really amazing food if you know where to go. I can show you this hole-in-the-wall Mexican place that's really nice if you like that kind of thing? It's pretty far out from the centre but if you're up for the journey then I promise it will be worth it.'

As little as I knew London, I knew enough to feel that eating Mexican food here was a weird, showy idea. But I didn't know what else to say so I agreed.

'Okay. Are we going to the Pret now?' I caught myself. 'I mean the Tate.'

He didn't laugh.

'Yes, we are.'

He wanted to walk the whole way there but I didn't. I found people always wanted to walk to places but I guess it was the Malaysian buried deep inside me. Why should I walk if I have a car/motor/bus/bicycle? So he let us take the tube but complained a lot about tourists taking short journeys when they could walk.

'I love this building,' Leon said as we approached the Tate.

The brown bricks made it look like the housing commission flats in Flemington we lived in when I was little. I wasn't sure what I thought of it but I felt I liked it, it was sort of overwhelming and that was the whole point.

'I love brutalist design,' he said.

People tended to assume they knew more than me about things. They took on the role of expert of the world around me. I let them. I let them because it meant that I learned new things about the world or else I learned things about their character. I grew up in the era of the bimbo, of girls taking on dog-whistle voices and making a big show of being dumb and laughing at themselves. This frustrated me at the time but I understood it now. You only really knew who you were dealing with when you didn't seem like a threat. It was like going undercover.

The first thing we saw was a brightly coloured and complicated-looking climbing frame constructed over a huge trampoline. Adults were scrambling up the frame and letting themselves fall onto the trampoline and laughing. Leon groaned.

'This is what it's come to here. Accessible art,' he said.

This development hadn't yet happened in Australia and it fascinated me. I would have gladly jumped inside and started crawling around if he hadn't been there, but I also saw his point of view. I suppose he found that kind of thing patronising to the public. He showed me to a room that resembled a black cave. Inside there was a glowing white cube that looked like it was a huge piece of agar agar. Ah Ma had made me agar agar in the shape of little pink teddy bears and strawberries and smooth half-spheres. And here there was a huge cube of something like it.

'I haven't had a chance to see this new commission yet,' he said.

I wasn't sure how to say that I was really here for the greatest hits tour of the Tate. I wanted to see *The Snail* and the Rothko room and the gift shop to find small presents for my family. But I knew that if I lived in London like he did I would come here every day and drift until I had seen everything, all 69,759 of the artworks, and if I had been every day I would want to see what I hadn't seen before. I tried to find a way out of the black cave.

There were banners everywhere advertising a special Georgia O'Keeffe exhibition and they seemed like a good excuse.

'Should we see it?' I asked. 'I like her.'

'You can,' he said. 'You buy tickets at the desk over there.'

I hadn't realised that the exhibition would cost and I regretted mentioning it but it was too late to back out now. It cost eighteen pounds even at a student rate. As I waited in line, I converted eighteen pounds in my head to thirty-four AUD sadly. Ikanyu would have gone further and converted it into ringgit. But I could only torture myself for so long.

The exhibition was smaller than I'd expected and there weren't even any Jimson weeds or skulls. But there were Santa Fe adobe houses and calla lilies and roses. I had never wondered how it would feel to walk into the enveloped mouth of a giant rose but now I did. I read on a placard that Georgia O'Keeffe had always denied that her flowers were images of vulvas. Had Georgia O'Keeffe been a bimbo? A person who plays games with what they do and don't know in order to get what they want. I wondered what had happened to all the bimbos and where they had gone. Maybe they'd dyed their hair back to brown and become CEOs.

After I left the O'Keeffe exhibition, it was almost closing time so I went to the gift shop. I saw *The Snail* as a small print wrapped in plastic and bought it for Ikanyu. He would probably say he didn't understand all of this art mumbo-jumbo and put it under his bed, but I bought it anyway.

We got to the Mexican restaurant, which turned out to have the veneer of a dingy, 'authentic' spot with its exposed brick, colourful flags and uncomfortable chairs but was really very expensive. Looking at the menu, I silently lamented that I hadn't made use of the free meal and drink the clubhouse offered that day.

'Why would you live somewhere where everything can kill you?' Leon asked me.

'What?'

'Snakes and sharks and spiders, all of that?'

'I've never seen a snake or a shark. I've seen a redback spider, though. It was really pretty like a red and black jewel.'

It surprised me how little British people knew about Australia and how much we knew about the UK. From the accents that I'd heard, it sounded like there were more Australians in London than in Melbourne. Or were they the ones perpetuating these myths? When we were in school, we thought we were part of the Big 3: The US, the UK and us. But this wasn't the case. We were actually just a country floating around at the bottom of the map by itself. Maybe this was the most Australian thing about me, the shame I felt about my country.

Feeling embarrassed about Australia's provincial personality – the trope of the Southern Cross tattoo, the happy immigrant, the magnets of Will and Kate's wedding, the disappointment with our political leaders – had always been automatic to me and everyone I knew. A sense that we were no one, that we had nothing, that spending your whole life secretly trying to get away from the huge yawn that was Australia made you somehow important. Sometimes I wished my parents had immigrated somewhere else; being a child of immigrants always made your birth country feel so random and unnecessary. What if the finger that turned the globe had slipped? But it hadn't. That was my country and everything that was awful and lovely about it was also mine.

'What do you do in your spare time?'

I wasn't sure how our conversation had become a laboured interview with Leon doing most of the work but I supposed I wasn't contributing much. I didn't have that many words inside of me and I had used up my day's worth of conversation at the Tate. And I was too distressed by paying twenty-five pounds for tacos to scrape for content. I said that I liked swimming and framed it as a hobby rather than as a necessity for stretching out my scrunched-up spine, a way to mask the pain signals emanating from my small nerve fibres with endorphins.

'If you like swimming you have to go to one of the lidos.'

'What are they?'

'You have to go while you're here. Muddy water and you'll probably get a lily pad or duck on your face. But if you're Australian, it'll be nothing.'

'Okay.'

'We should go to one of the mixed ponds. I'd have to go before work starts. Is seven thirty too early for you?'

'No, I love early mornings.'

I wondered what my parents would think of this. Men and women doing anything together that wasn't absolutely necessary was suspicious to Ma and Ikanyu. If a male editor of a literary magazine invited me to do a reading my parents called him ham sap. When it came to finding a supervisor for my dissertation, Ma told me it would have to be a woman professor not some ham sap male academic. The West is very perverse, they said.

Was Leon ham sap? It did seem strange to me to go swimming in a foreign place with someone who was managing the arts arm of the charity that had sponsored you to come there. Did he have some kind of power over me? Or maybe this was part of the programme, a kind of local tour guide thing? It was hard to tell if Jack and Blessing would have been with us had they been able to. Was it vain or prudish of me to think it was anything more than kindness? So, I did what I did when I wasn't sure about something, I texted Ma.

Don't go. These men are like wolves. Prowling around looking for pret. Her text said. I read that a few times over before I realised that she had meant to say prey.

We went swimming in the Serpentine Pond. It seemed rich to complain about hygiene as someone who swam back home at the Williamstown beach (where everyone knew that the sewers were emptied after storms and the sand was so full of broken shells you got cuts in your feet trying to get in the water) but it disgusted me more than I'd expected. There was a slimy green film at the top of the water that was probably algae and the indistinct colour of the water turned out not to be from mud but from some kind of animal faeces, possibly from the ducks. And of course, it was particularly cold that morning and of course, it began to rain so it was no use trying to keep your face dry and clean by holding it up above the water. I tried to tell myself it would be good for my back after the long plane trip but any benefit I was getting from being in the water was mitigated by the way the cold seeped into my bones and burned them. Leon seemed to be having a great time; he was swimming huge laps that cut the water in two behind him. Perhaps it was a cultural difference of sorts: a masochistic love of being cold versus ... being normal? At least it didn't seem like a good place at all to make a pass at someone. I felt relieved by that. I tried to stay in the water for as long as I could out of gratitude to him for not being a creep. That was the kind of thing I was never sure of. Would it be rude to get out early? Maybe not if it was only slightly before he did. What if it was ten minutes before? Fifteen? Thirty? As I was debating this, he swam over to me.

'Have you had enough? You can stay in if you want, but I'm knackered. I wish I had your stamina. I'd give anything to be in my twenties again.'

This confused me. I'd thought we were the same age. I'd based this on the fact that his hairline seemed to still be on his face. But I supposed it was possible, though not probable, that you could be a thirty-something male and still have lots of hair.

'I'm ready to get out anyway,' I said.

'Really, feel free to stay in if you want to. Don't leave on account of me.'

'No, no, it's fine,' I said.

When I got to the changeroom, I realised that I had forgotten to pack any underwear as I'd worn my bathers under my clothes. Ma would have said that a girl without any underwear on is easy prey for wolves, so I put my clothes over my wet bathers and tried to protect my neck by wearing my towel around it like a scarf. When I came out Leon looked concerned.

'Why are you still so wet? I'd lose my job if you got hypothermia and died.'

It seemed too late for him to be worrying about this given I had just been swimming in a pond in 4-degree weather at his urging. It took everything I had within me not to roll my eyes back into my head like an evil doll.

I took the tube back to the clubhouse by myself. I was shaking and I was sure that I looked like a large, wet cat to the morning commuters around us. It was peak hour but no one seemed to want to take the empty seat next to me so it was possible that I had started to smell as well.

At the clubhouse, I went to my room and took a hot bath. I loved emotional heating. A hot bath or shower always made me feel better. It was so warm and nice I fell asleep in the tub. When I woke up, the water was cold as a polite smile and it was lunch-time. I changed into the smart-casual clothes they insisted upon and policed at meal times (no sneakers or jeans) in what they called the Princess Maud room. I sat down in the corner and a waiter asked me if I wanted anything to drink so I ordered a double espresso because I wanted him to think I was smart. On my table was a leaflet that explained that the Princess Maud room had a rich plaster moulding in the Edwardian style. The very intricate details at the tops of the walls were dentils which looked like white blocks alternating with cornices which looked like flowers. The dentils symbolised teeth because, as the Ancient Greeks had said, architecture mirrored the proportions of the human body. This terrified me a little, seeing the huge, white smile that ran around the top of the room with flowers stuck in between its teeth. The big wide mouth looked like it might eat up the chandelier and the powder-blue chairs and the marble-topped tables.

The teeth made me think of Ikanyu and his big, Australian smile. When he had come to Australia, he had arrived with teeth that were tangled and twisted over each other and gums bloody with abscesses. The Australian Dentist had told him they could gradually drain the abscesses of the pus that was oozing out of them and that he should also gargle with salt water after eating. The Australian Dentist told him to come back once a week for the next month. But then Ikanyu got the bill for the first appointment and almost fell over and died right then and there when he saw it. The next time he saw The Australian Dentist he told him he wanted his teeth pulled out. It hurt like hell but what hurt him more was that the false teeth cost $500 AUD (1500 ringgit). But at least now he wouldn't keep having to see the dentist who he had decided must be a bad, money-hungry man.

The only problem was that The Australian Dentist was used to making teeth to fit big Australian faces not small Malaysian Chinese faces. This was how Ikanyu got his big, Australian smile. When I saw his new teeth I called him Ikanyu and it stuck because his huge white teeth really did make him look like a shark. He looked a little scary with that smile. I liked him best when he took his dentures out before bed. Then he looked just like himself. Less like a great white and more like a friendly, little, gummy shark. But he didn't like it if I called him a gummy shark or even acknowledged that his teeth weren't real, so I didn't.

I called him Ikanyu (that was my code word for him).

And he called me Girl (that was his code word for me).

Girl, he said, because what else was this child of his old age than the only girl in the world entire?

I really had no idea what I was doing wasting my time thinking of Ikanyu's teeth when I was finally away from my three parents and in that mythical place, England, which I had always dreamed about.

Australians go to Europe all the time to get drunk, see 'history', watch sports, eat gelato and throw a coin in the Trevi Fountain. But I wasn't like them. I grew up a child forested by grown-ups and they would never have let me go anywhere without them. They thought I might get mugged, kidnapped, assaulted or killed. And being by myself there would be no one to help me.

But because I was here on a scholarship from the British monarchy, my trip fell into the category of work and not pleasure. And my parents had reared me to work. Ma always said that if you were the best at what you did then even if they didn't *want* to reward you because of your face – her metonym for race – they would be *forced* into rewarding you. (In my experience, this was turning out to be less and less true. As I sat in my dark corner, accumulating accolades, I watched with jealousy as so many of my coevals moved further and further ahead of me until they were a tiny speck in the distance. But I never told Ma that. Because she thought that complaining, like unionising or protesting, was exclusively the privilege of the rich and idle.)

All of this to say that when I got the scholarship offer, my parents were not only permissive about the trip but excited for it. Ma even had an unstylish pair of black pants and matching twisty top made to my measurements in Footscray (in case I met someone important and needed something nice to put on).

But here I was just thinking of them instead of enjoying my newfound freedom. England had always been a dream of mine because we needed whole oceans between us before my parents would leave me alone. But now I just missed them, I guess.

I tried to practise remaining in the moment and staying aware of my surroundings, like all the meditations on this app on my phone said to do. I was here. Not there. I breathed in and out deeply. My parents had always said I was neither here nor there as a person but that didn't matter now because I was sat in the corner of this beautiful old room by the big Palladian window that opened up to Green Park. The waiter put my coffee on the table for me and I began drinking it. The caffeine went straight to my head like a power trip. I began to shake like a socially anxious greyhound, but I kept up the meditation as I sipped it. I reasoned that the meditation would cancel out the caffeine high and I would be back to normal soon. I tried to focus on my surroundings and what I could notice about them.

There were Scotch eggs on the menu which I'd never tried and curry which I was already beginning to miss from home but I ordered the steak frites because it was the most expensive item on the menu. In my head I converted thirty pounds to fifty-six Australian dollars. I was feeling the excitement of spending money that wasn't mine (whilst resolving to not order the steak again because I didn't want the bill for my food to come to Leon and for him to think I was taking advantage). Then the waiter asked how I wanted the steak cooked. I was terrified. I had never told someone how to cook something before; Ma would have whacked me with her spatula if I had dared to. But I also knew from movies that the pinker your meat was, the more refined you were, just as the blacker the coffee you drank, the more learned a person you were, so I told him medium rare.

The meat came out dripping with blood as if it had just walked off the set of a horror movie. I almost vomited when I saw it. Was this safe to eat? Didn't raw meat give you food poisoning? It seemed that it didn't but only if you were rich. I ate some chips while deliberating over what to do. The chips were well done and they were good. I sent the steak back with an unclear conscience. Normally, cosplaying being rich was my favourite thing but I felt terrible about what I'd done. A brand-new steak appeared on my table that was so well done it looked like a soft-leather shoe and I couldn't eat any of it. As I was playing with my food, an elderly woman with cauliflower hair leaned over to my table.

'That looks good,' she said. 'What's wrong with it? Not hungry?'

I told her the story of what had happened.

'Don't be silly, the chef isn't the one paying for the meat. He's probably finished off what you left and had a good lunch now thanks to you. It's an honest mistake. We all make those. Anyway, what are you doing here by yourself? I always notice you at breakfast eating over in the corner.'

I realised I must be an anomaly here. I never saw anyone who wasn't white or below the age of sixty-five. I explained about the scholarship and the thesis and the novel.

'Where are you from?'

'I'm from Australia but my parents were born in Malaysia.'

'My late husband was stationed at Butterworth back in the sixties and seventies.'

'My parents are from there.'

I was surprised by the coincidence and then it made me think about what my maternal grandmother had always said about the Ang Moh stationed in Butterworth. One fish feeds our entire family but the greedy Ang Moh can eat a whole fish by themselves. They eat plates of beef as large as the cow itself. Eat and eat and eat but still they don't know how to eat.

'What have you seen in London so far?'

'The Serpentine Pond, Oxford Street, The Tate Modern.'

'You haven't been to Oxford University yet? You must if you are a doctorate student. You should see Oxford before you leave.'

'That's not in London, though.'

'No, but there's a bus that takes you the whole way there. You must go.'

She seemed so insistent that I almost worried that she would suggest coming with me. To avoid this, I agreed that I would see it today.

'And give me what's left of your steak and chips if you don't want them, please, before you go,' she said.

Since forever, I more or less did what people said. Even if I didn't know them or trust them, I assumed they knew better. Maybe it was to avoid having to make any decisions on my own, to find the shape and contours of my own desires. But being powerless fit me like a well-tailored suit. So, I gave her my plate and went. As I walked away she began digging into my half-eaten food. Rich people were so weird, I thought. But I really liked her – she did whatever she wanted and I admired that in a person that wasn't me.

She seemed to expect me to leave and get on a bus straight away. Not knowing what else to do, I left the Princess Maud room and looked up how to get to Oxford University on my phone.

Being at Oxford University made me ashamed that I was only a student at an Australian sandstone university. It made me think of when I had learned that the old sandstone buildings our campus was so famous for were actually built in the nineteenth century in the Tudor Gothic Style to imitate the Cambridge and Oxford colleges that were built in the fifteenth and sixteenth centuries. Our university buildings were, in a sense, just like the replicas of the Great Pyramid of Giza and the Colosseum and the Eiffel Tower that you got in Las Vegas. Before that point, I had thought they were the real thing and had chosen my university based on their medieval design. By the time I found out it was too late to change. Was it possible for a building to lie to you? I felt ashamed of my naivety every time I walked past it after that. Then I felt ashamed of myself for being ungrateful. Cringing back at my own sense of cultural cringe. After all, there weren't buildings as old as that in Australia because colonisation was so recent. It made me sick when Australians travelled to Europe and admired the period architecture whilst lamenting that everything back home was so modern. It wasn't. It was just that the old had been destroyed. But here I was doing the same thing.

When my VCE results came in good Ikanyu had said I should apply for a scholarship to study at Oxford. But I didn't know how to apply for either a British university or a huge scholarship. I went to a public school where it was already special and rare to go on to my university or any university at all. Of course, my school didn't offer IB and I had no idea how to convert my score. I also knew such scholarships required you to be a community leader, but I didn't think I had a community to lead. I gave cheap piano and free English lessons to the other kids at the Chinese church I was raised in. But that was more because I didn't think I was a very good teacher and found it embarrassing to take money off someone who had earned it. I also knew my parents couldn't really afford to fill in the gaps that scholarships inevitably miss: rent and board, flights, knowledge of how the whole thing worked.

I began to explore Oxford without knowing what anything was. There were maps I could follow but I had no idea which way was north or south or east or west. When I happened upon a library I was excited. Libraries were the place I sought refuge until the storms in my heart passed. The door was locked. A security guard told me that it was only for students. I asked about visiting scholars and he told me that you needed a special card for that which would take at least a few days to receive. I could come back another day. But it was late by then and I had to make the last bus back to London.

On the bus I watched everything slipping further and further away from me until it was only a green and yellow blur. Seeing Oxford had depressed me so much that I just gave up. I gave up on my novel and work for the rest of the time I had in London. Instead, I walked around without any sense of where I was going, buying clothes and sandwiches from Tesco.

I felt that I would never amount to anything because I hadn't studied in buildings that were the right kind of architecture. And now what? I was the kind of person who knew more about Oxford Street than Oxford University.

It might sound strange to create a binary between these two things but you have to understand that anything that got in the way of my ambitions was my enemy, especially any desire within myself that didn't fall into the line of my plans. Ikanyu had been trained in the British navy as part of the colonial handover in Malaysia and he knew a thing or two about disciplining the self. Early mornings, cold showers, complete obedience to the task at hand. That was the person he brought me up to be. I needed to deny myself of everything I loved to get everything I wanted. The only problem was that I wasn't sure what I wanted yet.

Three

It was my last day in London and I had an early train to catch. Leon ferried me to the station in a cab and gave me my train ticket, telling me I mustn't lose it. As the train pulled in, he hugged me and said he hoped I would have a good time in Arbroath. I hugged him back and said thanks for everything because I was grateful he had showed me around and I had begun to feel guilty for having suspected him of anything bad. As we let go, his hands moved from the middle of my back to delicately brush against my coccyx. Before I could work out what had happened, the train conductor whistled and I ran onto the train, dragging my luggage behind me. I couldn't see his face from the window and I had no idea if it had been a simple accident and I was being too sensitive or if he was some ham sap after all.

The thing about these kinds of situations is how ridiculous they made you feel. I could see now how I had let this whole thing happen to me. Unlike the era of the bimbo I had grown up in, it was now the era of leaning in and empowering yourself. But I didn't know where the power was supposed to come from. It had to come from somewhere. I wasn't sure if I wanted power anyway. I just didn't want any more trouble. Every time I had taken under-graduate gender studies units, they just made me more aware of the different things that were expected of me as a woman and the kind of retribution I would receive if I didn't fulfil them. This was supposed to be my political awakening, I realised, but it only made me more afraid of incurring punishment and less likely to do anything that would upset anyone.

Once, when I was walking home from dinner after an undergraduate class with some girls from my class, I discovered that I was a coward. A car full of young men had slowed to yell obscenities at us. It was a scene I was so familiar with that it bored me more than it scared me but what surprised me was that one of the girls had stuck her finger up with one hand and started filming them on her phone with the other. I didn't do anything to back her up. I reasoned that my parents hadn't brought me to this country only for me to be found dead on a street somewhere near the university. This would defeat the purpose of immigrating at all. And unlike her parents, mine would never forgive me for dying on them. Hers would set up a memorial in her name and campaign for change on the news. Mine would probably use the investigation to retrace my steps and work out where I had taken an unnecessary risk. I couldn't work out whether she was just braver than me or whether not having this kind of thing in the back of her head meant she could take more chances than me.

I lugged my self and my things to the quiet carriage. After I'd sat down, I noticed a young girl sitting to the right of me reading *The Bell Jar*. She was totally absorbed by it. It was the copy with the controversial new cover which showed a woman putting on her lipstick. I thought I might have been the only one in the world who liked this cover. I didn't see what was wrong with so-called chick lit. I loved the old Mills & Boon books Ma had on the bookshelf from when she was training to be a nurse in

Margaret Thatcher's England. And I had always loved the glamour of the magazine internship scenes. I wished I could do such an internship in New York with crab meat sitting in an avocado (in my fantasies the food was good and it didn't make anyone sick). I wanted the pretty mirror with the daisies and my name written on it that Doreen had laughed at. I never told anyone this because it made me sound vapid given the darkness lurking behind all the false glamour in the book. But sometimes, I was vapid. Seeing the girl and the book with its bright cover cheered me up a little.

Like so many other adolescent rites of passage, I came late to *The Bell Jar*. When I read *The Bell Jar* for an undergraduate women's writing class, I felt something new, brand new. It took me in from the start with its woozy charm and kidnapped my mind clean away. Which meant that it hurt like hell when she wrote about being 'yellow as a Chinaman' and worse when a few pages later there was 'a big, smudgy-eyed Chinese woman ... staring idiotically into my face'. The hurt kept me from reading on for a while. This often happened to me when I was reading books I loved.

I felt betrayed because in the most routine, narcissistic, obvious way, I had thought that *I* was Esther Greenwood. She wasn't just my friend or my cousin. She was my mirror and my non-fraternal twin. When I reflected on this I decided to keep reading. I would see how I felt by the end of the book. The next line from where I left off said about the Chinawoman: 'it was only me of course'. It was only me. Perhaps I had been too quick to judge.

It still stung that she saw me in that unflattering mirror glow, that she thought I looked like her at her worst. But then I thought Esther Greenwood would have been *me* at my worst: self-involved, so much so that other people could only ever be the backdrop to her own suffering. In a way, she was the person I saw when I came home from a long night out smelling like sweat and smoke after having my heart broken all over again and looked right into the mirror. She was a 'big, smudgy-eyed white woman staring idiotically in my face' and yet she was only me. Of course.

After that I became the cliché of a girl who is obsessed with Sylvia Plath. It was embarrassing but it was true. I applied to do a PhD on Plath and the underfunded English department gave me a full ride, the only full ride they could afford to give out that year. This made it hard to make friends with the other students because they thought that I thought I was better than them, which was true. I also didn't really get them, though, because of our different backgrounds. They were the children of mathe-maticians and musicians and well-meaning middle-class parents that try very hard to understand you. They were the offspring of people who helped you with your homework when you were in school and paid for your therapy when you were in university. They didn't need scholarships for anything but the prestige of them and if they didn't get them then their plans to study some-thing as fruitless as English Literature would remain unchanged. And me, I was someone who started university knowing lots of fancy French words and names but I pronounced them all wrong (Barts, Flow-bert, in-genuine, en-new, juice-sense). See, I had been reading lots and lots but didn't have anyone to talk about what I was reading with. When I found out the right way to say the word, I would feel betrayed by it, that old friend that had always been with me, I hadn't known her at all. And then I would wonder why no one in my classes had ever corrected me and that silence was the most embarrassing thing about it.

I was supposed to be writing a thesis on the postcolonial in Sylvia Plath's poetry but I hadn't written a word. I told myself it was because the Plath estate was very litigious, and I didn't need to be sued. But really, that was only hubris, because who would sue a PhD student working on a thesis no one would want to turn into a monograph anyway? It was an excuse because I didn't know what to write. Her poetry made me speechless, which would seem like a good feeling to have as a researcher if only it didn't mean you literally had nothing to say on the subject at all.

When I was growing up, Ikanyu had worked at Monash University as an electrical technician. It was an unusual job – he made tiny robots out of ping-pong balls and little sets of streets with traffic lights that really worked when you ran a toy car over the cardboard pavement. They were for experiments which the doctorate students wanted to run.

From his perspective, professors did very little for very much in return, which is why he had decided that I should become one. He said he had been in the staffroom once and it had chocolates wrapped in gold foil and fresh flowers on the table and was very well heated. He thought this was a good place for me to spend my adult years. Ma wanted me to be a lawyer but her ideas of what being a lawyer entailed were from TV shows like *Law and Order* and *Judge John Deed*. So I decided it was best that I follow

Ikanyu's map for the rest of my life. But by the time I was a grad-uate student he had retired and I saw his sepia-toned memories were reflections of the golden years of academia. Now every-thing was underfunded, academics were harried and tired and the staff kitchenette was tiny and always smelled of someone's strange, leftover lunch. The sciences fought with the humanities for the zero-sum game of money and status and they usually won because what was an analysis of the different rooms in Henry James' oeuvre to finding the cure for skin cancer?

The shared office I was assigned had mice, mildew, an old broken chair and a dusty half-broken computer. My office mate was an art history student who was very tall and wore tasteful, simple clothes. She said my typing was too loud and asked me if I could only type when she was not in the office. I agreed to this because my typing was kind of loud. She also asked if we could keep the air conditioning off in summer because it hit her bare shoulder at a weird angle from where she was sitting. I agreed to this, too, because it seemed unreasonable that her shoulders get cold while she was trying to work. Then she asked me not to bring a packed lunch as she was concerned that it might attract the mice and also, she disliked food smells. This was the hardest request for me because I didn't have enough money to buy lunch on campus and the leftover morsels Ma saved for me after dinner was done were even more delicious microwaved in a Tupperware container the next day. My office mate left sticky notes all over the communal kitchenette and the door to our office that said things like, 'We have mice!' and, 'Great! We have mice again!' and once simply, 'MICE.' I never said what I thought, which was that the mice were kind of cute and it gave me comfort some-times watching their industrious little bodies running back and forth from one secret place to another. It became hard to work as I sweated, hungry and not typing any notes about what I was reading, just memorising it all as best as I could, but I tried to persevere anyway because that is what my parents would have wanted me to do.

Later it was discovered that my building – like all other Aus-tralian buildings built in the seventies – was full of asbestos, and we had to evacuate it. So for the rest of my studies I had no office and I read and worked on the lawn outside my old office. This made it awkward when I was supervising honours students who I didn't want to admit my displacement to lest they lose respect for me.

Ikanyu refused to believe my account of things and thought if I simply worked hard I would slip straight from submitting my PhD to becoming a professor with the chocolates and the flow-ers and the nice heating. He thought it would be a neat trick to pull if after all those books with the impractical mumbo-jumbo I read, I got tenure. He really was very naive about Australia; he thought that it was a kind of Western utopia in which everything was decided based on merit unlike in corrupt Malaysia where the racial quotas and the gomen ruined everything. And he thought that if he, who had come from absolutely nothing, had become something, then I, who came from somewhere with gifts he never had, should be able to become someone. It made me terri-fied of failing him because how could I? I loved him more than anything.

It might sound strange that a twenty-two-year-old woman should be following the plans her father had created for her life as if he was God and she were a devout believer. But you have to understand that my father had suffered greatly. He hated remembering those times and refused to admit that he had been a victim of his circumstances. But I knew that he had been born into a world of pain. And I. I was born to be his very great reward for his very great suffering.

Ikanyu preferred to start his story at the part when he applied to join the navy. He was a teenager when he saw an advertisement in Butterworth's local paper that said:

IT'S NOT A JOB, IT'S AN ADVENTURE.
JOIN THE NAVY.
SEE GREAT BRITAIN AND THE WORLD.

and realised he had found his way out. Being too young, he needed a signature from his father to apply. It was the first time he had seen him in fifteen years and Lai Kong was onto Wife Number Three by then. His only words were, *Boy, why do you want to join the Malaysian navy? Don't you know that's for the Malays? You are a Chinese. If you join, you'll never be promoted.* But he signed the form and Ikanyu scraped together the money for a postage stamp somehow and sent it in. When he went for his physical examination, they asked him to remove his shirt and saw that he was clearly malnourished, as well as asthmatic. They stood him a few centimetres from the wall. *Puff out your chest until it touches the wall*, they said. He breathed out as hard as he possibly could but before he could touch his bare chest to the wall he began to cough. They told him that he had failed the physical and that they would not be able to consider his application any further. He convinced them to let him do it again. He closed his eyes and thought of that mythical place they called England he had read about in school and the poem that the missionaries had made them learn by heart.

And did those feet in ancient time
Walk upon England's mountains green:
And was the holy Lamb of God,
On England's pleasant pastures seen!

He breathed in. Then he breathed out as hard as he could and this time, he felt the hairs on his chest stand up and touch the wall for him. That was when his youth really began.

They put him onto a Sabena flight to England. He wore his only suit onto the plane and they served him caviar and crab meat in some kind of special cocktail. England was the first good thing to ever happen to him. The second good thing was Ma. She was there as part of the same colonial handover programme – only the British were training her to be a nurse. She was a good girl from a good family from the good part of his hometown. And she was smart and knew how to stretch a dollar so it didn't matter that they were poor. When they had completed their training, they moved to Tawau where Ikanyu was stationed and Ma found work as a nurse at the local clinic. She ran their conjugal household with the precision of a drill sergeant and the shrewdness of a survivor and he submitted to her rule with his hand on his heart.

The only thing was that they were unable to conceive. They tried Chinese medicine and then Western medicine and then the laying on of hands at the church run by the young missionary couple. Nothing worked. When Ma fell unexpectedly pregnant in her forties, they thought I was their miracle child. They decided to pack up their life and move to Australia in haste. So I could live my miraculous life.

My supervisor at university, a short woman with frazzled hair, told me I needed to start taking Valium and stop barging into her office and infecting her with my anxiety. She also told me that writing a thesis is like putting an octopus in a jar, the head goes in and all the tentacles slip out, the tentacles go in and it squirts poison at you. But I found it cruel that we were being asked, even metaphorically, to put such beautiful and strange creatures into tiny glass jam jars they would surely suffocate in. I wanted to put my octopus back into the ocean and smash the jar on a rock but that would mean not having a thesis at the end of three years and losing my stipend which I badly needed. So, I kept myself busy with anything but the thesis, hoping one day I would wake up and it would be there, finished and bound in green cloth, lying under my pillow like a dollar from the tooth fairy.

I suppose that this is why, when I had been offered a scholarship to travel to the UK and work on the novel I had always intended to write, I felt it would be a way to escape my problems. The only thing was that I needed my supervisor's clearance to take a leave of absence.

I met with my supervisor to tell her about my plans to write a postcolonial novel and the scholarship. She told me to make sure I cracked open the bubbly. I said I'd never had champagne before and she brought a half-empty bottle of champagne out from somewhere deep, under her desk, and poured a little into a coffee mug she had. I had a bit of it and it tasted like I'd eaten a lemon, peel and seeds and all. It was a rare moment of connection for us and I was touched by this woman who I pretended didn't exist most of the time in order to cope with the fact that I felt neglected by her.

She asked me for the name of the organisation and looked it up on her computer. She inexplicably pulled up a photo of a bridal shoot done at the clubhouse and turned her monitor around so I could see it. There was a photo of a serious-looking bride in a puffy white dress splayed out across a velvet chaise longue in the clubhouse's library. She laughed and pretended to pose like the bride and I laughed, too. She asked when I was going and when I told her March, she said there was a postcolonial conference in London around that time and that I should send an abstract in if I wanted to get a shot at the job market after graduating. Then she signed off on my leave of absence and told me to come back with a novel and successful conference presentation in hand. I promised I would because I was feeling good about everything that day and I hadn't expected us to have a conversation that didn't make me just feel weird and sad.

I was meant to be writing a postcolonial novel. It had been an immigrant novel first but I learned the word 'postcolonial' at university and I had started to say that was what I was writing on grant applications and the like. It was also good to say to people who asked what my book was about because it intimidated them and made them feel so bad about themselves for not knowing what it meant that they dropped the subject altogether. Also, immigrant felt like such a threadbare, sad word to me. It even had the poor, beseeching word 'grant' in it.

So, I was supposed to be writing a ~~immigrant~~ postcolonial novel but writing was starting to feel more and more akin to flashing for me and Ma would never have wanted me to expose myself like that. She had always described any clothes I wore out that she thought were too tight or too short as 'exposing myself'. Now, I was supposed to seek out exposure as a young writer, but I was afraid that I would lose respect for myself if I did.

Everything about my book felt embarrassing to me. In my head I would go through a list of different ways it was the most embarrassing novel ever written:

- There is nothing more embarrassing than writing a book about girls and young women.
- There is nothing more embarrassing than writing a book about childhood.
- There is nothing more embarrassing than writing a campus novel and that university not being Oxford or Cambridge or at the very least Harvard or Yale.
- There is nothing more embarrassing than writing a *bildungsroman*.
- There is nothing more embarrassing than writing a *roman-à-clef*.

- There is nothing more embarrassing than writing a novel.
- There is nothing more embarrassing than writing a book about love.
- There is nothing more embarrassing than writing a book.

And everything I wrote gave me a heart attack over how politically suspect it might be seen as. Writing a yellow body meant everything you did meant something one way or another. But I couldn't help my body. It was just normal to me. Every time I wrote a word, I just wanted to disappear into the air never to be seen again.

Anyway, to put off thinking about my problems, I watched the scenery through the window of the train. When I got tired of that, I pulled out *Birthday Letters*. I had been putting off reading it because its clever but surgical tone made me feel like vomiting sometimes. I had a vague idea that as a fledgling Plath scholar I should examine her work in the context of Hughes'. But I had no idea what to do with it – how should I view their relationship and how it affected her work? If I thought of them as collaborators, as iron sharpening iron, then I would be idealising their relationship as so many before me had. But on the other hand, if I treated Hughes with a kind of suspicion, as the man who 'killed a genius', I veered into the territory of a particularly 70s kind of hysteria.

But this time when I read the Hughes, I was easily taken in. I read innocently, like an idiot rather than like a discerning scholar. I enjoyed what I read. His poetry was bare and naked like a gum tree with all the bark stripped off. There were no linguistic tricks for him to hide behind. He was there in plain sight. Sometimes this purity could feel brutal and at other times it felt beautiful.

I enjoyed it until it made me start to feel deficient as a writer. Unlike his, my writing was horribly florid and maximalist, like a white shirt with lots of lace ruffles and puffs. I hated it. It was as embarrassingly girlie as I was. I wasn't sure why I was so embarrassed of being a girl and it showing in my writing. When I was a teenager, I had thought that there was nothing more embarrassing in the whole word than being a teenage girl. Being a teenage girl was just one humiliation after another. And even more embarrassingly, no one cared about your humiliations because they didn't matter that much anyway in the 'grand scheme of things', as Ma said. But these tiny, childish humiliations still made me shrink and shrink until my whole adult body could fit right back into them. And when I crawled into the tunnel of memory, I was someone else entirely.

I was Vanessa Hudgens in a red dress. I also had a cardigan on, which was somewhat inaccurate, but none of my Google image searches were able to find a way that Vanessa Hudgens kept warm. I walked up to the front door and saw a sign in bubble writing that read: *Elly's High School Musical 14th Birthday!! Go straight through to the backyard.* I went straight through to the backyard. Zac Efron was in a purple shirt, chain tags and side-swept wig, eating barbeque chips out of a bowl. Behind him was a huddle of Zac Efrons in different coloured basketball jerseys. I saw Vanessa Hudgens everywhere: shivering in spindly heels;

taking shots of Fanta in gold dresses; dancing with hoop earrings swinging; holding onto synthetic black wigs; sitting on the laps of their corresponding Zac Efrons. Despite the broad theme, everyone had come as either Vanessa Hudgens or Zac Efron. What happens in a teen film with thirty protagonists and no clear sense of plot?

I moved towards a bowl of chips, so I had something to do, and spied a small crowd of Vanessa Hudgens on a picnic rug. As each new Vanessa Hudgens arrived, the rest of the girls made dog-whistle sounds and hugged each other. I experimented with walking towards the picnic rug.

'Hey.' I waved at no one in particular.

A sonic pattern of 'hi's at different pitches emitted from the different girls. I tried squatting on the edge of the rug (rather than outright sitting) so that I was close enough to standing to get back up if someone cut their eyes at me.

'Can I ask you a question?' Olive said.

High school had made me realise that people asked if they could ask something, creating never-ever-ending, opening and closing, matryoshka dolls of questions. At home, things were straight like arrows. Ah Ma grumbled, Ma yelled, Ikanyu placated, I stayed silent. There were no questions.

'Who did you dress up as?' Olive asked.

Her real red hair was obscured by synthetic black hair and it made me feel strange, looking at her. My black hair on Olive's red hair. Olive was the kind of person who described herself as being 'strawberry-blonde' so I made a point of always calling Olive red-haired to herself. In her hand she held a fake Coach clutch.

'Vanessa Hudgens.'

'Oh.'

'I guess,' I felt my tongue become bloated and soft on the floor of my mouth. With a huge effort I lifted it up, 'if you have to ask it's not a very good costume.'

'Vanessa's all in the hair,' Olive said.

The way she referred to her on a first-name basis stumped me. It was as if she knew her personally.

'Oh.'

I didn't know what to say. I'd been like this for a long time now. When I was small, I had a hot rush of anger that said what to do. The hot rush was my best friend, a friend I carried inside of me. It kept me company when I was lonely. It compelled me to push, pull, scream and run whenever anyone hurt me. Where had it gone? It had disappeared entirely. I used to think I was someone and that no one could touch me. Now I knew this wasn't true. I wasn't anything to anyone anymore anywhere anyway.

'Why don't you say something? Do you even speak English?'

The other girls were mostly spectating. Elly, the birthday girl with the best get-up, a dress made of champagne froth, smiled at me. I watched Jasmine stage whisper 'so awkward' at her as if I was not just dumb but deaf as well. I found it hard to make myself like Jasmine. She was, in a way, a symbol that these girls weren't racist, because they had a friend who was Asian. She was a symbol to concerned teachers that I was just bad at integrating and would always have to be the kind of kid that teachers try to 'care' about. But Jasmine was the kind of a Chinese girl who told everyone as loud and proud as she could that she hated rice and found Footscray 'gross' and thought her parents emotionally stunted. In some ways, I got it, I too wanted them to know I was more than quiet and rice and swotting down and all of that stuff, but I couldn't help but feel pleasure in hating her. My balance started to slip. I stood up and moved towards the sliding doors of the house as if I was going to the toilet. I felt that I was running out of purposeful gestures that obscured my solitariness. Snacks, toilet; after this I would be out of ideas about how to pass the time until Ikanyu picked me up. I walked into the lounge-room and there were a group of adults sitting around the dining table and a few mothers preparing snacks in the kitchen. In the lounge-room was a flat-screen TV and a purple feature wall. There were photos of the family all in tight black T-shirts in front of a white background which seemed to not have any depth of field at all.

'Are you all right?' It was Elly's mum, burying candles into a cake.

'Just looking for the toilet.'

'There's someone in the downstairs bathroom already but if you go upstairs and turn left, you'll see the upstairs one.'

'Okay,' I managed to say.

'You're welcome.'

I went up the stairs. I opened one of the doors. Elly's room. On the wall was a poster of Kirsten Dunst in *Bring it On*. She smiled sadly at me like she felt sorry for me and I smiled back. There was a single bed heaped with unfolded clothes. I climbed onto the bed and heaped the clothes perfumed with the bright scent of Cold Power on top of me. Lying under the clothes, I stared at the stars that had lost their glow on the ceiling. I closed my eyes. I closed my eyes and fell asleep.

Four

The cabbie had a tired face and a 360-degree belly. He hefted my bags into the boot and sat me in the back seat. I had never taken a cab on my own before and I wasn't sure if it was better to burden him with my conversation or risk rudeness by staring out the window, slack-jawed and afraid of everything I saw.

'Whererom?' he said, catching my eye in the rear-view mirror.

'Sorry?'

His Scottish accent caught me off guard and I tried to listen harder.

'Where. Er. Om,' he said patiently.

'Australia,' I said.

'I've not been down to China but I got some cousins who been. Pretty, no?'

'Yes.' The small stone houses, unsteady on their slope, and shops selling very specific things – Janet's Birthday Card Shop, Mr Wriggly's Balloon Shop, The Big Bean Bag Shop, The Olde Liquorice Store – blurred as they ran past me.

'I would have liked to have gone to China myself but I was always too busy running my own business. Used to own a metal-mongers.'

'What's that?'

'Sells nuts, bolts, tools, all sorts.'

It sounded like a lolly shop but for spare parts. It made me think of Ikanyu right away.

'Oh, my dad would like you. He loves that kind of thing.'

'Eh?'

It began to occur to me that as hard as it was for me to understand the cabbie, it might be equally hard for him to understand me.

'KFC, McDonald's, Asda, Chinese take-away down the road from the station. And this here is St Agatha's Convent,' he said as he turned into the strangest and most beautiful driveway I had ever seen.

The driveway to our house was just long enough to fit Ikanyu's car. The driveway to St Agatha's Convent was so long you couldn't see the end of it. Gothic brick pillars and shiny black gate. A gravel path that made a lovely rumbly sound when you drove over it. Trees and trees and trees on either side. Trees with leaves a wet green colour I'd never seen before. I was reminded of something I'd learned in my high school art classes: *The artists amongst the early settlers had to mix and make new paints to accurately represent the burnt yellow green of the Australian bush.* Now as we drove past the deep blue-green of the Scottish trees and mosses, I couldn't tell you the colour they were. All I could say is that I'd never seen them before, needed new words to describe them, to think of them. A new smell, too – sweet and gritty and thick and briny – the smell of a seaside town.

'And this is the convent itself.'

The convent was the shape and size of a small castle. It was built entirely from pink sandstone. Fat flanking towers with grey witch's hats for roofs. Pretty balconies; I later learned they were called machicolations. Huge French windows with white windowpanes. Strange details poking out of walls, the stone heads of greyhounds, flowers unpetaling and angry old men. Climbing clusters of thorns and rosehip buds and pink petals as big and thick as cabbages. And the front door, raw wood with a golden handle and two black metal greyhounds standing guard symmetrically. It was so beautiful it made me immediately want to take up my vows and become a nun. It seemed like a beautiful place to live an ascetic and aesthetic life. I wanted to be locked away in there and made pure from the big, ugly world.

'Er, excuse me. Could you fix me up with something?'

I had sat there just staring at the house for a good few minutes without realising it.

'How much do I owe you?' I said, trying out the language of a lady who took a cab in a movie.

'Three pound fifty.' He got out of the front seat and dragged my bags to the front door. He seemed so old and worn that I reached out to take them myself but then retreated. I didn't want him to feel as old as he looked. I counted out the foreign coins slowly and he helped me.

'Now, that's right, that's it, just twenty-five pee more.'

I waited at the door. When I turned around to look at the trees again, I realised he was sitting in the cab, waiting for me to be all right.

The door swung open.

'Oh, is that you? Hello! Hello!' A woman whose cheekbones bulged from her small face and eyes like big blue lamps under her weak, thin fringe. She gathered me into her arms as if I were a birthday present. I wondered whether it was exhausting at times to have to simulate delight at every new artist she met or whether she really always was ecstatic to meet us. I felt the same way about air hostesses' smiles and anyone that was made to call you 'sir' or 'ma'am'.

'I'm Penelope. How was your train? How was your flight?'

'Good. Both good,' I said with my scholarship smile on.

'What was it, twenty-four hours by plane and an hour and a half by train? But you Australians don't complain.'

'Yes.'

'You know, living down there with all those dangerous snakes and sharks and spiders!'

'Well.' I scraped for something about Australia that would fit into the picture she was painting of it.

'The beach kind of makes up for all of that,' I said, trying to sound convincing.

'I'll show you to your room.'

She walked in front of me, her legs hopping up the red-carpeted marble stairs. Moving past the strangest things, pink grouting in the marble walls. A lampshade on an antique marble table illuminating the decapitated bust of a Grecian woman, some fresh green apples on a broken branch, a large purple flower and some dried sea anemones. So many things I wanted to touch that I couldn't touch. Huge oil paintings of kings and queens and milkmaids and children with huge black eyes and incomplete smiles. I would later learn that these were perfect copies of portraits by Titian, Rembrandt and Velázquez made by artists who wanted to learn from the old masters. On the mezzanine level was my room. A room repainted International Klein Blue, varnished wood panelling and a strip of wallpaper with a design of little crosses near the ceiling. A red door. A big white window seat with huge French windows. A four-poster bed with tartan curtains and a little wooden roof fringed with bronze tassels. A fireplace. A green cut-glass lamp shaped like a grandmother's shower-cap. In short, it was the bedroom of my childhood dreams.

'You've also got a little bathroom to yourself round that corner. And a balcony beyond the window; see that door on the left leads you to the balcony.'

I looked at the door.

'But it says, "No access beyond this point."'

'I know.' Penelope's eye bloomed widely. Then she turned and ran down the stairs.

When she was gone I rubbed the places in my back that were glowing with a red-hot pain and then I lay down on the bed and fell asleep with all my clothes on.

I woke up. It was late in the morning and I was covered in the tangerine smell of my own sweat. I realised that someone had turned the heater on before I had arrived and it had turned the weather in my room tropical. I threw my jacket onto the ground and began ripping my things from my suitcase looking for my toiletries so I could have a shower. Before long, I had messed up the whole room. I had always been slovenly. I thought that it made me a modern woman. So different to my Ah Ma and Ma and even Ikanyu who were all driven half-crazed by my chaos. Now I could ruin a room with impunity.

After my shower I went downstairs and wandered around till I found the dining room. A floor of cool green and blue chipped tiles. Three big wooden tables of uneven lengths pushed together to make a great big dining table. White walls. Fresh bread, a commercial toaster, cereals and homemade jams in jars with torn-off labels. I opened a jar of what looked like bitter Seville orange and rhubarb marmalade and sniffed it. A thin and pale man, with a balding head transparently concealed with a wool hat shaped like a mushroom, walked inside and stared at me.

'Hi,' I said.

'Uhp ... hello,' he said.

We each waited for the other to speak.

'I'm Jack,' he said, putting out his hand. It was like shaking a wet rag.

'Jack,' I repeated.

'Jack,' he confirmed.

'Jack,' I said again.

I laughed but his eyes just kept staring.

'Weren't you sick on the plane to London? I feel like you missed so much.'

'I was sick. I usually get sick on planes. My Wellington-to-Singapore flight went okay so I thought I was fine but then Singapore to London was a nightmare. I stayed in bed for the first day I was there except for when I had to throw up. Then I was fine and I saw a bit of London. Performance art and galleries and the like.'

I was confused. Why hadn't he joined me and Leon then? To avoid thinking about it, I tried to move the conversation along.

'Did you feel as if the old people at the clubhouse were always talking to you at mealtimes?' I asked.

'No, never.'

'Oh, I felt like they'd tell me where to visit and all of that,' I said.

'Try being a balding man in his mid-forties and then see how many people come up to you in public.'

I laughed and he scowled in a friendly way at me.

'Do you know when Blessing's coming?'

'I heard he couldn't get his visa sorted in time.'

'Okay.'

'Where are you from?'

'I'm from Australia but my parents are from Malaysia.'

'My wife is Malaysian,' he said.

Sometimes this kind of pronouncement could feel like a red flag. A passive-aggressive prologue to a relationship with someone who felt they were exempt from treating me normally because they had already used up all of their colonial benevolence on their spouse.

But with Jack it turned out to be more of a white flag. He was one of those men who venerated his wife to the point of being afraid of her. He told me his wife had said that he should use his time at the residency away from his young family well or else.

'Or else what.'

'I'd come back, go to bed and wake up one morning with a knife in my back.'

I smiled. I knew then that he wouldn't see me as animal, mineral or vegetable but as a real, live human girl.

'Do you mind leaving your kids for so long?'

'I do. But I think even they get that this is kind of a big deal for me. I'm forty-two and I've never been invited to do a residency. So,' he said conclusively.

'So,' I agreed.

I liked Jack – he was everything Australians believe people from New Zealand to be. Harmlessly strange and awkwardly friendly. I have never been disappointed by anyone from that country.

'Hi,' a girl waved walking into the room.

'I'm Maeve,' said the girl. She had her hair closely cut in a behind-the-ears bob that bounced around when she walked. She was wearing the kind of clothes that made her look like a particularly lovely but still practical gardener – dungarees, leather boots, sensible thermal tops.

'I've already forgotten all your names,' I said, apologising sideways.

'That's all right, I'm terrible at names anyway,' Maeve said.

Maeve's cheerful and easy manner was already showing me that she was going to be the most socially competent person at the residency. Her role would be that of smoothing things over and being the easiest person to get along with. I hoped she wouldn't get burnt out before the residency was over from making conversation with people like me and Jack.

'I was actually sent down to fetch you both,' said Maeve. 'We have presentations and introductions now upstairs in the library with the others. There was an email sent out about it last night.'

We followed Maeve upstairs to the first level. The library was dark with intricate wooden flowers carved into the ceiling,

a different flower in each panel. Books lined the shelves, all leath-
er-bound with mysterious non-fiction names like *The Idea of
Evil* or *Big Cats*. The carpet was a mossy green. Sitting around
a big walnut table were Penelope, a man with lines so deep into
his forehead they looked like tilled soil, a greyhound with sad,
still eyes and a woman with expensively bleached white hair that
toggled somewhere between 'Nordic' and 'ghost'. She was wearing clothing that made you think of the royal family going on a
hunting excursion – tartan, of course, but also a turtleneck and
gloves and a weird beaver hat. Under her silly, ugly clothes, her
face poked out like a pale, serious flower.

'Did you get the email I sent out last night?' Penelope said.

I looked at Jack to see if he would answer first and get me out
of speaking but he was staring at the dog.

'No, sorry, I fell asleep,' I said.

'Well, it was just a little note to say that I thought we could
start the residency by introducing ourselves, talking about our
own art practice, and the like.'

'Oh,' I said, standing up. 'Can you give me a minute? I just
need to do something.'

'Are you going to change into a costume for your presentation?' the girl with the bleached hair said.

I wondered if I had said the wrong thing already.

'No. Just getting my laptop,' I said.

I didn't really need my laptop. But it made me feel safer, not
because it had anything useful written on it, but because it
functioned as a kind of shield between me and the world.

'It's just an informal thing really, but go ahead,' said Penelope.

I retrieved the laptop with the charger wound from under a pile of clothes and brought it back into the room.

'I'm Clementine and I—' began the girl with the bleached hair as I fiddled with my international plug. She stopped speaking and stared at me struggling to plug my laptop into the wall. When I sat back down she cleared her throat and began again.

'As I was saying, I'm Clementine.'

My computer made its Windows XP start-up sound. Clementine looked at my laptop.

'I'm working on a series of paintings called "Portrait of the Artist as a Young Woman". I'm painting portraits of female artists both dead and alive at work in their studios or natural habitats and really interrogating the idea of male artistic genius by giving it a new face.'

On her phone, she showed us photographs of her work. They were really very beautiful; the kind of paintings where skin texture was rendered so glossy and shameless that it looked plastic and made you think simultaneously of Victorian-era caricature and Instagram. The women were short and stubby and fleshy and all looked as if they belonged to the same family. They wore velveteen slip dresses and teddies and sports bras with high-waisted skirts. But their sexuality was undercut by something bitter and perilous. There was a kind of sly humour behind the paintings intermixed with a complete despair that was easy to feel but difficult to make out. And as she made a point of telling us, she had recently accepted an offer of representation from the Gagosian and the paintings were from her very first showing with them.

We applauded her. Excited at the commotion, the greyhound barked.

'Matisse ...' Penelope pleaded with the dog. 'Thank you, Clementine. I look forward to seeing what you come up with at the end of your time with us. Now. I suppose we'll go around the circle. She pointed her pen at the man with the wrinkly, soil-like face.

'Hello, I'm Otto,' he said, leaning back in his chair.

'I'm forty-one this year. I make stuff with my hands. Huge sculptural installations. Sort of pseudo-phallic sculptures. Parodies of phallo-centric culture,' he said.

He added that he had also 'done stuff' for Adam Swan, an artist who was known for his cartoonishly large sculptures of everyday objects and friendly, childlike drawings, all of which bore huge, unnerving googly eyes. I had seen the colourful artworks when they came to Melbourne and loved them – they were irreverent and funny and endearing. So, getting to meet someone who had met him excited me.

'What kind of stuff?' I asked.

'Basically everything. He comes up with the big ideas at his desk. I make the actual sculptures for the exhibit.'

'He doesn't make them himself?'

'Of course not. He has a whole factory of us doing it for him,' he said patiently. 'It was the same thing with his most recent show – the really critically acclaimed one. Where he collaborated and mentored children from refugee backgrounds and showed his work alongside theirs. The bits that were his work were crafted by us but thought up by him.'

It sounds so weird and maudlin now, but this was a kind of loss of innocence for me. I really thought everything was pure in the world up until that point. I'd had some very severe ideas about purity and artmaking. I had thought of the artist as a kind of pure and noble person, a person that floated above normal society and made things that came from the essence of their rare and beautiful minds. The idea of many dull hands making the one thing, the idea that the artist might never have even touched his own work, made me want to cry. To cry for the belief that had gotten me through the cold and lonely life thus far – that I was somehow part of a genealogy of special and misunderstood people who I would someday find. It was an embarrassing feeling to have but it was how I felt.

Jack told us about his existentialist movies, smiling and moving his big fingers and flashing his white wrists. I was not really listening. I was trying to look as if I was paying attention whilst thinking about what to say for my speech.

Maeve told us that she worked on these huge, large-scale tapestries that were based loosely on the images of calamity she found on the front pages of newspapers, natural disasters, human stampedes, wildfires, war, famine, protests, anything with huge crowds of distressed people and negative consequences. The people in her crowds were nude, blurry splotches and their pink, red, orange and yellow skin was the only way of distinguishing between them. Amidst these images of terror and death and sex were also tiny, poignant, things, two figures seemingly exchanging hats on each other's bald heads, someone sitting under a blasted and burnt tree and reading.

Penelope turned to me. 'Lucky last.'

'Please, could I have some water? Does anyone else want some water? I could bring up a jug and some glasses,' Clementine said suddenly, standing up.

There was a general murmur of assent around the room. The convent was overheated as a kind of backlash to the cold weather outside.

'Wait. Put up your hand if you're after a glass of water.'

We raised our hands obediently. Everyone except Matisse who looked on sourly. I wasn't sure why, but I resented having to raise mine.

'Right, I won't be a minute.'

Everyone turned back to me. I tried to use my big voice on these kinds of occasions, but always felt like I was wearing a huge coat that didn't belong to me. It felt like the small voice I usually used was hidden inside the big one and that everyone could see it poking through.

'I'm writing a novel.'

There was a long pause as everyone waited for me to elaborate but I didn't. Penelope looked at me with an encouraging smile.

'Here we go.' Clementine held the door open with her foot and came in bearing a wooden tray with upturned glasses and a fat jug of water. She proceeded to turn over each of the glasses, fill and pass them along to a Mexican wave of 'thank-you's.

'Great, sounds exciting. All of you. I'm excited to see what you each come up with over the next four weeks.'

There was a silence. And then we started standing up and stretching.

'Do you want to go see the garden?' Maeve asked me.

I was said yes because from the moment I'd met her, I had wanted to be friends with Maeve. I felt like she was the kind of friend you had in your adult years – rational, ordered and able to get along with everyone. Exactly the kind of person I could never be. She would make a time with you to catch up and stick to it and then you would say goodbye and repeat the practice again and again until one or both of you died. She would eat cereal for breakfast every morning because it was 'quick'.

Clementine asked if she could come too and Maeve told her, of course, that would be great. I wasn't so sure about Clementine – I was drawn to her as I felt anyone would be. I had seen her in the library commanding the room. I felt her power, the sheer force of her personality and her beauty, of course, was a part of it. It was hard to look at her because she had that kind of knowing beauty of a woman who has seen herself a million times through other people's eyes and knows she is being looked at. A kind of charisma, I supposed, that I was both wary of and yet irresistibly drawn towards. Who wasn't?

We went to the huge, meandering garden and moved among the fuchsias.

'You're Australian, aren't you?' Maeve said to me.

When I said yes, she told us that she worked for an Australian couple in London tending to the garden of their Melbourne-style café. She said that the sedentary nature of being at the convent was already worrying her; she had been used to working on her hands and knees and liked the physical exertion. I imagined Maeve deep inside a fecund garden, listening to the plants and giving them whatever they needed, and I smiled.

'I might have to take up running,' she said in conclusion.

'I don't think the lack of exercise will be so different for me,' I said. 'I'm a PhD student.'

'Do you like it?' Maeve asked.

'It can be a bit lonely,' I said, qualifying 'lonely' with 'a bit' so I wouldn't sound like a sad case. 'But on the other hand, I really like the solitariness of it as well.'

'I've always wondered what it was like to do a PhD.'

'It's like showing up to class but there's no teacher there and no texts or anything to study. In a way, there aren't really any chairs or tables. And it's up to you to make it all up yourself.'

'That sounds terrifying,' said Maeve.

'But making art sounds hard, too,' I said. I was doing the thing where if sympathy is given to you, you must give an equivalent-sized gift of sympathy back.

'Yes, imagine your task is to make something and it can be anything in the world at all. And it's up to you to decide what it is.'

'But that's the thing I like about it,' Clementine said.

I had forgotten she was there but she was. To make up for my forgetting, I tried to even out the conversation so more of it went to her now.

'Do you think you'll mind being in the studio all day?' I asked her.

'I'll love it. The only thing I'll miss is Henri. We got married just last year in our pyjamas. Beautiful silk pyjamas, though. He's my dealer, actually.'

I tried not to look surprised at this admission. I knew I could appear a bit prim to people like Clementine.

'Art dealer,' she added, reading my expression.

'Is he in London now?' Maeve asked.

'Yes. I'll miss him a lot; we aren't often apart given we're in the same business, you know? Even our work lives are tied up with each other.'

'What's that like?' Maeve said, because it was obvious Clementine wanted to be asked.

'Really nice. Well, I know I can trust him because he's Henri. I know he's protecting my best interests and actually cares about my paintings selling and all of that because we're in it together. But he also cares about my art and really nurtures me, doesn't pressure me into anything I wouldn't want to happen.'

'That's lovely,' Maeve said.

The conversation began to slow into silence. Maeve climbed onto the fence to look out at the sea. I stared at a statue of a woman in the middle of the garden. She had these soft curves like the sea and a face that had never known sadness. In one hand she held a sunflower. On the plaque at her feet, it said that she had jilted the Sun and he turned her into a sunflower. A sunflower so she would always have to turn her face towards him.

Five

The next morning, I was woken by a knock at my bedroom door. I wriggled out of my pyjamas and into a dress that was crumpled from lying on the floor and smoothed my hair with my hands. I opened the door, and it was Clementine. She was dressed in another strange outfit – that of a cowboy with a bolero and suede pants. It felt as if she was dressing herself like a parody of a person as if to question the very idea of clothes. They drew your attention and then made you realise that by giving so much clear information about what they meant they were giving you nothing at all about the wearer.

'Sorry if I woke you up,' she said.

'It's fine.'

'I wondered if you would mind if I painted you sometime during the residency? I mean, I know that you have your own work to do but maybe you could spare a few hours to sit for me.'

I was surprised and she watched as the feeling spread over my face.

'I mean, you're really very beautiful. Wonderful to look at. And your work sounds really interesting. It'd be amazing to paint not just you but your mind at work.'

I was flattered but I tried not to show it. I had always wanted to be considered beautiful and believed women to be better judges of beauty than men. It was for women that women made gold and silver glint at their wrists and necks and ears and fingers. Only other women could properly admire the lovely indent of a wrist, the contour of a neck, the round drop of an earlobe, the musical movements of a woman's long fingertips. Men famously loved to look at women but they got too much credit for their looking. Men saw the wrong things, couldn't discern intricate differences, were too easily fixated on their own point of view. And for some reason, the discernment of a beautiful woman like Clementine felt particularly wise to me.

'Sure,' I said.

'It's not going to be a vanity portrait. It's going to show you as you really are,' she assured me.

This made it sound like a kind of fortune teller's crystal ball, except that it was my present rather than my future self that was going to be revealed through it. I was excited to find out who I was. I was one of those embarrassing people who loved personality tests and daily horoscopes and being described. I wanted some other entity or thing outside of me to tell me who I was so I wouldn't have to find it out for myself.

'Sounds good,' I said.

'Really? I'm so glad you said yes!'

After breakfast, I dressed carefully in a simple, collared white dress with two buttons undone and I made my way down to her studio space. As I walked I remembered with a jolt that only the day before I had been suspicious of Clementine's charisma and wanted to keep my distance from her. And yet here I was finding her pull irresistible. It was like she had the original meaning of that word with her – charisma, as in gift or power or even, Holy Ghost.

I supposed that was why I was walking towards her now. The private studio space she had been allotted turned out to be a small grey concrete room with large, dusty windows. Clementine sat down on the floor with her easel and paints and gestured for me to sit on a wooden chair she had placed carefully under the soapy light of the window. She looked at me and feeling embarrassed, I looked down. There were so many bottles of paint splayed all over the floor. I hadn't realised that there were so many co-lours in the world. I felt sharp, shooting stars of pain in my back when I sat down and I couldn't get comfortable; I began moving around like an octopus that had been asked to sit on a stool. I kept moving my head this way or that, organising my limbs in some strange shape. I looked at her as she prepared her paints and found it strange that she was still wearing her cowgirl outfit. The other artists had come to the colony wearing typical studio attire: paint-splattered black hoodies; overalls; old, too big shirts. All of which swallowed up their bodies instead of drawing attention to them.

'Could you try and sit still, please?'

'Okay.'

I tried to still myself. Imagining that I was a statue rather than a person helped. I sat so still it looked as if I wasn't breathing but I was still, of course, alive.

'Thanks, that's great. Now, would you mind facing directly towards me, please?'

'Okay.'

I looked at Clementine and tried to hold her gaze.

'Perfect.'

She began her work and I. I held her gaze but it was harder to sustain than I thought it would be. I held her gaze but I looked at her with the resigned air of a person getting their picture taken for a new passport photograph at the post office. I made myself a kind of shell and you couldn't see the soft parts of me inside that casing. You couldn't even see that I existed underneath all of that. I began to feel the usual ache – a desire to disappear myself, to become the dust I came from.

She put down her paints and brushes.

'I can't paint you if you resist me painting you. I can paint your face and your body, of course. But I can't really paint you.'

'Sorry.'

'No, it's completely fine.'

I tried to commit myself to the portrait the way a person commits themselves to a relationship or a religion or a mortgage. I let the light back into my eyes, I smiled as if I wanted nothing more than to sit for Clementine. I tried to become the person she had wanted to paint when she knocked on my door this morning.

'I also can't paint you if you try and pose like a toothpaste commercial,' she said.

'I'm so sorry. I didn't know how hard this would be.'

'No, it's fine. Do you want to try again?'

'Okay.'

I felt my body become a balloon with no air in it. It was so exhausting sitting there trying to be some pure and clear essence of myself that I wasn't even sure existed.

'I think we're going to spend some time just you learning to feel comfortable and okay with sitting for me. What would make you feel comfortable?'

I shrugged.

'Do you want a cup of tea and some biscuits or something?'

'Okay,' I said.

She went into the kitchenette and moved about making tea. She came out with a teapot and some cups balanced precariously in her arms. And then went back for some packets of oatcakes. We sat on the polished cement floor together eating and drinking. I loved the hot amber liquid and the white whirlpool that the milk made and the crumbly, utilitarian feel of the biscuits. I had always loved buttery things with oats laced through them.

'I'm sorry. I didn't realise how hard this would be,' I said again.

'No, most people don't. They think sitting for a portrait is just, like, being there. But it's so much more than that. Anyway, let's not think about it for now. Let's just try and break the ice. Here's the customary icebreaker I have adopted over the years: my dad is the Queen's gynaecologist.'

I laughed. The false sheen of this shiny new thing fell upon us, and it made me think of other false intimacies of convenience. Sleepless nights at school camps, reality TV stars crying when another contestant is eliminated, shotgun weddings. I didn't resist it, though. I let myself be pulled along because that was what I always did.

'Wow.'

'I know. He got an MBE last year for services to the Queen. We got to go to Buckingham Palace and see him accept it. It was really amazing.'

I was surprised to hear a beautiful and successful artist in her early thirties boasting about her father like a private school girl. When she had initially brought him up, I'd thought the conversation would take a weirder, more specific turn. But it went back to this. It was difficult to know how to respond. Whenever someone tried to impress me, I tried very hard to look like I wasn't impressed by them, never mind what I felt inside.

'Okay,' I said.

'What about you?'

'I don't have an icebreaker at hand, sorry.'

'Go on, everyone does. What fact about yourself do you bring out at dinner parties and the like?'

'I've never been to a dinner party.'

'Please, just one thing.'

'I was born a day or two after my parents immigrated to Australia. I'm an Australian citizen based on a technicality.'

'I knew you had one in you. What was that like?'

'Well, I don't remember, obviously.'

'But you know.'

She was a good listener and she kept trying to unfurl me. So I told her things about myself, more than I meant to. I told her about those small, tender, sacred things I was usually afraid people might stomp on – Ah Ma and Ikanyu and Ma and Australia and school. We spoke for a long time and she took on a seriousness that was different to the way she had come across that first day and the way she would continue to come across in public – as someone who had a kind of social power because she was always willing to claim it and also as someone's eccentric and easily offended maiden aunt.

'Do you want to explore the area around the convent for a bit?'

'Okay.'

'There's a beach nearby, I think.' She got out her phone and opened Google Maps. 'Here.' She showed me.

'Okay,' I said.

'Okay, okay, okay. Is that all you say? You should be more excited. You're Australian. It'll make you feel right at home.' Penelope's office looked out onto the front on the convent and I thought about her seeing us leave the convent for a silly reason like the beach. I wondered what the other artists were doing. Probably spending all of their precious time in their box-like studios. What would I be doing if I weren't with Clementine? Probably spending most of my time sitting at the desk in my bedroom staring at a blank page while the cursor blinked at me like it was trying to silently say something but what, I could never figure out. I agreed to go with Clementine and she said that she would get changed into her bathing suit and meet me in the dining room. I hadn't expected that we would go swimming, but I went along with it anyway.

We walked through the fields of wheat and made our way through tunnels of green leaves. We came out onto to a caravan park with a playground, a small indoor pool, a firepit.

We walked on from the caravan park till we came across an abrupt beach. The landscape went from road to grass to beach with incredible compression. In Australia, the shore stretched out languidly until it dissolved into sand and then shells and rocks and sea. This was so different to me. As Clementine and I walked on the dunes and in amongst the sand reeds and the pastel grey and white and pink stones, I had the feeling that we might be becoming friends. We took off our clothes and made them into a little heap on the sand so they wouldn't blow away. And we swam into the grey-blue water. It was the kind of cold water that felt good to splash on your face in the morning, except that instead of just waking up your face, it woke up your whole body. I was awake, which is another way of saying I was alive and sometimes this felt good.

The next day, I went down to Clementine's studio after breakfast to sit for her again. I thought to wear the white dress again so she wouldn't have to start over in her vision of me. She was wearing a classic burglar costume – striped, black-and-white shirt and slacks with a beret. She wore the beret at an exaggerated angle on her head. It sat there with a kind of sly wit like it was in on the joke – 'I'm a beret!' it seemed to say.

Clementine had me sit on the same wooden chair under the same grey window and made me a cup of tea to sip on. As she cleaned her brushes and stretched her canvas, she spoke to me, performing our friendship like a seal balancing a ball on its nose.

'Dad was never allowed to tell us anything about the Queen. I think he signed something to do with that. But he would tell us everything about his other patients. Apart from the Queen, he was really bad with patient confidentiality.'

'What was his best story?'

'A couple came in to see him because they were stuck together. Not, like, metaphorically. They were literally stuck together.'

'Where?'

'Penis and vagina. With superglue.'

I laughed my real laugh. The ugly one I saved for special occasions only.

'Is that your laugh?'

'Yes.'

She mimicked it, exaggerating the low, rumbly sound, which made us both laugh.

'Do you think it was a weird sex slash romance thing? Like they wanted to be stuck together for ever?' I asked her.

She paused. Sometimes she did this, leave a little tear in the conversation so that she could work silently for a moment. She was painting in large, broad swoops at that moment. Then she would return to the world of us.

'I think it turned out to have been a mistake. They were in the middle of renovating the house. He mistook the superglue for a bottle of lube.'

'What did they wear?'

'I have no idea. It was such a long time ago when he told us. I was pretty young.'

She kept talking to me in that way until we were telling each other old stories with new words and it was like getting a lollypop after an injection as a child. It made me forget the painfulness of what I was doing – being seen, seeing myself being seen. It was like having your nails painted and being paralysed by the transformation you were undergoing, not wanting to touch anything in case you ruined it, except that in this case it was your whole body you had to keep still.

'Anyway. I feel like we're always talking about me. And my dad, weirdly,' Clementine said. 'What about you?'

'What about me.'

'Tell me what your PhD is about. Are you going to change the world?'

'No.'

'Well.'

I usually lied when people asked me what my PhD was about. Why? I wasn't sure. For one thing, liking Sylvia Plath was a truly embarrassing thing. When her life had been made into a flop movie starring Gwyneth Paltrow as Plath and Daniel Craig as Ted Hughes. When *The Bell Jar* cropped up in just about every coming-of-age teen film with a female protagonist, when Lisa Simpson made a diorama about her, when she came with a trail of associations with teenage girls who think they're 'dark' because no one invites them out on a Friday night. Or university girls who have their 'feminist awakening' after a tradie sitting on the back of his Ute wolf-whistles them. Or white middle-class girls with marketing degrees who think they're oppressed because they're not white men. But I felt like telling Clementine the truth.

'I'm writing a thesis on Sylvia Plath's work.'

'I love her. The colours in her work are very interesting to me as an artist. And of course, she kind of overshadows the work as like this, amazing, larger-than-life figure. You know, I wanted to be her when I was a teenager and I'd talk about putting my head in the oven when I was feeling melodramatic. She's just amazing, isn't she?'

'She is. But that's not necessarily why I'm writing on her. When people hear I'm doing a single author study they think I must be obsessed with Plath. But that's not really how research works.'

'But you do enjoy her stuff, right?'

'I guess.'

'I have an idea for the painting.'

Whatever Clementine's idea was – it alarmed me. Having a painting done of you that would somehow commemorate your interest in Plath and her writings fell squarely into the groupie camp.

'I don't know about that.'

'Nothing campy. We won't do the fifties clothing or anything. I'll just ... I'm thinking about it. Let me think about it, think with my hands.'

'Okay.'

'Sorry, I'm going to go quiet for a bit. I've got an idea. You don't mind, do you?'

'No, I don't mind.'

As I sat there letting her paint me as someone who I wasn't, I thought about my non-existent academic 'career'. Of course, I wanted to be a Plath scholar. But I felt the supreme detachment of the scholar was a kind of arrogant and very masculine pose in its own way. A way of eschewing the embarrassment associated with simply loving Plath, being moved by her work.

But then that was being a graduate student, wasn't it? An initiation into that place with the hard drawn lines we called academia. A precariously special group of people who sometimes needed to separate themselves from other people in order to feel like they were being taken seriously. Literary studies academics were people who had once sat alone in their rooms falling in love with books and now had the privilege of becoming professional readers in the public square of the university. But in order to distinguish themselves from 'amateur' readers and amateur ways of reading texts, had had to stomp hard on the self that had once loved books for banal reasons like their beauty or the way the books had made them feel. It wasn't entirely their fault – the humanities were having to constantly make a case for why they should exist in order to exist. And focusing on the utilitarian functions of books – the study of the human, the cultivation of empathy, the democratic importance of the critique, their ability to resist social structures, etc., etc. – was the best way to make an argument for the value of the humanities, for a sense that a novel had certain powers and was not exactly what it seemed: a limp, inert and superfluous object that did nothing of 'use' really. Just offered itself to you and let itself be loved.

The whole thing was particularly heightened by Plath scholars who were oftentimes preoccupied more with questions or taste and orthodoxy than with the texts themselves. There was a silent yet clear idea that Plath scholars had to continually distinguish and distance themselves from this other group that had also dedicated their lives to studying her work – the Plath groupies. And the Plath scholarship made it clear that there were sharp lines drawn between the two groups. In my head, I saw it laid out neatly in a table with two sides like this:

Plath Groupies	Plath Scholars
Read *The Bell Jar*	Read *Colossus* and *Ariel* and the Juvenilia
Mine her work for autobiographical detail	Understand her work as capital-L Literature
Respond with a deeply personal sense of recognition to her writing.	Read with a scholarly interest and are personally detached from the mythos of Plath.
Allow her work to permeate their lives and act upon them, thinking of her work as a sacred text with a set of precepts they must follow.	Act upon Plath's work rather than the other way around, apply literary theories to her work e.g. feminist theory, psychoanalytic theory.
Respond with hysteria and adolescent emotion to her life and death.	Read her work contextually, understanding it as a response to 1950s gender values.
Picket Ted Hughes' readings (when he was still alive), deface his grave, construe him as the 'murderer of a genius.'	Read Ted Hughes' work alongside Plath's and consider him an important influence upon her work and life.
Glamorise her suicide and romanticise her work as expressions of her mental illness.	Consider the way her suicide has impacted readings of her work and agree that while the way she died cannot be entirely set aside, are cautious about making her death the point of her life's work.

I felt the tug of both of these groups – there were some weird, sexist assumptions underlying the way Plath groupies were thought of. But I also needed to be able to take myself seriously as a person and sometimes that meant falling into step with some weird and sexist assumptions around reading. So, I always told myself that I was a scholar. Which was why Clementine's painting felt like such a terrible idea to me. As I sat there with my meta-phorical head in my metaphorical hands, working out what I was going to do, Clementine was painting with a renewed vigour. She was daubing her brush in new colours, ones she hadn't made before, and looking up at me as if she couldn't see me at all. She was clearly caught in the riptide of her own thoughts, letting the strong and sudden current pull her along. I recognised that feeling, it was maybe the only reason I had chosen this terrible laughing stock of a 'career'. And that feeling – it wasn't always there. Seeing her evident excitement, I didn't know how to tell her to stop and that this wasn't what I had been thinking of when I started sitting for her. So, I let her. I let her make me who she wanted me to be.

Slowly, without meaning to, I began to spend almost all of my time at the residency sitting for Clementine in that same white dress from the first day. We began in the mornings after break-fast, broke for lunch and continued all the way until the light evaporated from the sky. Clementine apologised sometimes for taking up my time in this way, but the truth was that it made me feel productive to be part of someone else's work – so much easier than figuring out what my own work was supposed to be.

At first it was a relief to be so completely out of control. To not have to walk through the continuous forest of decisions that would have come with working alone in my room. There was a certain kind of freedom in the passivity of sitting in a grey room watching myself being watched as the hours passed. But after a while it felt less like I was a bystander to time passing alongside me and more as if time was accumulating inside me, a load that my body carried in its chest. It turned out to be physically demanding work just sitting there all day. It was hard on the kneecaps and the spine and the neck and the shoulder blades. And it was psychologically exhausting to simply be in such a place of intimacy with another person for such a long time. To decide again to give yourself over to this gaze, to let yourself be truly looked at. To encounter periods of self-consciousness and other moments of vanity and self-importance and then periods of plain, stone-like boredom.

We would break for lunch and then go straight back to the studio to continue our work. Though I suppose it was her work not mine. But I began to think of it as ours in some way. I would always tell myself that I would start *my* work after dinner when I went back to my room, but as I moved towards my desk, I would inevitably fall into my bed instead. I worried about my lack of self-discipline, I wasn't sure where my own thoughts had gone to; I felt guilty for being so tired and unfocused. And then after the guilt began to taper, I began to feel the loneliness of missing my family, my Ah Ma especially. I wondered what she would do in my situation. When sitting for photographs as a young woman, her face would be blurred with misery, with her dry hands she would hold onto her knees and in her eyes was the bright light of her glare. I hadn't thought to bring any of those sad, brown photographs with me here.

Those evenings before I fell asleep, I often thought about telling Clementine that it had been enough – that I needed to turn now and focus on my own work – but I couldn't. Partly because I felt as if I was breaking my word, which I had given her and which Ikanyu had always said was something you could never take back. And partly because I felt as if I would be giving up on something which I no longer considered small or frivolous but a serious task that I already had begun and could not stop till it was completed.

With every new day, I became more and more involved as a collaborator and actor in my own right and not just a vessel which her colours would pass through. I began sitting up straight sometimes, and then at other times, turning my head a little this way and that. At her direction, I made my body's movements slow and pliable, I moved as if I was underwater. She had me rub olive oil over my arms and legs and face and neck so that the different corners of my body would catch the light better. In assuming this position of complete passivity, I now understood, there was hidden inside me an urgency, an electric undercurrent of activity. I had been disabused of that very old, very masculine notion that the artist was a singular, pure, creator of things and I had found something better. The sense that an artwork was the work of multiple people and forces. It struck me that that multiplicity suited me better than the solitariness of sitting alone in my room with a blank page on my desk.

Six

It was a Sunday, so I was free from my sitting duties. I decided to find the Asda the cabbie had told me about to buy some ibuprofen. After a week of being painted, the physical toll of sitting there was starting to hurt every bone in my back; bones I hadn't realised existed in my body felt as if they were aflame. Of course, back pain had been a constant companion since I started writing (which was since forever) but at times it got so bad it caught me completely off guard and I felt my soul shatter inside me. And this was one of those times. But I didn't want to say anything that would make Clementine's job harder. She had recently reached an impasse in her work; the material was overwhelming her, she said. And her face had taken on the hard look of a person who is second-guessing herself. I decided that I would try to resolve the problem myself. I would buy some over-the-counter drugs and maybe an ice pack.

Before I left, I thought I would ask Maeve if she wanted to come with me. Sitting for Clementine, I had begun to feel a little unmoored from everything and I wanted to be with someone who would make me feel normal after being looked at over and over again in this tiny grey studio. I knocked on the door to her room and she was sitting at her desk, embroidering a piece of fabric with a fine gold thread.

'Sorry to disturb you,' I said.

'No, this is the worst bit anyway, it's very tedious actually,' she said in her usual comforting way.

'Oh.'

'It comes out really nice but it strains your eyes and your fingers in the process. Isn't it so weird that you can't see all of that when it's done? It just looks beautiful or whatever – you can't see all of the boredom and self-mangling pain and disgust you felt making it.'

'I feel like it's that way with everything,' I said.

'I know. Why does it always have to be like that?'

'I wondered if you wanted to do an Asda trip but I didn't realise you were in the middle of something.'

'I'd actually really welcome a break from this.'

We walked through the field of wheat and I ate the heads while Maeve diligently checked Google Maps on her phone. We made our way through the same tunnel of green leaves Clementine and I had walked through and then the English pastoral faded and I saw a car park filled with assorted cars and a large grey building with its green, four-letter word pasted onto it. After the confinement of Clementine's studio and my bedroom at the convent, Asda seemed like such a wide-open space. There were bright lights like heaven and there was a cool blue air when you walked into the minty-fresh mouth of the shop.

When we got inside we split up silently. Maeve began by looking at the cheeses and I looked around with a kind of aimless love for everything I saw. I have always loved to drift in supermarkets. I smelled a honeydew melon. Not because I wanted to buy it but because I wanted to smell it. And I touched a few cabbages, letting their cool whale-boned leaves drift under my fingers. And then I plunged my hands into a box of chestnuts and felt their smooth, woody shells.

I found ibuprofen in the first aisle I tried and was surprised that it was only 99p a packet. I grabbed four packets, thinking I would take some home for Ma who sometimes got a shooting pain in her hands. I was disappointed at how quickly I had found it. I didn't want to leave so I started wandering in amongst the clothes racks and the snacks aisle, deciding that I would buy something to eat. I put together a meal deal: a packet of salt and vinegar crisps, orange juice 'with bits' and an egg and cress sandwich. Maeve joined me holding a bag of green apples and some crackers. She looked at what I had bought and made noises of approval at what I had selected.

'Do British people eat a lot of sandwiches?' I asked Maeve.

'I've honestly never thought about it.'

'No one in Australia above school age really eats sandwiches.'

'Really?'

'Yeah. But it looks like the sandwich industry is really thriving here.'

'I guess so. It's like that thing where you can't notice anything about your home country. It's just normal to you.'

I scanned my meal deal and ibuprofen as well as a punnet of strawberries. I had never seen such round and smooth strawberries before. Back home, they were huge, lumpy with boils and a dry maroon colour. Here the strawberries looked cute and bright like the love interest in a Shojo manga.

'Hello,' the self-serve check-out machine said.

I didn't respond to it – just scanned my groceries silently.

'Please wait for assistance,' it said as I scanned the ibuprofen.

A woman in a green polar fleece jumper with dyed black hair came over.

'Oh. You can't buy more than two of the ibuprofens,' she said.

I started to feel embarrassed. I didn't want to seem like I was hoping to OD but I didn't know how to explain. I glanced around me feeling self-conscious, worried people were staring – Maeve was busy at her own self-serve station. I noticed a person wearing a tennis player's outfit – or rather, a hyperbolic, satirical idea of a tennis player's outfit: white skirt and socks, knitted sweater – and I realised that it could only be Clementine.

She hadn't seen me or Maeve yet, she was bending over the nail polish section, completely absorbed in her task. Then I realised that she had one hand under her jumper and was stashing bottles there. I wondered if Clementine would become a kind of Doreen figure to me – an interesting girl who didn't think the ordinary rules applied to her. And like Esther Greenwood, I was drawn to the possibilities of being with this kind of person. A 'bad girl' who would lead me astray if I let her. I wanted to let her. As she looked up from what she was doing, I smiled at her conspiratorially, but she avoided eye contact with me and I realised she was ashamed.

'I said, you can only buy two,' the woman in the polar fleece repeated.

'That's fine, sorry,' I apologised to her.

She removed two of the packets from my bag and swiped her card over the screen.

Maeve and I headed back to the convent. She offered me an apple. I wasn't hungry but I took one anyway. I felt a different kind of emptiness in my stomach. I wondered what Clementine was doing and whether or not she had gotten away with it. I wanted her to get away with it.

When I got back to the convent, I took the ibuprofen which alleviated the pain in my back but turned my stomach lining to magma. Then I went down to the basement to do my laundry – a kind of novelty for me. Ah Ma had always done all of our washing. It was her favourite task to do while muttering consciously about how much we all oppressed her. Sometimes, even when there were no clothes to wash, she would pull them out of my cupboard and wash them seemingly for fun. We argued about this all the time, with her being of the opinion that I was a useless person who had never so much as touched a box of soap powder and me thinking I never had the opportunity to do so given how overbearing she was. But despite what I said, I suspected I was as lazy as she made me out to be. And I felt useless and guilty about it but didn't know how to change it. So, it was an embarrassingly big moment for me when I stuffed my clothes into the washing machine now. I sat on the ground and watched the washing machine turning, letting the sight of my things going round and round hypnotise me. I decided that I needed to ask Clementine for some sort of timeline, some way of knowing when my time in her studio would end. I needed to get on with my own work.

The next morning, I went to Clementine's studio ostensibly to sit for her but really to ask her when we would be done. When I opened the door, she was on the floor looking over her paints and she seemed tired. Mixed in with the usual tubes of oil paints were seven or eight bottles of supermarket nail polish in various colours – some of them solid colours, others shimmery or sparkly. She looked up at me watching her and I knew from her look that we had created a kind of pact. Neither of us would ever mention it. The grey walls of her studio sealed away the task we were undertaking together.

I wasn't sure how Clementine felt about it but pinching cheap nail polish from a supermarket felt very much like an adolescent form of petty crime to me. More 'petty' than 'crime'. Actually, I had done far worse when I was younger.

When I was seventeen, I had wanted nothing more than a blue velvet dress for formal. I had seen the dress in a shop window and thought of it as the colour of midnight, made from a woven piece of the night sky. I had tried it on and saw how it showed my bare shoulders and my neck and made me beautiful. It made me feel like I belonged in some dreamy other world – away from the life I inhabited at the time. A world filled with beautiful and interesting and clever people who understood everything about me and knew almost everything. I suppose I was in the world I had imagined now only it wasn't exactly as I had imagined it.

I thought about the dress I had seen in the shop all the time, I looked at the photos I had taken of it, I looked at the photos of it online with the model wearing it. But it was expensive, and at the time, I was making six dollars fifty an hour as what they called a 'sandwich artist', with my boss breathing down my neck, getting too close and asking if I had a boyfriend, telling me to finish my lunch faster so I could get back to serving customers. I was terrible at my job, I would charge customers the wrong amount, or forget to toast their bread for them, and I slacked off with my equally underpaid teenage colleagues every time my boss wasn't there. We used the industrial sink's high-pressure hose to have water fights, ate frozen cookie dough from the bag and shut each other in the huge walk-in fridge for laughs. I hated the smell of the meatballs and sauce that stuck to my hair and my body even after I'd changed out of my depressing uniform. But I loved money, which was why I kept showing up for work.

As the day of formal approached and I still hadn't accumulated more than a few handfuls of bills, I thought about stealing the dress. It was easy enough, a boy in my class, Cameron, who often took things, told me how. *The main thing is to have some scissors in your bag to cut the security tag off with. Though some smaller shops might not even have that. Do you know if it had a security tag?* I didn't know. *Check next time*, he said. *Also, they won't suspect you as much if you are a girl. They don't think girls can do much harm. Just try on a lot of similar dresses at once, different sizes, different colours, to confuse them and they won't notice if you stuff one into your bag. They can't follow you into the changeroom, after all.* He was an expert; he was the one who spread out his steals on the bitumen at lunchtime and showed us all the things he had taken over the weekend. He stole all sorts of things, chocolate bars from convenience stores, expensive sneakers from department stores, DVDs and video games from the video rental shop. He even had a folder filled with car badges of varying levels of prestige. A lot of Mercedes- Benz logos (they snapped off easily), Hondas, Mazdas, Toyotas and even an Alpha Romeo. He called it 'badging'. And I. I was one of the kids that gathered around the stolen things admiring them and listening to stories of how he was never caught. He would tell us nonchalantly that what he enjoyed most about stealing was how easy it was. And like everyone else, I thought he was very cool.

When I bumped into him in the city many years later, walking with a pretty girl who turned out to be his girlfriend, we began reminiscing about our high school years and I asked him if was still stealing, laughing at the memory. Cameron said nothing and was obviously embarrassed by me bringing it up. I looked at his girlfriend and she looked at him. It was clear that she didn't know about the period of his life I was referring to. I felt like an idiot for humiliating him like that.

In any case, this is what matters: I decided to steal the dress. I went to the store and did everything Cameron had told me to do. But what he hadn't told me about was how terrible it would feel when I noticed the storekeepers watching me, pretending to tidy things up near me, smiling if I looked up and saw them, and how I felt instantly degraded by this. How could I satisfy their image of me – as a bad, evil person, as person to be watched – by doing what they thought I would do? I left the shop, walked to the interchange and cried on the bus all the way home. Through my blurred, hot vision, I watched everything passing me by out the window and thought with despair about formal, which was only a few days away. I got home and lay down on Ah Ma's bed – the bed I had shared with her when I was still small enough to fit into it. I remembered what she had shown me when I was so small that I had appeared innocent – the way she had stitched $50 notes into the dusty curtains, into the hem of an old pair of pants, into a stuffed bear she kept on her TV. She had developed this approach after we had been broken into a few years back and all of her jewellery, jewellery she had loved – gold necklaces, jade bracelets, ruby and diamond rings kept as insurance against financial disaster – had been taken.

I took the bear and a fruit knife and unpicked the seams. Money burst open from its stomach. I put it in my pocket and cleaned up the mess of stuffing and fabric it had made. I sewed it up and put it back. Then I took the bus back to the store and bought the dress with the cash, relishing the expensive shock hardening on the faces of the shopkeepers. It was only when I got home that I felt like dirt. Formal came and I wore a borrowed dress from a friend – I never wore the blue velvet dress. I couldn't have. I hid it in my bottom drawer and felt like a fool every time I saw it poking out from behind a glut of old socks.

It was months after formal when Ah Ma realised her money was missing. The wailing and ranting from her room filled the house like smoke. I knew immediately. My heart turned to ash. I listened from my room as Ikanyu told her she had probably lost or misplaced the money and that no one had stolen it. When she couldn't be consoled, he offered to withdraw whatever she had lost from the bank and give it to her. *I don't want your money*, she screamed. *I want the money that was stolen from me. I want my money.* When I entered the room, Ikanyu told me to go back into my room and not get involved. But Ah Ma could tell straight away from looking at me. She looked into my small white face and knew I wasn't innocent. I decided I would confess – better to confess than be outed and I was sick of holding on to this terrible secret. But on seeing me her demeanour changed. She rummaged around in her drawers and suddenly pulled out a bundle of notes. *Ah, I've found it,* she said. *It was here all along and I forgot.* Ikanyu left the room in disgust, and I stood there just looking at her. I sat on the floor and we watched TV together as if nothing had happened. *I sayang you,* she said quietly.

In Clementine's room I sat down in my usual spot without saying anything, and she began painting with the nail polishes, mixing them with the more expensive artist paints. She worked silently and I thought about how I would ask her about when she might be finished with me. I kept saying what I wanted to say very loudly in my head, but it just sounded like silence to her. I finally got to the point of trying to say it with my mouth but she spoke before I could.

'You're not wearing the same clothes, are you?'

'No.'

I was wearing a striped shirt and a pair of old jeans. The white dress, having been hung up only the day before was still dripping wet. I had hoped that a shirt would be more or less the same to her.

'Can you change back into the same clothes please?'

'I'm sorry, the dress is still wet. I washed it yesterday.'

'Why did you wash it when you knew I needed it?'

'It's been a week. It was pretty dirty.'

'But I need to paint now. I've just got everything out. Could you wear the dress wet? It'll only be for a little while.'

I hesitated. 'No, sorry.'

'Well, I can't paint then,' she said.

'Actually, I was going to talk to you about that,' I began, ready to throw myself into asking her the question but she interrupted me.

'How long will it take to dry?'

I said I didn't know. How long did it take clothes to dry in a damp basement? I wasn't used to washing my own clothes generally, let alone washing them in a cold country. Clementine said nothing. She began packing up her things, shoving paints and brushes and cups and everything into a wooden box, displacing her anger at me onto the random objects. I said nothing. I wanted to hold each object in my hand and speak tenderly to it. But I didn't. I left the studio and closed the door behind me quietly.

Alone in my room, I found myself with no real reason not to work on my novel or at the very least on my research. I realised with a jolt that I was free for at least the day, or a couple of days, maybe even a week. I bolted the door to my room, locking myself in to working at my desk, and sat expectantly at the desk waiting for the writing to happen to me.

I decided to start by working on my paper for the postcolonial literature conference in London. It would be adapted from the first chapter of my dissertation on Plath and the postcolonial.

When I had first started working with my supervisor she had told me that I needed to start by writing a literature review. The point of the literature review, she said, was to clear space in the forest of other scholar's work to make way for my own, which sounded terribly similar to deforestation but I didn't say anything like that to her. As I reviewed the literature about Plath, I found that there wasn't a lot of existing literature that dealt with Plath through the lens of race, which was when I knew I had found my clear, white space in the forest. My supervisor was excited when I told her about this; she encouraged me to pursue Plath through a postcolonial lens saying she thought it would be the best way for me to find a job in the oversaturated academic market after I had graduated. As for me, she said, smiling, I am a white woman who specialises in postcolonial studies, so it's amazing that they let me have this job at all. But for you, it will be easier, they won't have any problems with you. I never asked her who 'they' were. All the academics specialising in postcolonial literature at my university – scratch that, all of the academics in the English faculty – were white, so I didn't know why she thought being white posed such a problem. Then I worried that by 'they' she meant me. But that couldn't be it – she had invited me to her house for lunch and cooked me a roast baby potato salad with lots of butter and herbs because I had once professed a love for potatoes to her. And I had eaten the potatoes because I was a huan chu. Huan chu was what Ah Ma called me whenever I ate potatoes because I loved them so much. Huan chu meaning potato in Hokkien. It also meant idiot or fool, but I didn't know about that doubleness until later.

The thing with working on Plath through a postcolonial lens was that what I actually meant by that was that I was interested in looking at representations of race in her work. But I didn't feel like I could use a word like 'race' straight out so I used the very professorial-sounding word 'postcolonial' instead, even though it didn't quite fit the subject matter. A postcolonial reading of *Jane Eyre* or *Mansfield Park* was one thing but a postcolonial reading of Plath didn't make as much sense. But I didn't want to use the word 'race' or 'critical race studies' because I noticed that the word 'race' made people awkward around me. And 'critical race studies' sounded, well, critical and I didn't want to sound as if I was criticising anyone, least of all Plath who I knew was considered sacrosanct. 'Race' felt like a crude, simplistic word said with brutish emotion but 'postcolonial' sounded theoretical and distant and impressive.

I opened up my copy of *The Bell Jar* with all of its sticky notes and highlighted sections. I started by tracing the origins of the shantung sheath Esther Greenwood wears in New York on that sweaty night out with Doreen. I looked up the word 'shantung' and found that, as I had suspected, it was an orientalist reference. I noted that in the late nineteenth century the word 'shantung' denoted a type of coarse silk from the Shantung province in China where the fabric was made. Then I made a note of the way the cut of the dress gives Esther a boyish, hipless form. In it, she has the 'odd colour of a Chinaman." The dress was a costume of sorts; with it she was transformed into a skinny, androgynous-looking Chinese boy. On the other hand, her more sexually daring friend Doreen, though white, was described as a 'dusky bleached, blonde negress'. So together, Esther and Doreen represented two ends of a racially constructed continuum – Esther was a sexless Chinese boy, a 'good' minority, and Doreen was an oversexualised Black woman, a 'bad' minority. I didn't describe this in my notes as racist, though it was. I described it as 'familiar' or 'constructed' or 'the reverberations of a colonial discourse in an era of segregation'. Then I brought it all back to the passage that haunts me – the one where Plath looks in the mirror of the elevator and sees herself as a 'big, smudgy-eyed Chinese woman'. This all fell under a chapter called 'Plath's Doubles' because of how Esther was writing an honours thesis on 'doubles' in *Finnegan's Wake.* I kept going and going at 797 horsepower, skipping lunch to keep going, working all the way up until dinnertime. It felt great and a relief and so much more satisfying that sitting in a studio with Clementine all day. It felt like all the windows being open in the house to let the cool air in after a hot, airless day in the Australian summer. I felt grateful that I had washed the dress and she had gotten angry at me and I got to be alone again for a while.

Dinner that night was huge tureens of yellow soup, purple salads, herby green pastas and lots of fresh bread. I was indecisive at the best of times; I often felt in cafés that I only knew what I truly wanted to eat after the waitress had left our table with our orders. And what I truly wanted to eat was usually the opposite of whatever I had ordered. If I had ordered poached eggs, I really wanted them scrambled. If I had ordered a sandwich, what I really wanted was granola, and so on.

My indecision hovered and heaved over the dinner options, as I watched everyone else heap their plates high. I ended up with three filled bowls, one for the soup, one for the salad and one for the pasta so I couldn't go wrong. In the end, I ate a full-sized meal of everything so as not to miss anything. Perhaps I wasn't indecisive, I was just greedy. I wanted everything life could give me and wanted it at all times.

I always ate my meals at the corner of the big wooden table, so I could look out the big window that showed the garden and the sea and the sky. Jack and Otto sat on the right side together, Maeve sat on the left and Clementine sat opposite me.

Otto got up from the table and brought out a cheap white wine from the fridge and began pouring glasses.

'Do you want some?' he asked me.

I tried a little but found the taste as sour as a jealous ex and I couldn't get used to it. Ikanyu's years spent in the navy and Ma's years spent on the night shift of Sunshine Hospital's ED ward had made them believe that alcohol was only good for casual violence and spiking the drinks of innocent young girls, so we never had it at home.

The conversation had turned to MAS370. There had been some kind of new discovery in the news that day. Some debris had washed up on a beach on a small island near the Indian Ocean.

'Do you think they'll find the black box?' Maeve asked.

'I don't think so. The ocean's like space, they say. We don't know anything about it,' Otto answered. Otto taught art classes part time at a high school in Dundee. I got the sense that he was used to explaining things. It was a very comforting presence to have about the place.

'Someone said that everyone on the plane is actually living on an island together and creating a new community,' Clementine said.

'I read the other day that one of the new theories is that there was some kind of fruit in the cargo. And also tonnes of lithium batteries. They could have somehow mixed with the fruit and created a fire,' Maeve said.

'That doesn't make sense of the different flight pattern, though,' Jack said. 'The pilot pivoted into a totally different direction and flew around for hours before the plane disappeared.'

'I hate to say it but I think Malaysia is covering something up to do with the pilot,' Otto said. 'He flew that exact same path on the flight simulator they found at his house. They keep trying to say what a happy, stable family man he was. But the rest of the investigation has been made classified. They don't want to share what they discovered.'

I began to feel a little sick. The whole thing made me feel so sad. But I didn't say that. I felt there was nothing stupider or more superficial to say about a news report than that it made you sad. I didn't think I had the right to insert myself into the story in that way. But I also didn't know how else to feel about it.

'Do you know anything about it?' Clementine asked me.

'No,' I said.

'Aren't you from Malaysia?' she asked.

'My parents are.'

'Are you covering something up for the government? We can't trust them. How can we trust you?'

She started giggling and I supposed she must be a little drunk. I wondered if what she was saying was a kind of retribution for seeing her pinch the nail polish, or for not sitting for her that day, or washing my dress, or doing my own work for once, or something else I hadn't even realised I'd done.

'I don't know,' I said at last.

'You wouldn't know anything about something that sordid and messed up, would you? You're perfect.'

'I never said that.'

'No, but you act it.'

I was surprised and I wasn't surprised at Clementine for turning on me in this way. I had initially been suspicious of her and then I had decided that maybe I had misjudged her. I had even wondered if the funny feeling I'd had about her initially was nothing more than jealousy. But no, it was disappointing to return to my initially banal conclusion: Clementine was not to be trusted. But surely, someone else at the table could be? I waited for someone to stand up for me but no one did. I had been led to believe, by the rather grandiose lectures from my undergraduate years, that making art was about standing up for something and for having an ethical framework that meant something. I started to feel that growing older was just a thousand losses of an innocence that had never really existed. I thought that someone might have said something, especially Maeve who seemed to like me or Jack who I obscurely thought I had a connection to because he was from my hemisphere.

Finally, to re-route the conversation, Maeve began speaking for the sake of speaking. She started playing the role of moderator on a writers' festival panel. The rest of the group continued the conversation as if nothing had happened.

I began to realise that as much as I thought of Clementine as a kind of Doreen figure, she thought of me as a sort of Betsy type – a type and not a person. That was the problem with always identifying with the protagonist of a coming-of-age novel, no one else but you ever got to come of age. You got to be an actual person and everyone else was just a symbol of a particular type of person or pathway. To Esther, Doreen and Betsy were not actual people, they were a fork in the road. Doreen showed Esther the kind of life she would have if she let herself 'go' and became like her: a salty-sweet 'bad girl' who did whatever she felt like and ended up passed out in her own vomit, half-naked and alone on the rug outside Esther's room. Besty showed her what her life would have been like if she did what everyone else wanted her to do: be a stupidly happy 'good girl' who smiled and followed the rules without ever questioning them and was rewarded with good health and modelling contracts and housework.

I couldn't imagine myself like this – as a 'good girl' who lives an obedient and airless life and accepts things without questioning them. But I was used to interesting and disobedient white people thinking of me like this. I knew how they saw me in their mind's eyes: as a tidy rule-keeper, as a pathway that showed them what their life might be like if they were dumb and cowardly enough to let society tell them what to do. Yes, I was an (ostensibly) obedient person but all the while there were unruly and strange things inside of me that were completely invisible and undefinable. And those were the things that mattered to me. Those were the things they would never be able to see.

When I was young, I thought I would escape my life. I was stupid enough to think that I would wear a blue velvet dress and become a part of the beautiful and interesting and clever people who would perfectly understand me. Now, I knew that these people would never understand me because they were so busy being beautiful and interesting and clever that they didn't have time to understand other people.

I got up from the table and went to my room. I could hear everyone still talking and laughing downstairs even after I'd locked the door. That was the most claustrophobic thing about residencies, you lived with these people you hadn't chosen and if you didn't like them, you couldn't escape them. I supposed that was the same as families in some ways. I didn't brush my teeth as a treat to myself. Then I lay in my bed, a weak person who didn't know what to say, and thought about calling my Ah Ma. But I didn't. What would I have told her anyway?

Seven

I woke up wanting to make things right with Clementine. The idea of having to put in the emotional work of having an enemy in such close proximity was exhausting to me. I supposed it was a little weak of me but I wondered how I could turn the other cheek. I went down to the basement and brought my damp white dress upstairs.

Wet and cold things were bad for me, I knew. My Big Aunty in Malaysia had chastised Ma for being too busy to cook fresh food for me as a toddler, preferring to batch cook vegetable congee, freeze it in small portions and leave it for Ah Ma to microwave while she worked. She had told Ma that I would end up with bone pain here and bone pain there. And when I started having back issues, twenty years later, she had chastised Ma again for not having listened to her. They had a Martha and Mary dynamic which was always confusing to me growing up because my mother was like a mountain to me. But there was this one person Ma lost all of her warm dominance and ice-cold impressiveness with – her older sister.

I took the wet, cold dress into my room and tried to put it onto the heater to dry, turning it every ten minutes or so to make sure it didn't get singed. Eventually it was dry enough. Not dry enough for a Chinese girl with bone pain exactly. But it would have to do. I put it on and made my way down to Clementine's studio. When I looked into the big mirror in the hallway as I passed by it, I saw that the fabric of the dress was especially white, having just been washed. It looked alive.

Clementine was crouched over her materials with big headphones over her ears, stretching out her canvases. It took a while for me to get her attention and when I finally did she jumped as if she was afraid of me – which I was starting to realise she was.

'I got the dress to dry more quickly,' I said, expecting my words to be a kind of apology and gift all at once.

'Oh,' she said. 'Don't worry about that. You can wear whatever you want to; I'm starting over, actually.'

'Will you still need me then?' I asked, already regretting that I'd framed it as a question.

'That'd be really great, actually. Thanks,' she said.

'Well, here I am,' I said.

I sat down in my usual spot in the sun and she sat opposite me as she always did. She painted silently, without cracking jokes and telling me stories as she had done before. She looked serious and focused; it was as if the persona she had put on the night before was just that – a persona not a person. I could tell that whatever she was doing was working for her. She painted with quick, dry brushstrokes, sometimes looking as if she was punishing the white space of the new canvas. I sat there in silence, giving her as much of myself as I could, choosing not to check out or let myself leave my body like a ghost. Looking straight at her and holding her gaze. My back hurt and it was unpleasantly cold in the studio that day, especially with a damp dress on, but I reasoned that if I didn't think about how unpleasant it was, it wouldn't be so unpleasant after a while. This thought experiment didn't work but I kept at it anyway.

'Thank you for sitting for me,' she said, breaking the silence of the last few hours.

'That's okay,' I said.

I was glad that we seemed to be friends again.

'No, I really, really appreciate it. I know it's your time and everything.'

'Don't worry about it,' I said. 'It's all good.'

'No, seriously, this is kind of collaborative. I want to do something to make that clear when it's done. Like name the painting after you or even list you as a collaborating artist.'

'It's fine.'

'No, really.'

'Thanks,' I said.

'It's like this more feminine way of thinking about creative work. The idea of the singular, male genius is such bullshit. And what if a way of deconstructing that in art practice is through collaborations and plurality. So that an artist is more than one person and an artwork isn't this thing that shoots out of you, a pure essence, and it's actually something else – something more generative and generous. And so what if my original vision is,' she raised her fingers in the shape of sardonic quotation marks, '"contaminated", by other people's thoughts?'

'I know. I've been thinking something similar,' I said.

'Figurative painting is so out of vogue, isn't it? But I secretly love it. Especially, formal and sat portraits like this,' Clementine said.

'I love them, too. But I know what you mean.'

'There's something almost too sincere about painting light falling on a human face.'

'Right. There's something about the honesty of that that feels really earnest. Which I love so much but which doesn't feel, like, cool?'

'Yes.'

'There are a lot of really bad portraits out there, though,' I said.

'Oh.'

'What?'

'I just wonder what you'll think of mine now.'

'I was actually thinking more of the Archibald. It's this huge Australian thing but gives me a really weird feeling sometimes.'

'I haven't heard of it.'

'No, you wouldn't have. But it's like Australian artists have to paint famous Australian people and then they go up for this big prize that gets covered by all the media and stuff.'

'That sounds really interesting. Like how we have the Portrait Gallery in London.'

'Right, yeah. But we don't really have huge celebrities in Australia. And the portraits that get made feel like they demonstrate everything that can go wrong with portraits ... they're kind of traditional and boring and a bit servile.'

'Like the portraits that get done of monarchs or presidents?'

'Exactly. And then there's always this big debate when an artist who has done something new wins. Like, "Is this really a portrait? Or is it a caricature? Is this too abstract to be a real portrait?" The only good ones are the self-portraits because they aren't beholden to anyone but the artist.'

'That makes me think of sixteenth-century patronage stuff. Like this rich person supporting an artist and then the artist having to make these portraits that toe the line between being sycophantic and beautiful. Or something.'

'I think of that when I see celebrity book club endorsements. Not that I wouldn't sacrifice my firstborn child for one but it's sort of the modern equivalent.'

'You'd want one? Even if it compromised your artistic integrity?'

'I'm kind of too desperate for integrity or ideals.'

'You're one of those? I wouldn't accept anything if it meant I lost autonomy over what I made or did. Don't you feel like you need to protect your creativity?'

'I don't think I have the luxury to think like that. I'm a second-generation immigrant. I don't have all of this family money to fall back on.'

There was a strange silence, in which my brain felt soupy and thick.

'You think I'm only an artist because my family's rich. We're not. But whatever.'

'I didn't mean you.'

'Who did you mean?'

'Most of the artists I meet went to private school and are trying the whole bohemian thing as an interesting pose. Maybe I'm just, like, jealous, though. Being jealous feels like a big part of being an artist or a writer. I find myself literally hating people for doing well and nit-picking little things about their work that I find so undeserving. Then I hate myself for doing that and the hate cycle goes on.'

'You use the privilege thing to justify that jealousy.'

'I don't think I use it. It's not a card I can pull out of my wallet and put back at will. Unfortunately, the card is printed on my face.'

'Do you think of me as privileged?'

'I don't know. I think that's more of a question that you have to ask yourself. I don't think anyone can put that on another person.'

'But you just did.'

'In an abstract way. I don't think it can be pointed. I don't think that achieves very much.'

'My parents really had to skimp and save for me to go to private school. And even then I never fit in with all of those prim and perfect girls. I was a kind of outcast.'

'I didn't mean you.'

'Okay.'

'Okay.'

We worked all the way till dinner when the wooden dining table was covered by an industrial-size tray of potato dauphinoise and a large silver pot of risotto made with Arbroath smokies. The food was good, but I was afraid of how rich and full of fat it was. Sometimes it felt like the only thing I had left was my thinness. I knew that, paradoxically, frailty and weakness in the body of a woman was a kind of armour, sword and shield against the scorn of the world. So, I had made a special discipline out of disappearing my own desires. It was the era of curvy women being called 'real women' as a part of the body positivity 'movement'. If that was the case, then what I wanted, I thought, was to be a fake woman. A person so unreal they barely even existed.

Otto was telling everyone how his old boss, the artist Adam Swan, had just been cancelled online for his work with school children from refugee backgrounds. Swan had worked with these children for a number of years, helping them express their feelings about their traumatic backgrounds and teaching them the secrets behind his accessible and charming googly-eyed paintings and sculptures. Recently there had been a showing of the children's artworks at a small gallery in London along-side Swan's own signature goofy and cartoonish artworks. Until recently it had been much lauded by critics and was popular with the public – school groups would fill the rooms of the tiny gallery to see these startlingly beautiful, darkly comic and very moving artworks. Swan had then been approached to publish a coffee-table book of these artworks and had, it now transpired, made quite a bit of money from it. It was this last step that had led the masses who had venerated Swan and his work with the refugee children to turn on him and expose him as colonising, profiteering, self-interested scum. Swan's good name and repu-tation had been ruined and he was said to be in the middle of a poor mental health episode. A small group from the larger group of refugee children he had worked with had come together and signed a letter explaining that they had consented to the use of their artworks in the book and that they believed his intentions to be sincere. At the end of the story Otto shook his head sadly as if to express general confusion and disapproval at the world we lived in these days.

'It's just like how people say we should remove Gaugin's paintings from galleries because he was a racist,' Clementine said. 'So was everyone in those days.'

'Context is everything,' Otto said wisely.

'What's wrong with Gaugin now?' Maeve asked.

'Only that he abandoned his family, moved to Tahiti where he became a "savage", took a thirteen-year-old girl as his child bride and gave syphilis to most of the other young girls on the island. And his paintings look like postcards home of all the women he got to bed on this exotic heathen land,' I said in my head.

'But to go back to Adam Swan,' Jack said. 'The children themselves don't have a problem with him so why should these people online? Cancellation feels so primitive. Like that book about how public humiliation has always been part of our culture except it used to take the form of public executions and whippings. The point of them is creating fear, which in turn creates conformity.'

'I don't see how Swan learning about how to see things from the perspective of some people of colour can be comparable to a public execution. If anything, he should be paying the people educating him for their emotional and professional labour,' I said silently.

'Everything these days is racist. Like, tell me something I don't know,' Clementine said.

'I can see how hearing about the pain of others, pain that they never asked for and that you benefit directly from, could sound boring or passé to you, Clementine,' I said silently, so quietly and so deep inside my mind that no one heard.

The silence stretched like chewing gum across time. It might have been only a few seconds, or a few minutes, but it felt like a length of time that couldn't have been measured numerically. And then the conversation turned to other things.

That night, as I lay in bed, my parents called me. They said it was to see how I was. They had to mask their actual desire to speak to me with concern because real desire would have been too embarrassing to admit. I hadn't told my parents about Clementine or the other artists. Racism was the easiest thing Ikanyu had ever faced and he considered it nothing to complain about. He felt much the same about women complaining about being tired when they were on their periods, or getting emotional when they were pregnant, or all of these modern parents saying having kids was hard work. That was the thing about surviving against the odds, you began to be personally offended by the weakness others regularly displayed. In our family's world, the idea of putting the word 'suffering' into my story was always a little maudlin, a little feeble. It was inappropriate for me to mind anything given what had come before me.

What had come before me. It was this thing that we never really talked about. I knew, of course, that Ah Ma had been a maid, *no in those days we didn't use the word maid, we used the word servant, and I was the servant's son.* Ah Ma took the boss's children to school and walked them home. She nursed them on her lap all night when they were sick. She poured them soft drinks and made them breakfast. When he was in the right mood, she made jokes with her boss while she made him his coffee. She sang the songs the boss's wife liked while she did the laundry. She was always smiling, seemingly having the time of her life. Everyone that employed her said she was the best servant they had ever had.

But when she turned her face to Ikanyu it was a face of stone. A child was a burden and he was sickly, which made him a double burden because of the doctor's fees. She was lucky to have even gotten work given that she had this small, wheezing boy with her. She was angry about how this lot had fallen into her lap every moment of every day and every night.

It wasn't something I was supposed to ask about. There were a lot of things I wasn't supposed to ask about. Ma would say *you dare ask*, and that was enough to stop me. But once I did dare ask Ikanyu about it and he couldn't tell me anything about how he felt or what went through his mind in those times. It was as if he had no consciousness and asking questions about it frustrated him. He would say things like, *Ah Ma chained me with a dog chain to the bottom of the staircase so I wouldn't get in the way of her work*. And then almost before I could ask how that felt he would say he felt nothing about it. Was he angry? Of course not. So, he understood her motivations? No, not that. There was just nothing.

- *I had no anger.*
- *I had no preferences.*
- *I had no thoughts.*
- *I had no money.*
- *I had no happiness.*

- *I had no unhappiness.*
- *I had no desires because I knew I couldn't have them anyway. So, there wasn't any point.*

Ikanyu told me that there was no such thing as good and bad in those days. There were just days. There was just a raised piece of wood where you slept and a beating if you asked for anything and sometimes there were a few cents in your father's pocket and he gave them to you when he came to visit and Ah Ma's bitterness towards him for what he had done and she was a maid – *no in those days they didn't use the word maid, they said servant – and I was just the servant's son and I knew my place. I knew my status. I knew my world. I didn't mind school but I wasn't good at remembering anything so it was hard for me. And everyone else could afford tuition and toys and stationery and all of that. And I had nothing. Not that I minded. No, I don't remember what kind of things they had. Maybe spinning tops or balls or marbles. You know those days what toys were. They would all be playing with them and I would wonder why I didn't have any and they did. But I wasn't jealous.*

And then suddenly there was England. He couldn't have afforded a newspaper but one day he found yesterday's discarded on the road and it said join the navy and he did. Did you tell your friends you were going? *No, I didn't know what to tell them.* So, it wasn't a big deal? *It was. No one I knew had ever been on a plane. Flying was as unlikely as raising your arms and lifting off into the sky.* But no one cared? *They were jealous. Very.* What did they say? *Nothing. Good for you. Oh. Actually, I had one best friend, the rich man's son. The son of Ah Ma's employers. I slept over at his house the night before I left and we talked all night until the sun came up because we knew I was going. But a month after I went to England I got a letter saying he had died. Motorcycle accident.*

But before that we had three months of basic training at the base in Malaysia. We were a group of forty boys and twenty of us would go to Australia and twenty to England and the guy who trained us hated us he was so jealous. He made us do our marching at twelve noon everyday when the sun was at its highest. He made us march to get our payslips and salute and if we didn't salute right he would make us run circles with the fire extinguisher held over our head just to humiliate us. And then we could do it all again, march and salute. All of that just for seventy ringgit. The day before we left he got out a pair of scissors and gave us all haircuts but only on the right side of our heads so we would look like fools when we got there. Lots of boys were crying as they got their hair cut. But you know me, I never cry.

And then London, we got there just after Christmas and I walked around in the snow with no money and no friends in the thin jacket they had given us, freezing. I was curious about everything. I hadn't seen a picture show of England; I hadn't even seen a drawing of it. Of course, people called me names yellow what? Yellow Peril. And Slant Eye and Chingchingchingchingchong-chong. And when we started out training. There were the things the seniors did to us juniors they aren't allowed to do any more. Initiation, you know, you had to climb up on the metal beams of the dormitory and hang there for hours and sometimes they'd even sharpen the beams so the edges cut into you. But I didn't get picked on much because I was smart. I said nothing and they couldn't report me. It was all so wonderful to me. The food they gave us was one hundred times better than what they gave us in Malaysia. I ate rabbit and stew and fish and chips and roast and spaghetti and you know all the Ang Moh stuff. The kind of rich food they eat here. I got stronger; that was all I wanted. I got strong on gallons of milk, the most expensive kind we could order, with the cream on top, and I ran and ran and ran and ran till I couldn't run any more.

I told my parents I was good and everything was fine. This was the kind of conversation we were adept at having. I had grown up amongst people who had believed that talk was the cheap currency of the Ang Moh. It was the overprinted paper money of a self-satisfied alien race. And as for expressing the self, which seemed to be the great project of the Western world, this was simply embarrassing given the sacred otherness of another person's interiority. It didn't make any sense to put one's interior self on the market via an open house inspection. This didn't mean that you couldn't sense how another person might feel or think; on the contrary, it made you more perceptive to the way small things signalled at bigger things and how language was not the only way to think through it all. How anger masked love, for instance. My parents and Ah Ma were always so angry at me growing up because they articulated their love for me through fear of losing me to something or someone else. Perhaps this was all wrong, but it was the way it was. I said goodnight and they told me to be good and I gave into my dreams and fragmented sleep.

I woke up from a dream about Ah Ma. We were eating noodle soup out of plastic bowls and I was small again. I wouldn't eat so she traded the fish balls in my bowl with the peh chai. I ate all the meat and she ate all the vegetables. I woke up and thought: Ah Ma would never have been than indulgent. But then again, maybe she would have been.

I got into my white dress and went to the studio to sit for Clementine again. And it was as if the night before hadn't happened or if it had, it had happened a very, very long time ago. She painted vigorously, as if inspired by my silence.

Eight

I was starting to feel so tired of sitting for Clementine. It had been a whole fortnight now and still she hadn't let me go. She worked relentlessly, as if possessed by the idea she had of me. Sometimes we skipped lunch and worked all the way through till dinner, and I felt my stomach acid splash like lava against its lining.

The only thing that gave me some comfort was that on the weekends she didn't usually work so I turned the heater in my room up to the highest setting and lay in my bed with the sheets twisted around me like a spool. The warmth felt like a kind of immobilising love. My back was hurting, my shoulder blades cut into me – it felt like they were bursting out of my skin sometimes. The pain was an unpleasant soundtrack to my life that I couldn't switch off or turn my attention away from.

It was Sunday. Mother's Day. I thought I should give Ma a call but instead I lay in my bed and read Plath's *Letters Home*. Reading Plath's letters to her mother from when she was away at Smith College was like watching YouTube video tours of celebrity homes or scrolling the Net-a-Porter website – they were a very comforting genre of fiction. Except that I sometimes let myself be carried away by their pull and saw them as realer than the so-called reality I lived in. I felt sedated, calmed, made forever happy by the idea that there were people out there who had succeeded in insulating their life from suffering entirely. The false brightness of Plath's letters flickered like a strobe light in a dungeon. She was so convincing. And I recognised myself in them. Like Plath I had an intelligent but thwarted mother who pursued life through her daughter. I moved so quickly from that first idea to the second one sometimes – from mother to daughter – but that day, I paused on the original idea – the mother. My mother.

My mother's gifts were like instruments that no one had ever taught her how to play. They lay in the corner wondering what to do with themselves.

My mother's gifts were like instruments that no one had ever taught her how to play. She made her own janky, loud-mouthed, difficult, angry music from them.

My mother's gifts were like instruments that no one had ever taught her how to play. She used them to make unheard of sounds – the sound of water rushing from the tap as she washed rice to get the starch out, the cymbal clash of her spatula hitting the pan, the soap opera opening theme song after she woke up from night shift, the sound of her laughing and pocketing the coins when she won another game of mah jong.

My mother's gifts were like instruments no one would ever dare to teach her how to play. She did whatever she wanted with them and made life dance for her over and over again. She had a natural charisma that made her seem taller than the sun. Some-times it felt like she had by the mystery of transubstantiation made something out of nothing and that something was her-self and the nothing was what she had. She was never joyless or afraid. At least that's what she wanted me to believe and, for the most part, I believed her.

Still, I recoiled from her sometimes. She couldn't completely understand me because she only understood me through the lens of herself. I was her double, her antagonist and her everything. It made me want to vomit and rise to the occasion. She considered me her difficult, Australian child. Her only child who knew how to despise vegetables and complain that things were 'unfair' and whose primary school teacher had told them that in Australia parents that hit their children could be reported to child services. I remembered that day – armed with my bright, new knowledge. *You can't hit me any more*, I had said. *My teacher said that the police will take you away for that*. My mother had told me to call the *polis* then. Call them. And I had realised how futile it was to think I could get away from her.

When I felt most sad, I thought about all the ways I would be a different kind of mother – one that let their kid off the hook too much and spoiled them and didn't expect anything of them. I fantasised about all the opposite ways in which I, too, would one day destroy my child.

Then I thought about how on my birthday, she would let me skip school and she would call in sick to work and we'd watch a movie and go to McDonald's and then I would only have to practise all my pieces on the piano three times over that day.

Then I would think about how I had once asked my mother if she liked hearing me play the piano and she had said no, not really, and that it was pretty awful hearing a child practise and make a million mistakes.

The thing that my mother didn't realise is that by placing little ticks and crosses next to my name as I went about my life she had taught me to do the same thing to her.

I was my mother's avatar and her greatest ambition. She wanted me to be clever and successful but not a swot. She wanted me to be beautiful and well groomed but not vain or made up. She wanted me to always win but be gentle and humble of heart. In other words, she wanted me to be perfect. And for such a long time I was. But now there were cracks in the mirror when I looked at it. It started with a small line in the corner of the glass. And then it became a long line across my face. And now there was a starburst at the dead centre that made it look as if a high-speed object had been hurled at it. And now, like the nurse at Esther's mental asylum told her: I was just seven years of bad luck and a shattered mirror on the ground.

Children are born to be boasted about so what happens if they shatter like a mirror? Immigrants are imported to work so what happens if the useful little engine breaks down? Then I started thinking about how boring and useless it was to be thinking of my family – my three parents and me – when I should be working on my novel or on myself or something.

My phone began to buzz; it was Ma, of course. She called almost every day, which made me feel special and smothered at the same time. I picked up the phone and wished her a happy day. I told her everything was fine and that I was going well, and she told me she was so happy for me. She told me how everyone was and then she laughed and said that Ah Ma was worried for me.

'Worried how?'

'She thinks you're exhausted and in pain all the time, that you're so sick you can't even get out of bed. She told me off, you know. She said, "Your only child is sick, and you don't even do anything for her." Maybe you should call her to tell her you're okay.'

'Okay.'

I didn't call her, but I thought a lot about her. How much she telepathically knew about me and how little I had always known about her. As I lay in bed feeling sorry for myself, I moved towards thinking of Ah Ma and wanted to write about what had happened to her but I didn't know if I had any right to it. Ah Ma hated photographs of herself and talking about her life. She disliked people who asked too many questions. I had been to lectures during my undergraduate years where the lecturer talked about things like the ethics of representation and said wise things like 'art without ethics is only an accessory', which we would all write down in our notebooks in acknowledgement of the knowledge that was being passed on to us. And Ah Ma was not only reticent about her past; in the last few years she had also begun to forget it wholesale. Where once her constant anger had been a vestige of that time, a self-respecting sense that she refused to let go or forgive, she had begun to move from scowling to absently smiling, from violence to strangely timed laughter. It made me miss those days when she chased me with her bamboo stick and screamed at me for no reason. I missed the times when she refused to let anyone forget how furious her life made her, even if it was nearly over, even if it was long ago.

Ah Ma's doctors had told us something that I didn't understand: that the hippocampus and the amygdala, those strange foreign place names, were becoming unmoored from the rest of the brain. The frontal cortex was shrinking, its nerve cells were blinking like bad lights, then their bulbs were blowing altogether. I couldn't understand it. They said the brain was damaged. But how could something undamaged become damaged without cause.

This was what I understood: Ah Ma would never forgive what had happened to her so long ago. But she could forget it. She was forgetting more and more these past few years, forgetting even to be angry, to judge, to yell, to be herself. And this hurt me because she had had such a long memory for everything that had gone wrong for her. And that was what I had loved about her, her honesty about how much everything hurt her. Ma and Ikanyu said what's past is past and let bygones be bygones and water under the bridge and their favourite: move on.

I thought about something Ikanyu had told me – that Western civilisation is about history, that the colonial fetish for administration, for taxonomy, for detail meant they kept records of everything or, perhaps, the way they saw everything. But that Chinese history had been destroyed with every new dynasty. Our history fails us, he had said. But then he would think of this as a kind of contradictory magic and tell me about language and how it shaped us. How there aren't any tenses in Chinese, how left and leaving and leave are more or less the same word. And how that had shaped us, made us able to survive, to wear our past lightly, to move through time more flexibly. And I thought about what bullshit that was.

It was a falsehood and nothing more. It was a falsehood because they had always told me about their past and buried it inside me like a time capsule. And they had thought I was their bright, clean and perfect future with my heap of shiny trophies and important-looking pieces of paper. But that futureness comprised completely of their pastness.

It was only now that I was flung far away into this future away from my past and my family, lying in a four-poster bed in a strange and foreign land, that I saw the book I wanted to write so much more clearly. I saw Australia and I saw Malaysia and I saw myself and my family in my mind's eye. I pulled myself up and sat at my desk expectantly, ignoring the fact that my spine was aching. I wrote on a piece of paper, *Pillar of Salt*, and drew a line under it that felt very final. *Pillar of Salt* because that would be the name of the book I was writing and anything I had written before this point could be thrown out completely. *Pillar of Salt* because I was like Lot's wife – always looking back with a secret longing for a place I could never return to: the past. The book would be a way of preserving that, of preserving myself really. I was obsessed with remembering the moment before everything had changed. Lot's wife had sinned by looked back for a half second and was punished by being turned into a pillar of salt – so she would be looking back for ever, stuck in that attitude of longing. A longing she could never come any closer to fulfilling – a sickening feeling of tasting nothing. That was me.

I wondered if it hurt to be made into a pillar of salt or if it was all right or like you were dead.

I googled 'pillar of salt' and was surprised when a photograph came up of an actual pillar of salt standing at the shore of the Dead Sea. I tried to work out if it looked at all like a woman but it was hard to tell – what did a woman look like, anyway? Archae-ologists said that 'salt floes in the Dead Sea had likely thrown up surging water creating this vaguely female form'. I liked that phrase 'vaguely female form'. It sounded like me – with my thin hips and straight down-the-line body, I had a vaguely female form.

I was thinking about Lot's wife and Genesis even though I wasn't really religious any more. I was thinking about all these things because the thing about being raised religious is that you could tell your parents you didn't believe any more, you could stop going to church and Bible study group and potluck nights at people's houses and all of the many activities that made up the so-called Christian life, but you could not outrun God. If he had been imprinted onto you as a child in a Chinese church, as he had been on me, then Yesu was always with you in some way, even if you hated him or thought he was nonsense or mean or an evil idea or a form of control. Even if you fall out of love with God, the bitterness you felt towards the bad ugly things about the Church, the rage at religion in all its forms, the heartbreak, in short, still remains. For me the most beguiling thing about faith was the Bible – I'd loved the stories as a child and been even more impressed by the writing of it as an adult. I was what my parents and the other church members would call a 'lost sheep' now but secretly, the Bible was still one of the most beautiful books in the world to me.

There were so many mysterious things about God in that book when it was really meant to reveal him to mankind. Like no one in the Bible being able to see his face without dying. I thought that if I saw his face and didn't die I would ask him what it was like to make the colour blue and why he chose it. Then I would also ask him why he had punished Lot's wife. Was she really so wicked for looking back just once? I thought she had made a pretty human mistake – one I knew I would have made under similar circumstances.

The novel I was writing was going to be called *Pillar of Salt* and it would be made up of the past, of my family's past, and how it felt to always be looking back at what happened. How it felt when it was your job to remember and carry everything and how painful it felt sometimes to be born with a perfect memory for things. How hard it was for me to exist or live when I remembered everything and everything I remembered made a place that I wanted to live in for ever.

I had never been the kind of person to fight something. I let things happen and waited to see what would become of me. It was going to be the same with the book, I realised. I could let the past happen and allow it to overwhelm me completely, and that would be the book.

I started writing, happy because for the first time in my life I had a book in my head and now all I needed was for my hands to write it out.

Pillar of Salt

I go. I go back in time and place, Ikanyu on the plane with me. Ikanyu doesn't speak much about the things that happened to him: what's past is past. But he has the self-righteousness of someone who has seen and suffered enough. He thinks people are to blame for their own problems; if he could escape everything in Malaysia then why can't they escape in Australia? Me and Ikanyu, we argue about this on the plane, we argue about it in the airport and then we are driving through Penang and on the bridge to Butterworth in silence. He thinks Australia is too soft, too good, like a big bed with lots of pillows. Everyone is half asleep there. This sounds like scorn, but then think. This is what he wanted for his girl.

We are driving slowly past the sea, half unseeable behind a green and blue block of flats, tall green fences in that pandan colour, empty stall shaped like a young coconut, Protons parked parallel, bougainvillea, a Tropicana Twister vending machine, a temple, high-rise flats and construction sites for more high-rise flats, the sound of someone starting their motorcycle, abandoned parking lots, the rust fences taken over by lush weeds, a small playground in dirty pastel, a Malay woman with a Mayo Magic apron and plastic gloves on staring at us. Last time there was only one temple around, now there are so many.

Then we are there, back in the place he left. There is a wide-open space, dirt driven on, there is a tree with green mangoes clustered on it, all alone. A Tiger beer and a Guinness ad, both upside down, used as what? I do not know. There are roosters in cages and there's a small rust covering over a car. *Oh ga-u garage kee. Last time boh.* There's even a garage now. We walk through their garage to a narrow walkway stuffed with pot plants, dusty plastic chairs, those glass windows shaped like large blinds that you could shut in or out. There's the sound of a baby fussing, a Bollywood song playing from somewhere inside, miscellaneous yelling, glimpses of lit-up shrines. A red letterbox, 2940 hanging on a fence covered in clothes and leaves. A house just like all the others, wood, white, rust, with a motor out the front and a Manchester United jersey hanging from the line.

There it is. We are walking and an old Malay woman, at once one hundred years old and thirty years old, with the face of a soothsayer, hits Ikanyu hard on the arm. He looks at her. He is looking at her and she is saying his name. She was there then and she is there now. She is ninety-five, she says, but she is still having children. She has eighteen children and eighty-seven grandchildren. She hits him again in disbelief. Annie is dying, she says. She doesn't say it like gossip or like a message; she says it like a prophecy. Ikanyu nods but says nothing. They keep talking in Malay.

I wander off to the back of the house, looking at the deep-down street drain. A fat rat runs past, rubbish floating along in the water. A voice creeps right up behind me.

'Hello, Ah Girl.'

'Hello, Aunty,' I say.

It is an auto-reply, I say it without even turning around.

'Not Aunty, Grandma.'

Her hands are grasping my waist as if afraid it might unfurl. She kisses me on the cheek. There are kisses that are given and kisses that are taken. This was a kiss that had been taken. I say nothing about it.

Later I would ask Ikanyu who the woman was, and Ikanyu would say that Ah Ma was Wife Number One and that the woman who called herself Grandma was Wife Number Two. Before this moment, I had thought that 'first' meant the Olympic athlete on the podium, the one who held a gold shining place that no one else could claim. It was the opposite way when it came to wives, I now knew. First meant the one who was not enough, the one who was cast out. Ah Ma became a maid in a big, strange house after Wife Number Two moved into her house. She cared for other people's children, cleaned other people's houses, cooked other people's food so that her children could play with the boss's children; she lived in a corner room of the big house and ate the scraps that fell from their lips.

Wife Number Two looked ordinary. No one looked like Ah Ma with her dark skin, sad eyes and bitter mouth. Her hunch and bad leg drifting over floorboards. She was happiest when she was angry and making other people angry. The second wife was a woman like other women. Fresh perm and hair dyed a blue-black colour. She liked to be likeable. Her glasses were darkening in the sun. I was often surprised by the unremarkableness of the women men left their wives for. Often, they were younger but uglier, fatter, shorter. Other times they looked and sounded identical to the first. In my view, men had bad taste in women and women had bad taste in men.

As I turned these things over in my mind, I felt anger blooming in me like a sudden flower. An anger that I had never known I had before and which I knew I would forget again. This was the sin that fell upon the third and fourth generations. The anger that would mark me and my children's children for ever. I was afraid it might kill me one day. I had found Ah Ma's rage monotonous and heavy as it pressed down on my childhood. Her casual violence and her hard face, her self-pity. Now I knew something else. No maid raged and grimaced like Ah Ma. A maid is the angel of the house, wordless, smiling stupidly, nodding, eating last, agreeing. She is the perfect mother no one ever has. And so, Ah Ma didn't think of herself as a maid any more. She had come into my childhood as a real mother, angry at her son, resentful of her daughter-in-law, a grandmother chastising her grandchildren, a matriarch demanding the best of the best for her and for her alone.

We are already leaving, the back way, walking to the beach. There, I see a boat turned over, abandoned, purple flowers and green leaves growing all over it. There, I see a broken aquarium with a motor helmet in it like a large round fish. There is a sign faded from the sun, advertising Satay Ayam, Satay Daging and Ketupat Nasi. A wheelbarrow and a bicycle are turned over on the path. Then there is the beach; it used to come all the way up but now it is only this. Still, it is beautiful, it was always beautiful. You can see Penang Island from here, crowned by its heavenly cloud of smog. And the little boats with the fisherman and the big blue emptiness. This is where Ikanyu used to watch the fisherman catching the tiny sweet fish, bringing the haul in, selling, bartering. Now not so much of that, but still.

When I was small, Great Aunty Annie used to live in a big house in Singapore with shiny tiles and a china cabinet filled with a backlog of all the different McDonald's toys released with Happy Meals each week. She lived alone there and bought us fried noodles wrapped in brown paper when we came to visit her. She would unwrap the noodles, slide them into a bowl for me and give me a metal fork because I was the Australian cousin and what did I know about chopsticks. The noodles would be red with a sugary chilli sauce and white with their essential blandness. And Ikanyu and Ma and I would complain about Singapore food on the flight all the way back to Penang. And then they would turn to complaining about Singaporeans themselves with the kind of specific xeno-phobia that people direct towards a country that is almost but not quite their own.

Now that I am big, Great Aunty Annie is living in Johor in the house of Ikanyu's cousins who I have only seen once or twice. The family are thin and brown and grasping. The kind of rich people that never buy a new jacket, who just like the feeling of the money being there.

After the soothsayer tells us Great Aunty Annie is dying, Ikanyu and I, we go and visit her. I sit with Uncle, a small man in glasses with a thin, undecided moustache. His daughter,

Helen, moves so slowly as if her limbs are always thinking before they speak. I dislike Helen and the slow way she raises a cup to her lips, the way she walks with a slow hunch as if she cannot support her own body weight. More to the point, I dislike Helen because when she and her dad visited Melbourne on holiday, they stayed with us to avoid paying for the cost of a hotel and Helen became Ah Ma's obsession. Ah Ma gave her money, food, even items of my clothing hoarded from the washing basket, cleaned and wrapped in paper as if they were store-bought gifts. Seeing Helen wearing my sweaters, even the ones I'd outgrown or didn't like all that much, was an insult I nursed even now as I sat with Helen and her dad, drinking tins of Kickapoo, eating groundnuts.

'How is your study, Girl,' Uncle asks, wiping his glasses, pedantic as an Iman.

'I'm working,' I lie.

'In what? Art or what?' Helen asks.

'No, media.' I don't dare make my lie more extravagant than that.

'Mediacoms?' Helen says, with genuine confusion in her voice.

'I might go and check on Ikanyu,' I say to escape conversation I have unnecessarily overcomplicated.

I walk down the hallway to a little room with a Chinese calendar on it. It is frayed at the top where the days have been ripped away. Ikanyu is sitting on a chair near a bed. Great Aunty Annie is sleeping.

'I think I tired her out,' Ikanyu says.

'So, how?'

'Not good.' He sighs and he gets up. 'I better go and say hello to your uncle. You stay here, is it?'

'Yes.'

I sit with Aunty Annie and watch her sleep. Great Aunty Annie is still Ah Ma's opposite: younger, fairer, sweet-lipped, with round eyes rimmed by blue. But the things that made her beautiful when she was young are now the things that I think are taking her body away. now Ah Ma is still dark, robust, solid, cruel, she will survive anything and anyone. Great Aunty Annie, gentle and thin, is smaller than small in the face of death. She begins coughing and sits up. I pat Great Aunty Annie on the back and pass her a glass of water.

'Gam sia,' she coughs and drinks.

'That's okay.'

'Har? Is it Ah Girl?'

'Yes, Ikanyu is just outside.'

'Girl?'

'Girl.'

'Ah. How is your Ah Ma?'

'She is good, she's losing her memory.'

'Ah, ah.'

'But she's healthy, strong. She can still eat.'

'Be good-good, okay? Take care of Ah Ma.'

'Yes.'

'She is just like that, you know?'

'Yes.'

'She ...'

'Yes.'

'I couldn't help her, Girl. I was just a small girl, there was nothing I could do.'

I look down at my empty hands. I'm not sure what to say. Any time I want someone to keep telling me something, I sit very still and try to make myself as inconspicuous as possible so that I don't do anything that might make them stop.

'Do you remember what it was like for her?' I ask.

'Yes. And no.'

'I saw Wife Number Two yesterday.'

'Yes. But not only that.'

Great Aunty Annie, she told the story, it was a short one. Lai Kong, he was tricked into marrying Ah Ma and never loved her. He had been promised Aunty Annie, Ah Ma's younger, fair-skinned sister, but the family had tricked him into marrying their elder daughter with her hard looks. So he left her for his second wife. It had always been like that. First, Ah Ma's parents had preferred her sister to her, giving her the good bits of the meat and the few eggs they had, and calling Ah Ma greedy for raising a spoon to her lips. Then the husband had wanted the younger sister and not the older. Who had Great Aunty Annie been then? Was she Rachel, indifferent to Leah's suffering, or was she someone else?

Great Aunty Annie falls into the mysterium of sleep after this. I leave her and Ikanyu says goodbye to his cousin. In the car, I tell Ikanyu about her revelations. He surprises me by being willing to speak about them. He doesn't think the story is true. He thinks he knows the story. He knows where the story has ended for Girl. The philandering man leaves for another woman. Later he takes on a third and even a fourth wife. The bad man and the woman all alone.

It was true that Ah Ma's parents hadn't liked the sight of their firstborn daughter much. They had beaten her for the misdemeanours of her younger siblings. They treated her more like a maid than like a daughter then they married her off to the town drunk. He gave her two children and spent his payslip on alcohol on the way home from work. She became a maid, washing other people's clothes to feed her children. But he would beat her, take her small money and guzzle it. Both her first and her second son died of starvation. Lai Kong, he heard about Ah Ma. He had had compassion on her, married her and drove off to Penang with her to save her life. Then they had Ikanyu and she saw that she loved him but he had never loved her. Pity, empathy even, was not the same thing as love. Lai Kong had left Ah Ma for his second wife. And Ah Ma? She became a maid again.

Great Aunty Annie is gone by the next morning. We receive a slip of paper titled

'O B I T U A R Y' that indicates the date of the Leaving Behind Loves Ones Ceremony, Night Service, Cortège Leaving and the Cremation. We go to the church which is built in the modern religious style with the geometric wall-feature at the front, backlit and tall, wood-panelled ceilings that make the pastor look small. The crowd overflows into a small tent at the side for latecomers with plastic chairs and a screen with a digital image of a white cross bursting into light and clouds. People wear clothes in the smart Johor style, jeans, dark polos, white T-shirts with slogans, fresh perms and sneakers. Ikanyu and me are ushered into the latecomers' tent and given a full-colour pamphlet with a hill, a starburst, a rainbow and the words: WHAT A DAY THAT WILL BE WHEN MY JESUS I SEE. After this, the cremation hall. There is the coffin in the centre, surrounded by lit-up orange walls. I see Annie's still face through the glass of the coffin and wonder if this is how the cremation occurs, right in front of the guests. Will those orange walls light up and devour the body right there? The family put a new set of clothes in the coffin. Then the mourners place flowers, sandalwood and clove in the coffin, too. Then the body is taken away. I am relieved; I did not want to see the body burning bright with death.

The trip ends on a sour note. As we pack in our hotel room, Ikanyu and me are fighting. Ikanyu is angry at me for not tying my shoelaces properly and letting them be trampled in the mud under me, for leaving water around the sink, for not packing early, and angry that now I have crushed my clothes into the bag instead of folding them, for being nuah, for being wet mud that can't stick on the wall, which just slides off, lazy, as it is, for. For, for, for. I am strong with anger and crying absurdly. My tears are sad but also red, welted with the hot rush, and I think: *This anger, then, is my inheritance.* My anger is the sin of the father falling to the third and the fourth generations; my anger is my inheritance, my gold, my power in weakness.

Nine

I woke up improbably early in the morning the next day. It was still dark when I sat at my desk and read over what I had written of *Pillar of Salt*. When I read what I had so proudly written just fifteen hours or so before, I felt so ashamed. How had I thought that memories and pastness and myself would be all that a novel needed to be? I was bad at writing Malaysia – everything I wrote sounded like it had come straight from Lonely Planet even though my family and I had come from there.

I put my face in my hands and pretended to disappear so I could have some reprieve from myself.

Whenever I felt bad about my novel, I pivoted to my dissertation (and vice versa really) so I opened the online catalogue of my university's library on my laptop.

I borrowed the e-book of Plath's unabridged journals. I began reading from the start and then I got to the famous quote from Plath's time while she was at Smith: 'And I sit here without identity: faceless.'

I thought about how Plath had been lost without any sense of clear identity and how the opposite had been true for me. I was overburdened by the overdetermining of my identity. And 'faceless': no immigrant in the West has ever thought of themselves as faceless because that would be to think of oneself as raceless. And, as Ma had always made clear to me: the face is a metonym for one's race. The Chinese face, with its physical markers – eyes, nose, mouth, cheeks, chin, hair – confirmed to those who looked at me that race was physically inscribed upon the body. The markers argued against the idea that race was merely a construct created alongside racism itself. The markers said, Hello I am indelibly me, an identity I cannot shed. There is no blank canvas for the person of colour. And yet this was all about how the white gaze saw me. What about how I saw it?

The word faceless made me think of the Chinese idea of losing face, of having no face at all and, conversely, of having face, saving face. 'Face' as a metonym for one's dignity, pride, social standing – for your ability to face the world without lowering your gaze to your shoes. Losing face was in some ways the worst possible thing that could happen to a person. It made me think of T. S. Eliot. It made me think of a person peeling their face off their skull so all that remained was a gluggy mess of blood and bone and brain. It was a difficult thing to articulate even to myself because despite the way 'face' referred to outward appearances and, in some ways, superficial markers of success or happiness, the idea of face sat so far beneath the surface that it felt invisible to me. It was part of the culture's preconscious, it lived where our worst fears and pettiest resentments and most painful memories live. The problem with face was that it made you beholden to other people – I gave my three parents face when I was pretty, well groomed and well mannered, quiet and deferent before my elders, self-effacingly successful. In some ways, this was what Plath seemed to give her lone mother with her shiny trophies and little gold stars and healthy all-American looks. If Plath had been a Chinese girl, feeling small and alone and mentally unravelling in that big college, she would have felt as if she had no face. She had no face because she was poor, awkward, swotty and sick. And it took her everything she had to mask these things about herself. She was, as she wrote, faceless.

I wondered what the right way to read Plath was. Plath scholars were possessive of and protective of her work – each believing they understood its true essence more than the others. Whatever the right way to read her was, I was sure that I wasn't doing it.

But this had nothing to do with the paper I was supposed to be writing for the postcolonial conference. It was completely beside the point. And the conference was supposed to be important for me. My supervisor had told me that it was filled with sweating PhD students and academics who had not yet experienced the protection of the institution, networking as if their lives depended upon it – because they really did. She told me she had actually seen someone being offered a job on the spot there at that conference after a particularly successful paper. I couldn't tell if this was truth or hyperbole.

I needed to work out how to read Plath now because I needed to finish my paper for this conference because I needed to network as if my life depended upon it. I needed 'connections' if I wanted to do a postdoctoral fellowship and I needed someone somewhere in the Northern Hemisphere to put their name on my application form and write me a letter of recommendation. I needed a job. And I needed to find a job outside of Australia so that the universities back home would respect me. They didn't want to employ another Australian who had done their dissertation at an Australian university. They wanted an Australian who had studied or worked in America or England at the very least, shedding some of their Australian-ness so that they became a 'big name from overseas' not a 'small name from the university down the road'. It was all so strange and unlikely and grotesque. It made me want to lie down on my bed for a long time and not get up, so I did.

I thought about the word 'connections', a word that made other people into links on a long, fine chain that led to where? I didn't know. I didn't want to go somewhere and 'make connections'. What a bad ugly word for a soft, lovely thing. I wanted to be more than a connection; by which I mean, I wanted a connection. But really, I didn't know anything about other people. I think when I was young I was too busy feeling misunderstood to make any real friends. It was funny to be flung into this place with lots of other people who felt the same way and realise I couldn't pretend I had nothing in common with them. My back hurt and I rubbed it as if my hand were an eraser that could remove the pain from the surface of my skin. But it was deeper than that, buried so far down that I couldn't reach out and touch even the tip of it. I burrowed my face into my pillow and fell back into the pale, quiet world of sleep. I woke up to the sound of a knock at the door. I tried to reorient myself in time and space – the windows were bursting with light, the knocking was continuing, I pulled on some normal clothes and slapped at my face to wake it up. Clementine was at the door – she was wearing a blue spacesuit with a black trim. The only thing that was missing was a bubble-shaped helmet.

'Oh,' I said.

'Are you okay? You didn't come down to the studio today, so I got worried.'

'What time is it?'

'Half ten.'

'I must have slept in.'

'Is sitting for me becoming too much? Do you need a break?'

'No,' I lied because I didn't know how to tell the truth. 'I can come now if you want.'

'I was thinking of taking the day off anyway,' she said. 'I'm pretty tired, too.'

'Oh,' I said. I was unexpectedly disappointed. The idea of facing my work again was ghoulish to me. 'Should we just hang out?' I said.

She was surprised by this and I was too. The thing was that I was feeling so lonely and, perhaps, she was part of that loneliness, by isolating me from the others and making me feel like an idiot in front of everyone whenever were together as a group. But she was also the only person around who could alleviate my loneliness. She was the only person I felt like I knew. The greedy, bad parts of her I knew. And the soft, lovely bits of her I also knew and loved.

'What do you want to do?' she said.

'I'm so sick of the convent,' I said.

'Should we go to Edinburgh?'

'Are we allowed?'

'Sorry?'

'Penelope said at the start of the residency that we weren't really supposed to use it for travel. She said previous artists had done that and it hadn't been as good for the cohort. They made a rule about it.'

'It was probably pretty good for them, though.'

'Yeah, it probably was good for the artists that got to see a bit more of Scotland.'

'No, I mean it was probably easier for Penelope and the other administrators of the residency. That's why she said not to leave.'

'Oh.'

'Do you want to come?'

I considered this. I supposed I was halfway around the world and I shouldn't be here for nothing.

'Will you be the one to tell Penelope?' This was a very important point to me. I didn't want to be the one to tell Penelope we were going. The moment of discomfort when she realised we were going against her wishes and the rules of the residency almost meant more to me than breaking the rule itself.

Clementine shrugged. 'I can.'

'How long were you thinking of going for?'

'A couple of days,' Clementine said.

'I can get ready by eleven,' I said.

'See you downstairs,' she smiled.

On the train, we sat opposite each other and disappeared each into our own private worlds. I was reading the copy of *Johnny Panic and the Bible of Dreams* I had pretty much permanently checked out of my university's library and trying to work it out for the thousandth time and she was watching something on her laptop. After a while I wandered to what they called The

Shop, a red kiosk that sold sandwiches and magazines and chocolates, and asked for a cup of hot water. The hostess handed
me a large paper cup of hot water. I took it back to my seat and
then when no one was looking took a teabag I had stolen from
the convent out of my pocket and made myself a rushed cup of
tea. Eating on a train was a kind of fantasy for me, born of too
many movies of people sitting in the dining carriage of a train
and eating complicated-looking salads and watching the world
go by, and having a tea on a train was pleasingly adjacent to this
fantasy. While I waited for it to cool, I balanced it on the table in
front of me. The train came to a sudden stop, jerking my body
back into the seat and then the tea spilled all over my book and
jumper. Clementine smiled and then laughed at me and I liked
that she did that. Together, we mopped up the mess on my lap
and the table.

'That was a library book,' I said, looking at the soggy rag the
book had become.

'It'll dry out, won't it? If you leave it near a window or something.'

'It won't. But thanks anyway,' I said.

'Do you want to watch something with me? I can come over
on your side and we could take an earphone each.'

'What are you watching?'

'*Keeping up with the Kardashians.*'

I laughed.

'No seriously, it's great. It's the best show that was ever made.'

'That's such a strong recommendation.'

'I'm not joking.'

On the laptop, we were watching an older girl with blonde hair jumping onto a younger girl wearing combat boots and pretending to strangle her.

'This is weirdly wholesome,' I said. 'Are they sisters?'

'The girl on top is Khloé and the younger one is Kylie.'

'There's a lot of fake tan,' I said. 'I wonder if it gets on their clothes.'

Kylie screamed and pretended to be dead. *Suck my blood*, said Khloé. *You're abusive*, yelled Kylie and they both laughed. *Kourt-ney!* Khloé yelled in a British accent when another girl, presumably also their sister, arrived at the house. They picked Kourtney up and span her around.

'I love them,' Clementine said. 'I wish I had sisters.'

'I know. I feel like this is *Little Women* but with sex and cultural appropriation.'

'Yes!'

The camera cut to a scene of three girls and their mother dining out at a dark bistro.

'Who's that?'

'Kris – that's their mother. And Kim. And Khloé who you saw before.'

'Oh. Kim got engaged, didn't she? It was in the news so much that my dad was, like, *Who's Cane West and Kim Cajun?*'

'Yeah. You have to re-watch the engagement with me.'

'That salad is so weird with the lettuce stacked up like that.'

'It's to get you to think their beauty comes from salads.'

'Rather than what?'

'Plastic surgery.'

'Oh.'

The scene cut to the swimsuit selfies that Kim had recently posted on Instagram, her body glistened with a professional gleam.

'Sometimes I worry that self-portraits can't be a thing any more now that Kim Kardashian exists. Like they've been made redundant by the selfie. I'm afraid that no artist could be better at representing the self than she can,' Clementine said.

'I think you're right. It's hard to replicate or compete with that kind of immediacy. But you could do something different from it. Have you ever done one?'

'A selfie?'

'A self-portrait.'

'Yeah. I just feel like it's hard to be honest when painting yourself. It's so tempting to give yourself a little makeover. It's hard to stare at your own face for that long and be totally transparent about what you see.'

'But you're gorgeous, Clem. You look like that Gilot painting, *Blue Eyes*.'

'I hate Picasso,' she said. 'I'm so glad Gilot had her own career and got away from that creep and their forty-year age gap.'

'My bad, secret thing is I think I'd rather be the muse for some great male artist than go to the trouble of being an artist myself.'

'Oh no.'

'I used to actually think: Would I rather be beautiful and have my beauty inspire men or would I rather be the man, the artist? And I would always settle on being beautiful. But I never felt like I was.'

'Oh but you are, of course.'

'Thanks. I wasn't trying to get you to say that.'

'No, I've always known this about you. Like, instinctively.'

'What?'

'You don't feel entirely comfortable with your face.'

'No. I have a boring complex from high school about being called, like, "fat face" by some girls, blah blah blah,' I admitted.

'Honestly, you have to move on from those issues – being a muse for a male genius artist is so stupid as an idea.'

'That's why it's a secret thing. I've never told anyone before. But you're not exactly encouraging my vulnerability,' I laughed.

'I'm so over vulnerability.'

'I know.'

'Like, what about invulnerability. What's so new or bold about being a broken woman crying into her pillow and then putting that on Instagram,' she said.

'Do you think I'm weird for what I just said?'

'Extremely. But that's, like, you're thing. You're so honest. Like, you never shapeshift at all. You're the same in every context, every day.'

I thought about Clementine's shapeshifting – how she was one person when I was with her in the studio, another when we were on the train together going to a different city, and still another at dinner with the other artists. The thought of it sat there like a levitating balloon hovering uncomfortably in the air between us. Then we moved back to watching the episode in silence.

Khloé was packing up her ex-husband's possessions into boxes. He had disappeared completely and left her to work out the minutiae of their divorce on her own. Her sisters told her she needed to expedite the process of moving out but she was reluctant to leave the home that she and her husband had made together. Though I had never been married, I felt her loneliness.

'Do you honestly not feel like you just need someone to guide you or tell you what to do sometimes? The fantasy I have is of having a super-wise, eighty-year-old guy pass on all of his knowledge to me, an old master,' I said suddenly.

'I actually get that,' she said.

'Really?'

'It's hard to be an artist sometimes. It feels like it's all down to you.'

'And a person.'

'What?'

'It's hard to be anyone, surely. I always feel so awkward about the whole "it's hard to be an artist" thing. Compared to what?'

'Compared to how it used to be. Artists used to have guilds and apprenticeships and patrons. I mean, we have art school but that's whatever. It just gets lonely,' she said.

'I get that, actually,' I said. 'I feel that. I just feel bad about feeling that.'

'But it's okay to feel sorry for yourself every once in a while.'

'Do you sometimes feel like it's so hard to tell if what you're doing is amazing and perfect or completely awful and pedestrian?' I asked impulsively.

'Yes.'

'It's never somewhere in the middle, it's always somehow one or the other extreme.'

'It's like that with painting. You look at something for so long that you struggle to actually see what you're looking at.'

'I find the longer I stay with a thing the more I hate what I'm writing and find it really embarrassing. I can't even make it better because just looking at it makes me so full of shame. And then I abandon it and start a whole new project which feels really, like, pure and perfect at first. But it inevitably goes back to feeling awful and terrifying and humiliating again.'

'Totally. I think paintings are more like discrete objects, though. They're more material than a Word document. Which helps somehow. It's perhaps easier than writing a whole book because you can stop and finish something and move on from it. But I do feel that way towards the end of if, say, I'm doing a whole bunch of paintings for an exhibition and they're "themed". You just feel like you're ready for the next thing.'

'But I feel ready for the next thing after one day of working on something.'

'It's like falling in love versus being married.'

'What's it like being married?' I asked.

'No one's ever asked me that. Usually, if I mention that I'm married in certain company it feels like I've just put on a plastic red nose.'

'Like a clown?'

'Yeah. So, I don't know. I feel like I would think of it more as being with a specific person than the relationship being in a different category because of the legal paperwork and the institution and all of that. Henri's a really nice person, basically. My parents divorced when I was, like, ten so I've seen relationships that are pretty much the opposite and I know what I prefer.'

'Weren't you cynical about marriage because of your parents' divorce?'

'No. I think the opposite but I don't mean that in a good way. I feel like I idealised my relationships for the longest time even when they weren't great because I don't know. You feel like so long as it's perfect it won't go bad and like it saves the childhood part of you that watched a relationship go bad. It's almost like a redo of your parents' marriage.'

'The whole thing – marriage and kids and suburban life – fills me with abject terror.'

'I know – the whole domestication thing. And a lot of artists worry about their time being impinged on. I worry about that. I'm in my mid-thirties and I'm starting to feel like I want kids but it just feels super late.'

'Oh. My mum had me in her early forties, so.'

'Stories like that make me feel so much better.'

'They told her I might have a disability – it was a different era ... They considered her a geriatric mother. It felt kind of shaming, like it was her fault for not having me earlier. But she always said she figured it doesn't change that it's your child.'

'I'd be terrified if someone said that to me, honestly,' she said. 'I'd want to prepare myself, read lots of books, make myself a better person for that child. I couldn't just be cool with it and say whatever, you know?'

'Same, actually. But I always found it kind of lovely.'

'No, it really is.'

I fell asleep for the rest of the trip, rocked by the gentle motion of the train.

'I've found an Airbnb,' Clementine said.

'Oh. Where?'

'Slightly outside of the city proper but still very close – in Leith. The check-in's a bit later but I could get it for three nights. What do you want to do while we wait?'

'I'm pretty hungry.'

'Yeah, let's get something to eat.'

Me and Clementine wandered from the station to a small, Sicilian deli on Leith Walk. It was a nice place to sit a while, with its wood-panelled walls and chairs covered in brown cloth and striped cushions. I ordered a cappuccino and a pasta alla Norma. Clementine ordered a little cold plate of cheese and fruit and a half chocolate, half ricotta cannoli.

The cappuccino came out with a huge mushroom of froth growing perilously out of the cup. I licked the chocolate powder off it. It melted onto my hot tongue and created a tiny lick of fondue there. The food came out on yellow and teal plates and as we ate I thought how it was so nice to feel the aimless desires of the tourist and, what was more, to follow them to their natural endpoint. Everything tasted more vivid and more real. I was hungrier here and I was more satisfied when I ate and wiped my mouth. I felt that I could do nothing wrong. Me and Clementine did not have to speak to each other all the time to feel okay. I liked that about us. We could just say something when we felt like it and stay quiet when we had nothing to say to each other. It was good.

We went to an op shop which they called charity shops over here. The thing about charity shops in Scotland was that they were named after the cause they were raising money for. You weren't just buying clothes, you were supporting the Edinburgh Dog and Cat Home or Cancer Research or people with diabetes or macular degeneration. I found a painting of a rose in a cheap gold frame. I bought it. I bought it as a souvenir for someone – I hadn't decided who yet. This was my way of telling myself I was buying something for myself. To create a nebulous imaginary other person that the gift was for so that it wouldn't sound like I was so reckless and greedy as to buy useless things for myself. Clementine bought a canvas printed image of a bowl of fruit. It was very ugly. You could feel that the image was supposed to be bright and happy but it just looked strange with the soft glow and glue-like droplets of water meant to indicate the freshness of the fruit.

'I have to have this,' she said.

I saw that she was going to use it for something, so I didn't say anything because I knew how it felt to want to keep strange little secrets inside yourself for no reason.

It was late by the time we got to the one-bed flat Clementine had booked. We walked up the cement stairwell with its ancient grime and gum and up to a little blue corridor with a red stripe. We could hear someone on the telephone in another flat with a raised voice. Clementine unlocked the door and I saw inside: a sashimi-coloured carpet and an egg-yolk wall. We lay down on the squashy bed and said nothing.

'Do you want to do anything tonight?' I asked.

'Do you?'

'I was thinking of going for a swim, honestly. It's been so long since I stretched my body out. And I feel like just being out and about for so long makes me feel really sticky and gross,' I said, framing my idea as quirky and fun rather than as a necessary thing to do for my pain-ridden, ailing back which responded well to being in the water for some weird reason.

'It's weird how inactive we've been at the convent. I think there's a pool near here, actually. Should we go now?'

At the swimming pool, it was the women's hour so only female lifeguards on duty and women swimming. We changed and got in. There weren't any lanes – just a large square space. Women criss-crossing, swimming slant-ways, adjacent, horizontally across, vertically, this ways, that ways, making up their own rhythms. A woman who was trying to swim little half laps at the edge asked me how to swim. I told her I wasn't good at swimming at all – actually, my technique was terrible and she shouldn't copy me. *You're so so happy when you swim, which is why I think you're good at it,* she said and waited for me to instruct her. Blowing bubbles is a good place to start, I said, and she blew and blew and I watched her breath growing from something invisible to something I could see.

The next morning me and Clementine decided to go to the National Gallery for an exhibition of Marina Abramovic's photography. I fell into my usual predilection of thinking everyone in the photographs was me. It was me, the woman holding the bow and leaning back as the man held the arrow. It was me, the lover slapping his face and being slapped. I saw my features morph and melt into hers. I felt this also when I saw the photos documenting her and her long-time lover and collaborator Ulay's catastrophic walk towards each other on the Great Wall of China. I felt her grief and her anger and exhaustion when Ulay did the opposite of marrying her – impregnating his translator instead and asking her what he should do about it. She told him to marry the translator. I could never have done that. But I also wondered what had happened to Ulay's translator. I couldn't find anything about her in the gallery brochure or even in the Google searches on my phone. I wanted to know about this Chinese woman who had carried a baby and a language while walking the Great Wall of China with the man who had impregnated her. Where was she now? Had he married her? Had he been faithful? And how had it felt to be that baby? She was not in any of the photos but as much as I was Abramovic, I was her too, and I wanted to know how the story had ended for her. In the middle of the exhibition, I got a phone call from a number I didn't recognise. I left the gallery space and sat outside the foyer on a huge, grey boulder that had been welded into the ground.

'Hello?' I said.

'Hi.' It was a male voice with a kind of flatness to it.

'Hi?' I said questioningly.

'It's Leon.'

'Oh.'

'Penelope said she had lost you and another artist. Are you still at the convent?'

'No – I'm in Edinburgh,' I said.

'Why didn't you tell anyone you were going?' he asked. 'I'm supposed to be responsible for you and the other scholars. I get blamed if you fall off the face of the earth. Did you think of that?'

'I didn't know,' I said. 'Sorry.'

I felt stupid apologising as if I was a teenager who had played hooky from school. But then I had always responded to authority by being deeply convicted of my own guilt.

'When will you be back?'

'I can book a train for tomorrow morning,' I said.

'Okay,' he said. 'I'll let Penelope know.'

He hung up and I stood and stared at my phone in an accusatory way as if it had been the thing that had gotten me into trouble in the first place. I went back inside to find Clementine – she was still staring at one of the portraits.

'I thought you said you would tell Penelope we were leaving the convent for a bit,' I said.

'I did, didn't I?' she said.

'You didn't. I just got a call to say Penelope couldn't find us.'

'Oh, I guess I didn't,' she said.

'You said you would.'

'It's just so infantilising, the whole thing, the idea of having your meals done for you at specific times and not being able to leave without asking and everything. I didn't think it was that important.'

'But I got in trouble with the programme that sent me here. They called me and I have to go back.'

'I'm not part of the royal brigade thing or whatever the fuck it's called. That's you and Jack and that other guy that never came.'

'Blessing.'

'What?'

'That was his name but yeah I don't think he's going to come now.'

'Right. So what do you want to do?' she asked.

'I'm going back tomorrow.'

'But the Airbnb's for three nights.'

'I think we should split up for the rest of the day at least,' I said. 'I can't really be around you right now.'

'Okay,' she said. 'It might be good to do our own thing anyway.'

I saw that she was unaffected by our conversation; in fact, she was already thinking about how it might be for the best. And this made me feel worse somehow.

I walked alone past the shops selling tartan scarves and Shetland wool jumpers and thistle-flavoured chocolate. And I started to hate Edinburgh with its crumbling beauty and quaint cake shops and carefully laid cobblestones. I hated the drama of its grey cliff faces and green hills and tastefulness of its streets and UNESCO-protected buildings, unbroken by the ugliness of the present day. It made me long for real cities made of glass and towers and stockbrokers in ugly suits that were actually transparent about their motives, honest about how much they wanted you. The only thing that made sense about it was the constant sound of bagpipes playing 'Auld Lang Syne' – yes, that was the only thing that told you that you were being marketed to and fed a narrative of Edinburgh's essential Edinburgh-ness.

Amidst all of this, it was a visual relief to descend into the glass-roofed Waverley Market searching for bottled water. My childhood had been comprised of deserted shopping centres in the suburbs and I could smell the cinema popcorn, the corn-starch-gleaming Chinese takeaway and the savoury stench of pet shops for ever. Me and Ah Ma, we would drift through Glad-stone Park Shopping Centre for potato cakes and dim sims and for nothing really. It was just a place to go to pass the time and no one minded if you stayed for hours looking at everything.

And then I remembered how me and Ikanyu, we would drive to Highpoint on hot summer days for the free air conditioning. And I would lie on the floor of Borders, reading any book I wanted and not having to pay for it, and he would read the newspaper from cover to cover at the book café and no one would bother us. And then we would drift to Myer and there, in that store, white as heaven, Ikanyu browsed the buffet of electrical goods.

'Do you need a hand with anything?' A man in a black polo approached.

'No, no, just looking.'

'Well, let me know.'

Ikanyu never let him know. He approached the vacuum cleaners. He picked up the different attachments and examined them. A catch fell open in the body of the vacuum and he looked inside to see its wiry intestines.

'Oh. Is that so?' he said to a secret part of himself, examining an inner mechanism. It was the same with the blender ('very sharp'), the electric steak knife ('rubbish'), the massage chair ('this is the life') and the big headphones like Mickey Mouse ears ('a bit loud'). Ikanyu, he was a gourmand of the electrical, his hands moved quickly as he dissected and put back each product. And as he looked at each shiny object, perfect as the future, I saw that Ikanyu was just like me. His eyes weren't on things seen but things yet unseen; he knew that this world would pass away and the next would come and that new world was me. This was before parenting in this way was seen as pressuring or a load you made your children carry. At the time, it felt like Ikanyu thought I was the sky.

'I'm bored,' I said at last, squatting on the ground like a kampung boy.

We went to the top floor of Myer where there was a loud room with no lights. In it, Ikanyu sat on a plush chair and we watched The Lion King II together. Ikanyu fell asleep in his chair and snored loudly. I kept waking him up but he kept falling back asleep.

'Ikanyu, wake up.' I shook his shoulder.

'Huh?' Ikanyu sat up quickly, his eyes flashing red and white. He started to sink back into his chair.

'Ikanyu, the movie's finished!' I shook him until he stopped blinking.

'Ohwatchagain?' Ikanyu's words were the formless texture of baby food.

'I'm hungry.'

The fog in his eyes seemed to clear up and I was pulling at his collar but then he fell asleep again and started snoring. I pulled at his pockets and two fat gold coins fell out. Ikanyu loved to collect two-dollar coins out of shopping trolleys. I picked them up and went downstairs, gliding along the escalator and down to the food court with the hot biscuits in paper bags. There were families out for their Saturday lunch and men in old suits eating sandwiches alone. I went to the ice-cream counter and a girl with all of her hair drawn back like she was bald smiled at her.

'Poison berry ice cream in a waffle cone.'

'Boysenberry?'

I ignored her comment and handed over the coins. She passed me a cone with a serviette curled around it. I tried biting the ice cream with my teeth and the cold shock hurt me. I rubbed my mouth and felt the red sticky all over my face.

'Girl!'

Ikanyu was awake at last and his skin was a colour I had never seen.

'Girl,' he said again and it came out like a snarl.

Ikanyu ripped serviettes out from a box on the counter and cleaned my face the way Ma and Ah Ma so often did. They thought the rougher they were the cleaner I would be. Ikanyu didn't do it like that, though. We walked back to the car in silence and Ikanyu stopped us halfway to help me finish off the melting ice cream, shaking his head. *Girl*, he was saying, his fingers red and sticky. *Girl*, he was saying it again.

At home, Ma was awake in her pyjamas, sweating in the big fire of the kitchen stove. She was frying five little fish filled with sambal and one little fish not filled with sambal for me.

'What? Gallivanting all day without me?' she asked.

I worried that Ikanyu would tell Ma, in that mysterious communication line of theirs, that I had done something wrong. I snapped off the tail of one of the fish cooling on a paper towel and munched on it like a chip.

'Yes.' Ikanyu smiled. His skin was clean and brown again.

'Kah the rice,' she told him. 'Call Ah Ma,' she told me.

I crept back into happiness again, tentatively, as if I might break something if I went too fast. We sat down and ate the fish and the rice and the turmeric cabbage. I went to grab another spoonful of cabbage and knocked over Ma's mug. Tea spilled richly over the table and onto the floor like a blessing from heaven.

'Girl!' both Ma and Ikanyu were yelling.

'Ho ho ho,' Ah Ma gloated, pointing at the tea.

'Alamak! You are always creating more work for me,' Ma said.

'Ma's a grouch, isn't she?' I said conspiratorially to Ikanyu.

'Why do you say that?' Ikanyu said, shaking his head.

I looked at Ma and saw her small pink face. I was surprised by how small it was. Ikanyu picked me up out of my chair and carried me into the bathroom. It was cold in there. Ikanyu smacked me and the black hexagons and white squares of the lino jumbled together like pieces of Lego in a bucket.

'Ma is very tired,' he said after he put me down. 'How would you feel if something happened and that was the last thing you said to her? You have to think.'

I was crying as was customary in these kinds of interactions.

'To hit you is to love you,' Ikanyu said as he left the bathroom.

Afterwards I went into Ma's room to lie beside her before her night shift. Her face was wet and her body was still. She wasn't asleep but she wasn't awake. That was when I realised that there was no code word for Ma like there was one for Ikanyu. There was just Ma and maybe she should have one too but. But Ma was a woman unlike other people. She didn't smile and speak in secret languages when she was angry. She didn't show one face to your face and one face to your back. It would never have made sense to give a person without passwords a code name. Then as suddenly as she had gone still and quiet, she got up and packed her bag and changed into her scrubs.

I went to the window and watched the lens flare of Ma's car headlamps reflect against our house. Ma didn't look back. She was a woman who never seemed to look back through windows. I didn't know then that anything could hurt her.

As it got dark, I went to a restaurant and sat down by myself. I was surprised to hear my voice leaping out of my throat like a lobbed tennis ball as I ordered a fish curry. You never know how quiet you can be until you've gone overseas and walked around all day and the only person who hears your voice is standing there waiting with his pen and pad.

I didn't want to go back to the apartment because that would mean facing Clementine. I was afraid that if I saw Clementine I would say something and then it would lead to Clementine saying something and we would keep accumulating things to say until we had another argument. I thought about going back to the pool because conveniently, my bathers were still lying in a soggy heap at the bottom of my bag from the night before. I took the bus there after dinner. The pool was restored to its usual state – it no longer calibrated itself around the idea of women's hour and looked like an ordinary public pool. Public pools everywhere, it seemed, were a mix of the sublime and the repugnant. The feeling of a large square of warm water enveloping your body and healing every ache and pain like a modern-day Pool of Bethesda. And yet the omnipresence of balls of dead hair floating to the top of the water like seafoam, balletic pieces of tissue, miscellaneous pieces of dust or dirt which had to constantly be put to the back of your mind. The sound of parents screaming at their children as they horsed around in the showers or refused to put their soggy clothes on. Elderly people walking slowly from one end of the rehab lane. Invulnerable young lifeguards, curly-headed men and serious-looking women, who were almost always beautiful and who seemed to belong to a different kind of human – tall as trees, clothed in the colours of the sun and capable of saving you. When I saw them, I always thought of being twenty again and having never known what insomnia was or pain or any distress that wasn't in some way delicious and exciting. For me, there was such a chasm between being twenty and twenty-one. That was the year I started hurting and my body began to break down on me in a million invisible ways. The self-affirming feminism lite that was in vogue at that moment often told young women that they should think of their body as a tool rather than a spectacle. I read somewhere that girls who used their body as a tool, e.g. playing sports like tennis or soccer, were statistically less likely to develop an eating disorder than girls who used their body as a spectacle like dancing or doing gymnastics. But if my body was a tool it was a broken one, a blamed one, one that would have long been discarded and thrown in a scrap-metal heap if I could have managed it. And I had never danced or done tumble turns, but I had learned my body was a spectacle, as every girl eventually does. Before I even knew it was mine, I knew it was a thing to be watched and looked at.

I was too tired for laps so I went over to the Jacuzzi and sat submerged watching the bubbles animating the water. The Jacuzzi occupied a marginal position in the suburban aquatic centre – it was always off to the side and a place from where you could watch the central action. It smelled a little of cleaning chemicals and a little of guilt – to be sedentary and slow when you could be redeeming your poor, maligned body by flinging it as quickly as possible through water.

A man with grey hair and self-tanned skin lowered himself into the Jacuzzi. He was handsome and made me think of an expensive pair of oiled leather shoes. He looked at me knowingly. Men started looking at me when I was maybe twelve or thirteen. I didn't know how to handle the stares or smiles or small talk, and I still don't really. I thought of myself then as an essentially repulsive and useless person so for someone else to desire me or desire to control some part of me didn't make any sense to me. Ma would always tell me I should just lie and say that I had a boyfriend, and I did, but something about this rubbed me up the wrong way. I understood that 'boyfriend' was a kind of shorthand for men who couldn't respect me but did respect the abstract but overbearing entity of 'the boyfriend'. I hated that girlish word, *boyfriend*, with its gasping excitement, its essential immaturity and how it made me seem stupid. But I wanted love one day and to be left alone otherwise – is there anyone in the world who doesn't? So, I said the word *boyfriend* to the men who approached me in public and they left me alone but smiled a little as if despising me, knowing they were superior to me, a stupid girl who did nothing but dream of love.

'I could never do that,' he said.

'What?' I asked.

'Sit in the Jacuzzi for so long. I saw you while I was doing laps – you've been here since almost half eight.'

'Oh. I like the Jacuzzi,' I said lamely.

'You do?'

'Yeah.'

'It is nice, isn't it?' He groaned as if to demonstrate how nice it was.

'Yeah.'

'Do you live around here?'

'Yes,' I lied because I began to think I should make up an alternative life to tell him about.

'I moved here five years ago. It's changed a lot but I really like the area.'

I noticed his wedding ring then. It was a thick, titanium band, quite matte and angular so that it looked like the nut part of a screw or maybe a washer or some other industrial thing a man would fix. I noticed it because I found contemporary men's wedding rings fascinating – how they seemed to be proving that they weren't jewellery or meant to be aesthetically pleasing but were instead necessary and functional. Ikanyu's wedding ring didn't follow this pattern – it was the plain gold band of the past. Ma had lost her wedding ring a long time ago and never replaced it ('waste of money!'). I wondered if I should bring the man's family up in some way, perhaps he had forgotten them.

'For the schools?' I said.

'Sorry?' He looked startled and for the first time a little bit scared.

'Do you like the area for the schools?'

'Oh. Yeah. My daughter goes to school around here. Fettes. Really good school,' he said.

'I know,' I said, although I didn't. I assumed it was expensive.

'And all her cousins go too, so she likes that.'

I said nothing because I couldn't think of anything to say to that.

'Did you go to a good school?' he asked suddenly.

'Um, it was a public school,' I said. 'It was all right, I guess.' The first true thing I had said to him.

'Oh.' He seemed disappointed by this.

Again I said nothing.

I wondered how long he would continue telling me about how rich he was in increasingly obvious ways and if I should just come out and say it: 'You are rich.' Was that what he wanted me to say to him? I had read on the internet that there were now pick-up artist boot camps – weekend long workshops that resembled in some ways an academic conference but were for men who wanted to learn how to talk to women. They were given useful tips like 'don't boast about your salary'; or if a woman asks your age don't be ashamed to tell her the truth because your age is actually an asset. They were also taught to 'neg' women, which meant to say lightly mean things to them which would count as flirting. When I read about this phenomenon, it made sense to me because I had been so confused by the mix of shyness and hatred with which men seemed to approach me. I wondered if that was what they were told to do: to seem both sweet and scary. I thought that maybe this man should go to one of those boot camps – it might help him.

'Do you have a boyfriend?' he asked.

'No,' I said. I forgot to lie and regretted it.

'Really?' he said and leaned back with his arms behind his head to look at me.

'I'm actually married,' I lied. 'So he's my husband, not my boyfriend. I know I look young, but I've actually been married five years.'

'You do look very young,' he said with a mixture of disgust and excitement.

'I know.'

'You know what?'

'I know,' I repeated dumbly.

'Well, *I* know a thing or two about Asian women,' he said and winked.

I felt a kind of abject joy when he said this to me. It gave me, for one moment, some clarity over what our interaction was about. As I got older, men would approach me and tell me how much they earned, flex their muscles at me, lick their lips at me; occasionally they told me they knew a thing or two about Asian girls. But mostly, this knowledge of 'me' was implied, setting the scene for the conversation rather than embodying its contents.

It hovered there invisibly behind the veil of plausible deniability. His forthrightness made me feel like I was a baby and I had been bathed in a scalding but ultimately cleansing water. It hurt but it was honest about how he saw me and that made it so much easier for me.

This was about the only thing I appreciated about the regressive historical context that *The Bell Jar* was set in – the honesty with which people treated each other. Esther's college boyfriend, Buddy tells her she will stop writing poetry when she becomes a mother. Later in the book, Esther describes the black man who wheels the food cart into the dining room at her psychiatric ward as 'the negro' and kicks him when she doesn't like the food that he brought her, believing that he has some strange plot to make her eat two kinds of beans at dinner. Of course, Esther has just had a breakdown, but Ma had always told me that the hospital was where you saw people as they really were. People in terrible suffering and people watching their loved ones suffer – these were the moments in which people told Ma that they didn't want to speak to someone like her and spat at her or even threatened to harm her. The pain was like a drug that made them say what they really thought. There wasn't much that America in the 1950s had to recommend itself but at least it had this: an embarrassing honesty about who mattered to white America and who didn't. There were none of the terrific mind games of inclusion and diversity and, before that, 'multiculturalism' and 'tolerance' that I had grown up with and that made you think you were crazy if something happened to you and you 'made it about race'.

'You can take it as a compliment,' the man in the Jacuzzi said.

Sometimes men would tell me things about myself and then, while waiting for my reaction, say 'you can take it as a compliment', which made the whole thing even stranger. It was supposed to ascribe value to my body, but it just made me feel the opposite – like a worthless person. An Asian body or a female body or both. But not more than a body. I thought about the word body and how it was mostly used for dead people, unidentifiable people, and I thought it made sense to think of myself as a body.

'I'm sorry,' I said. 'I have to go home.'

I left the pool and walked back to the Airbnb in the cold and dark. Whenever I walked alone, I felt the clarity of the air as it rushed through me and my limbs sliced through it. I looked around and, seeing no one, felt the world belonged to me. But this feeling was often followed by a kind of dread of what I could not see. Ma had been afraid to emigrate to the West *because, you know, they are very perverse there*. Sometimes, she would say, they will even like that you are Chinese. And it was so obvious who 'they' were to me. Ah Ma, she had no euphemisms in her vocabulary and she would scream at random if I left the house: a man will liat you and then he will take off your teh kor and then cham. Trouble. In the many eyes of my family, me walking alone with my body was a liability. If a girl is assaulted and no one hears her then did she really scream?

So many times, I had confirmed their fears. When I was still in school, I'd go on these long walks in my neighbourhood, even in the cold and dark, because I thought my legs were too thick for love. One day, a man with something missing in his eyes blocked the road with his car as I went to cross it. He pulled over and wound the window down. The headlights cold and white. And he asked me if I wanted to come with him and I walked around his car, no words in my mouth, and then I was running and looking back at him and he was just staring at me. Something was still missing from his eyes but I wasn't sure what it was. When I told Ma about it she kept tossing the cabbage and turmeric and mustard seeds in the pan with her hands. With her mouth, she blamed the time of day, my too small school dress, my aloneness. I was wounded because on some level, I knew, she blamed even me. If it was my fault, it gave her some sense of control over what might happen and what might keep me safe. As for the man in the car, I realised the thing he was missing in his eyes was shame.

As I was walked now I started to feel my abject joy turn to a kind of terror that felt unsubstantiated but real. I realised that the sick elation I had initially felt was the pretty foil over an Easter egg and once I had gotten around to unwrapping it, I saw that what was inside was not a chocolate egg but an empty, dark well of feeling.

I thought again about how women were supposed to think of their bodies as tools but how my body never seemed to actually do its job. It was always hurting – misunderstanding normal things as painful, weak, puny and not at all functional in so many ways. If my body was a tool then the only thing it reliably did was fool people into thinking it was a thing to look at. All I had ever known about my body was that it was the spectacle of myself.

I crept back into the apartment, hoping not to wake Clementine but she was up watching an old episode of *Keeping up with the Kardashians* on her laptop in bed.

'Are you okay?' she said.

'Aren't we in a fight?' I asked.

'You don't look that good,' she said.

'Oh,' I said.

I told her about the man I had met at the pool and the thing I had been thinking about – how my body was more spectacle than tool and how that was messing me up.

'I'm really sorry,' she said. 'What a dickhead.'

'Yeah.'

'When you said the thing about your body not being a tool. Are you in a lot of pain?'

'Yeah.'

'I'm so sorry. You should have told me.'

'I didn't want to burden you.'

'Oh, you're so brave and refined. You're so strong and smart,' she said with a venom that I didn't expect.

I was caught off guard but then I felt like the anger she had was towards the idea that she couldn't help me more than at me.

'Come on. You know better,' she said.

'Okay. Which episode are you watching?'

'The proposal one. Look how happy Kanye and Kim are.'

'Oh, you said I had to see that one.'

'You have to see it. I'll go back.'

I lay down next to her and we watched the episode together. When Kanye proposed to Kim, I cried because they looked so happy. And then we fell asleep.

The next morning, I woke up late and ran to the station without having any breakfast. I got to the station hungry and tired and realised my train was delayed. So I bought a takeaway meal from a burger chain near the station. As I waited for the train, I unwrapped my burger, enjoying the rustle of the thin paper with its tomato sauce and mayonnaise lining as if I was unwrapping a carefully chosen gift. I savoured the pickle half and beef patty and cheese. Eating meat again after so long made me feel like I could run up and vault myself over the bar with a pole at the Olympics. It was sweet and burnt and creamy. There was a packet of chips and I marvelled at the variety of textures in a single packet – from soggy and sweet to crispy and bitter to brown and gold. I sucked the fizz from a Coke though a plastic straw and felt like a helium balloon filled up with anti-gravity.

On the platform I sat next to a heavily made-up woman. There was no one else on the platform apart from a Vietnamese-looking woman sitting cross-legged on the ground. She closed her eyes and glowed in the warmth of the sun. She looked like she was meditating. Then she began taking her clothes off with the same serene face. First her T-shirt then her pants. Then her underwear and her bra. When she was nude but for her necklaces she began meditating again. She breathed in and out. I wasn't sure what it meant or if it meant anything at all.

The train was coming. I stood up. But the woman on the platform, she jumped. She hit the side of the rushing train and flew back onto the platform. Her naked body lay still on the tarmac. Her eyes were open and the expression on her face had the calm look of the dead. I had a brief moment of wondering if I should be the one to go to her. I didn't want to be the person who is secretly repulsed by death or infirmity, who puts their own ease and comfort, their own so-called normality, above the suffering of others. But here I was, scared of another human, and because I was scared, repulsed by that wide-eyed corpse. And moreover, I didn't want to wait another twenty minutes for the next train, I was so tired and weak that surely I wouldn't be of much help anyway and wouldn't it make more sense for the people getting off the train to help than the ones getting on? And actually, I was ashamed to admit this even to myself but I was afraid of Leon calling me again if Penelope told him that I hadn't yet returned to the convent by the end of the morning.

I watched as a man ran over from another platform and crouched over the woman. I heard the beeping of the train doors to indicate it was pulling away soon and I ran on board. I collapsed into a chair and once I was seated I saw that I was sat opposite the woman with the make-up. Now that I was opposite her, I found myself admiring the way she had shaded in her face to give it dimension, as if it were a painting. The make-up clarified her facial features, narrating her eyebrows and telling her lips.

'I knew what she was going to do as soon as she sat on the platform,' she said.

'Really?'

'Yes. I already knew.'

I wondered why the woman had said nothing if she'd known. Then I remembered that I myself had been unable to bear the delay which tending to the woman's body would have meant. In the black nothingness of the tunnel that the train barrelled through, I found that it was easier to bear the still small voice of an injured conscience than it was to tend to the physical wounds of another. How easy it was to create small, office-desk partitions around myself and the selves that were not me. The worst thing was that no one would think worse of me, that I lost nothing by doing what I had done. In fact, I knew that if I told anyone what I had seen, it would be me they would pity and not the woman. My metaphysical pain would hurt them more than the woman's death and the pain which had led to it. Much would be made of the unluckiness of my presence at the woman's death, not the woman's irrevocable absence from the world entire. And I hated that even thinking about her now was a kind of mental atonement for the lack of physical help my body had given another body. That I was a so-called good person for having these thoughts in the safety of my own head, in the warmth of the train carriage with its pleasant forward motion that took me away.

I got off at my stop and stood at the platform looking at nothing after the train had left. I vomited a black liquid onto the tracks that I hadn't known was inside me.

Ten

After I got back from Edinburgh, I was tired and slept all day but when I woke up, I still felt crook. I got up and vomited into the bathtub and felt briefly better but then I cleared my throat and felt as if there was a spiked glove inside it. I knew then that I was sick in the ordinary, difficult-to-complain-about-plausibly, makes-you-want-to-die way. Of course, pain poured into my back in a way that took up all of my attention like a boring and aggressive rant that never seemed to end. I fell asleep and this was the only consolation I had, that I could still trick my body into going quiet if I closed my eyes and lay there long enough pretending I didn't exist.

I woke up and someone was sitting at the end of my bed – it was Clementine, looking like a mournful flapper with a drop-hem skirt and a sparkly headband and pin curls and everything. I never mentioned her silly clothes to her – because they always seemed to grow from her, rather than be on her. They made sense and it was as if she was born with multiple costumes from different eras and movies and mentioning one would be as rude as mentioning a mole on someone's face or a birthmark on their arm.

'I thought you still had another night at the Airbnb.'

'No, I got confused by how it looked on the website when I booked it. It turns out I had another *day* – which meant I had to get out, like, immediately after I woke up.'

'Oh.'

'Otto said he hadn't seen you yet at meals or whatever so I thought I'd pay you a visit.'

'Thanks. Yeah – I've been throwing up.'

'I think you ate something weird,' she said.

'You're not sick, too? But we ate all the same stuff.'

'No, I never get sick,' she said.

I instantly felt annoyed at her stupid, superior tone and remembered why I disliked her all over again.

'Never, like you wouldn't get sick if a person with leprosy touched you all over. The leprosy would just bounce off you?'

'I take a lot of vitamins.'

She pronounced vitamins in such a weird, clipped, English accent. Vitermins rather than Vaitermins. I knew English people could work out from just an accent where exactly a person came from. I wondered if Vitermins was a universal thing here or if it was particular to one locale. Then I realised I had gotten lost in my thoughts and let her absurd statement pass without saying anything. So, I moved on.

'Does Penelope know I actually came back this morning? I need to timestamp that somehow.'

Clementine rolled her eyes.

'Penelope doesn't care, all right? Like, she said nothing about it to me when she saw me today. Just stop worrying. Seriously.'

I closed my eyes – it began to occur to me that the light of the lamp on my bedside table was glaringly bright.

'I asked the cook if she could make you some soup. It looks a bit watery but it'll be easy to eat at least,' she said.

'Thanks,' I said.

She passed me the bowl and I sat up to drink some of the soup – it was a cloudy yellow thing with bits of celery and carrot floating around in it.

'It tastes like heaven.'

'I'd hate to go to your idea of heaven.'

'No, seriously, thanks for this.'

'Do you need anything else?'

'Maybe a book so I have something to do while I'm lying in bed with a deep desire to die. I have loads of books that I brought with me, obviously, but I'm a bit over all of them.'

'Okay, give me a sec.'

She went downstairs and I waited for the door to open again. After a few minutes she returned.

'I found this in the library. I thought you would like it, though you've probably already read it given you're such a Plath fan. So, you have something to do while you rest.'

'I'm not a fan, I'm a scholar.'

'Yeah, right,' she said.

She put a book on the bed. It was *Ariel*.

I first read *Ariel* the summer before Year 12 started. Like all Australian summers, it was hotter than anyone had thought was possible, quiet because everyone was away at different times. But it also had an anticipatory hum to it, the feeling that it was the summer before anything real was going to happen to me. *Ariel* was on the list for my English Literature class and I read it in that January lull inside my oven-hot bedroom. It really hadn't made sense to me at first. I was confused about why I was reading about death when I felt totally removed from it – when I had nothing but life inside of me. And the word 'confessional' – which followed any description of her poetry – had a sense of forthrightness and accidentalness, like water spilling from a vase. It didn't seem to bear any relationship to the actual felt texture of these poems. The poems were set in formal, tightly wound lines with a clear, bell-like voice. They felt as neat and tidy and impenetrable as a house that has been hastily cleaned before the arrival of guests. The obscure and mythological imagery, the settings which veered between the pastoral and the surreal. They were difficult and I felt a sense of shame at how much I felt I was standing at the outskirts of these poems, not daring to really approach them and feeling as if they were even further away from me the closer I tried to come.

I knew that this was the last summer before I would become a Year 12, which was both a terrifying and an exquisite thing to me and to all of us really. This year, we would be the ones in the school who got to use the microwaves and sit in the common room at lunch looking effortlessly cool; we would be treated by the teachers as something closer to equals; we would be the ones picking out our clothes for Valedictory (and Ma had said I could get my make-up done at Myer); we were the ones walking around the yard, tall and authoritative in specially made bomber jackets that said Class of '09. I loved that jacket and the nonchalance of the apostrophe that swung in next to the 09. It was so effortless; like, we don't even have to write the whole year out because we already know what year it is: the year is ours – it belongs completely to us.

By then, I had loved school for some time because I loved being clever and knowing I was always the cleverest person in the room and having that confirmed by exact percentiles and letter grades written in red pen. I loved the feeling I got as my brain let off tiny fireworks in class when I learned something I didn't know existed before. I looked forward with carnivorous anticipation to my Year 12 exams and the sense of racing, knowing what to do, cramming the night before and feeling the lightness of having finished them. I relished the sense of being in a state-wide competition in which I would get a ranking to tell me, at last, how smart I really was.

But I tried not to show how much I cared. I spent the classes I really liked trying to impress the teacher but spent the classes I thought were beneath me mucking around with my friends, laughing at the teacher, not even doing the work I was assigned so that I could show everyone how effortlessly brilliant I was. I wanted everyone to know that I wasn't just a swot, I was *gifted*, and nothing could ever hurt me.

Some of my teachers hated me, my arrogance and my indestructibility, but most of them loved me, called me perfect, told me I was the best student they had ever had and this was enough for me. I wanted always to be a student and loved. I had been predictably bullied and isolated in the early years of high school by Ang Moh girls who called me racial slurs or told me my body was unworthy of love and laughed at me. But we got older and time moved us along and our role models changed, silently and imperceptibly. We went from idolising pop stars and actresses with straightened blonde hair, who giggled a lot and bragged about their eating disorders, to idolising irreverent brunette models who wore lots of winged eyeliner, cut their hair into shaggy bobs and carefully concealed their eating disorders. I felt instinctively that while on the outside I was always going to be 'Asian', on the inside I was the brown-haired girl whose clothes spoke of a woman with a conspicuous and interesting inner life, and I began dressing myself in a miscellaneous jumble of pastness and obscure references to movies that suited me. I thought of myself as being obliquely cool and misunderstood. After this, I occupied a weird new position in the school hierarchy – as someone abject and still Asian, a nerd and a loser essentially but also cool and interesting and smart.

Sometimes this fell apart – as it did when at a seventeenth birthday party themed simply 'America', I came dressed as Annie Hall in an ill-fitting shirt, vest and slacks and was mistaken as the unnamed 'Asian nerd' from basically every American teen movie. I stood immobilised by fear as over a hundred drunk teenagers stood in the approximate shape of a circle around me and chanted a song that just went 'you're my token Asian friend, you're my token Asian friend' over and over again while pointing at me as if the fact of my racial difference was still not entirely clear. I left early and Ikanyu picked me up and I told him what had happened and he told me I overthought everything.

All this to say, I couldn't sleep the night before the first day because everything about it was going to be perfect. Monday would start with homeroom then double English Lit and we were to have a new male teacher no one knew anything about. I wondered if he was handsome.

It turned out that the new teacher was indeed handsome but that wasn't the only thing that impressed us. He also told us that he thought in Latin, had achieved a perfect VCE score when he was in school and had a photographic memory, which we believed. He told us that he had family members in the IRA, which made him seem vaguely violent and interesting as well as the genius we believed him to be. He also told me that I was *gifted*. I used to believe that, too.

The teacher was tall and broad. He wasn't big like a Mack truck or a slab of meat. He was big like a personality. He wore a suit and it didn't make him look anonymous. He wore a suit in the kind of public high school where the teachers' clothes (jeans, nice sneakers, surf-brand T-shirts) were less formal than the students' uniforms. The teacher was everyone's favourite; we said his name like a broken rosary and he liked that. Sometimes we called him 'sir' and he really liked that. When he came into the room, his voice was deeper than the darkest night and we loved that. Most of our teachers were kind, older women with eccentrically dyed hair, and where was the fun in that? We wanted something like something from the movies. And we got it.

The first we laid eyes on him he walked into the room, placed his wool hat on the table, sighed hugely and began writing on the board. He wrote in huge letters, ARIEL. Then he asked us what we thought of it. The other kids began telling him they liked this or that poem, wanting to please him. He said yes, yes, yes. But I could tell by the contour of his lips that this was exactly the wrong answer. I put my hand up and told him I hadn't liked it at all. This was not entirely true but I sensed that it was true to him and as Pilate had said to Jesus: 'What is truth?'

He pointed at me to speak and his finger went right through me. I decided that I would tell him what I thought he thought about the poems.

'There's something obvious about the poems, there's not the playfulness or mystery or the free fall that poetry should have. They have a prose-like quality to them, at times. It's as if Plath doesn't trust us to go where she leads unless she spells it out for us.'

'Exactly,' he said. 'As Harold Bloom writes: *These are poems for people who don't read poems.*'

I nodded and he looked at me then smiled ironically at the class, looking at them as if they were the people who didn't read poems. And none of us knew who the hell Harold Bloom was, of course. I decided I would look him up later.

'Sir, is it true that she killed herself?' a girl sitting up the back asked.

'Yes, she killed herself in 1963.'

The sound of twenty-something pens writing in their notebooks filled the room.

'Which is part of her relationship with popular culture, the mythology of Plath and her death,' he said, looking at me like I was the only one who understood. 'In the end, very little of why Plath is read today is because of her poetry. It is because of her person.'

The class, it continued like this. The teacher, who still hadn't told us his name, would speak to me about *Ariel* and Plath as if the other students didn't exist. They vanished into the backdrop of our conversation. At the end of the class, he picked up *Ariel* with its shiny new cover, its bold red title and its skinny spine.

'And this is what I think of the texts they've set for Year Twelve this year,' he said. He opened the window and ripped the book into four pieces. What was left of the book fell from some height into the bushes below.

The class was laughing and some of the boys ran to the window to look down.

'Get back to your seats, you idiots!' he yelled, his voice cracking like a whip.

It was the loudest voice we had ever heard. Like a herd of cattle, the boys ran, panting, back to their seats. The bell rang. Still in their seats, the class looked up at him. We still didn't know his name. He wrote out yellow detention slips for the boys and gave them to me to pass to them. On them, he had printed his name: Bishop.

We handed in our essays on *Ariel*. Mr Bishop sat there with a red pen and a stack of pages torn from exercise books. He called me over with his finger and brought a chair over to his desk for me. We sat there opposite each other, and he found my essay and began reading it. He wrote so hard that his pen punctured the thin-lined paper I had written it on. I hoped he would like the paper – it used the 'black shoe' in 'Daddy' as a metaphor for the 1950s female oppression which Plath had encountered. I continued not to understand *Ariel* and because of that I had begun to believe what Mr Bishop had said about Plath, that she was in some way unworthy of our notice, should never have been made 'canon'. But I could still write an essay that impressed a teacher about something I didn't really understand or believe, with a detachment that alarmed even me. Mr Bishop hunched over the essay for almost a whole hour, reading it with a frown and an intense level of absorption and annotating it constantly. But halfway through the double period, he looked up and saw the rest of the class mutinying and he turned the open colour of a blood orange.

'Alec, I am going to rip off your head and shit in your throat!' he said.

Alec had played a trick on Patrick that the boys called 'pick up the soap'. It was a sort of game where the first boy would knock over another boy's possessions so that the second boy was forced to pick them up off the ground. While the second boy bent over, the first boy would begin thrusting joyfully into his buttocks. Which was what Alec had been doing while Patrick giggled and gathered up the contents of his pencil case on the ground. Now, looking up into Mr Bishop's red face, Alec flattened out his rubber-band lips into a straight line. The other boys who had been spectating and laughing slunk into silence.

'Do you want me to do it?' he asked him.

'No.'

All the colour in Alec's eyes went quiet.

'Then sit in silence and do your work.'

'I don't have any work to do. You didn't give us anything,' Alec said, small-voiced.

'Then sit there and look at the wall,' he said slowly, giving the 't' in sit and the 'k' in look their own stabbing sound.

Mr Bishop turned back at me and it was as if all of his anger had just been a mask. His face transformed into a sloppy, smiling thing. I felt strange.

'Let's continue then, now that that's been dealt with,' he said to me in the silence.

Then he added, 'This essay is the best I have ever seen. Compared to most of the students, I have to teach, this is *Tolstoy*. But there are a few things I still want you to work on.'

It took him the rest of the class to mark up my five-page essay and when he was done it was covered in blood-coloured arrows, crossings-out and annotations. I felt grateful that he had spent so much time improving me. I squinted to read his tiny, medieval-looking handwriting and wondered what the words 'catharsis' and 'apotheosis' meant. The bell rang and the rest of the class filed out silently, it seemed that even the sound of the other students packing up had been drained from the room. I got up and began to leave when he said: 'Stay back. I want to talk to you.'

'Oh.' I sat back down.

He stood up and began walking around the room as he spoke, the essay was in his hand.

'This was absolutely brilliant,' he said, pointing to the essay.

'Oh,' I said, trying not to show how much it pleased me to hear that.

'It was just ...' he exhaled, 'really, really good. Have you ever thought about becoming a writer?'

'No, not really,' I lied.

'You should.'

I said nothing because there was nothing like this feeling. For the longest time, I had listened as teachers spoke to me in slow-motion voices that made me think they had language difficulties. I had said nothing as classmates asked if I could even read. If I had any English. I had been mistakenly put in ESL classes by my high school. But I knew I had English and I wanted to be someone who didn't just have English in the sense of possessing it but in the sense of having it the way a lover has the object. I had a sadomasochistic fascination with English: it hurt me, and it gave me acute pleasure. But I also wanted to be the one to hurt it back, to teach it new tricks, to stand over it, to win its favour, to know it better than it knew me, to mangle it and deform it and re-make it into my own image.

'Has anyone ever said that to you?'

'No, no one's ever said that to me,' I said.

'You should come to my office. I have something you might like to read.'

His 'office' turned out to be a small wooden desk shoved next to a cramped maze of other desks in staffroom 6. Feeling elephantine in the tiny space, I tried to make myself two-dimensional whenever another teacher rushed past. Mr Bishop rummaged till he found a thin book with a stringy spine. *The Anxiety of Influence* it said.

'I want you to have this,' he said.

'Why?'

'So you can become a strong writer.'

'Thanks,' I said, trying not to smile all of my feelings at once.

I took it home and read it. It was about poets wrestling their poetic forefathers to the death. They needed to kill their fathers to become strong men themselves. But I didn't think patricide was really for me. I loved books and they loved me right back, some opening themselves up to me straightaway, some needing to be coaxed open before all their secrets fell out. Some you needed to speak tenderly to, some you had to be firm with or they'd walk all over you, some you had to respect their shyness before they broke open like a Fabergé egg. Sometimes they flirted with you, standing in the doorway, asking if you liked their furniture or their shoes, and you were driven crazy not knowing if you'd ever be let inside. Some were straightforward as a sibling. Others complicated as a still beautiful ex-lover who looks at you the wrong way. The books were my mothers and my fathers, my grandmothers and grandfathers, they were a place for me to lay my head. They gave me piggybacks, they gave me long looks, they packed my lunchbox for me. No, I could never kill them.

Perhaps this made me what Bloom would call weak, but weakness was one of the qualities I most valued in my life. Weak like when I was tired and falling into the arms of my favourite book. Weak as I lay in bed, watching movies with a hot-water bottle while feeling sick on my period. Weak when a drunk man alone on the pavement yelled racial slurs at me on Christmas and feeling everything for him. Weakness as in sipping on the delicious sadness of having my heart broken again. Weakness as in swimming in the ocean and letting the water take me where it wanted. Weakness as in being a person.

The next morning was double English, which meant double the amount of time that I would spend sitting at the front of the classroom with Mr Bishop. The first thing he said after he took his hat off and sat down was:

'Did you read it?'

'Yes.'

'The whole thing?'

'Yes.'

'I knew it.'

I smiled.

'And?'

'I wasn't sure ...'

His face hardened into a stone tablet on which his displeasure was carved.

'I wasn't sure I understood it but then I did and I loved it.'

'Good,' he said and his heart of stone turned into flesh again.

'Good,' I said.

The thing that made my soul shake sometimes was that despite Mr Bishop's obvious belief that I was gifted, smart, whatever, I still didn't understand *Ariel*. I felt defeated by those poems and in some strange way, intimidated by them and by Plath herself. The thing that I had initially understood about her from reading about her online was that she was a straight-A student like me, a girl with promise, a person who sometimes rather grandiosely believed she was *gifted* and who was carried by this self-knowledge. Perhaps she was simply too clever for me, I began to think.

Then there was the Saturday when I was watching stupid YouTube videos on my laptop in bed and thought to see if there was any existing footage of Plath on YouTube. There weren't any videos but there were radio interview and, more importantly, I found some recordings of Plath reading her poems – 'Daddy' and 'Tulips' as well as 'The Applicant'. It was in the immediacy of her voice that I heard the black humour, the floating grin I imagined her wearing. The way the strange and abject images felt stranger and uglier when housed in their neat lines and near rhymes. The appropriation and gross exaggeration of 'Daddy' began to feel like both satire and yet an entirely sincere, real thing. I realised how far her comic and knowing voice felt from the humourless and dead ideas we have of her. And I realised I had fallen in love with her and would, in some way, always love her. She wasn't the kind of writer whose writing you could love but whose person you could ignore. When you loved her poetry, you loved her.

I went to class on Monday, armed with this new knowledge – it was knowledge because loving Plath was knowing Plath to me. Looking back, I see how this made sense because all real love is a kind of knowing. And it was Plath I was in love with now.

Mr Bishop had written two stanzas and a lone free-floating line from 'Daddy' on the whiteboard in his spindly, archaic script.

He described the poem to us as a pastiche of references to wildly disparate things: World War Two and the Holocaust, the wave of anti-German sentiment that swept America; the Colossus of Rhodes, a thirty-metre tall statue of Helios which had domi-nated Ancient Greece that Plath had named her first collection of poetry after, the interest Plath and Ted Hughes had in the occult.

He wrote feverishly on the board, annotating different things, and when he wasn't writing, he paced and spoke to us. Some of the other teachers disapproved of his method of teaching, less Socratic forum than university-style lecture – they sometimes spoke with vinaigrette voices about how they, too, had honours or masters degrees in literature and science and history and pure maths and yet they didn't feel the need to make themselves the centre of their classroom. But I loved it – I loved how it felt like the sheer reserves of knowledge that were pouring out of him fell directly like a rainstorm upon our still plastic, spongy little brains.

'And at the end of the day, we're reading a poem that seems to be about all of these huge ideas when really it's about a girl with very literal Daddy issues who mixes them up with her sorrow that her husband is having an affair with another woman. And seems to use the very real tragedy of the Holocaust as a rather inappropriate and overblown metaphor for her own sense of "persecution" by the men in her life,' he said as he concluded his lecture.

I realised then that Mr Bishop hated Plath, not just the idea of her or her work or the fact that he had been made by the school and the Board of Examiners to teach her to us but that he seemed to actively despise her as a person. And for the first time, rather than finding his cynical comments about Plath to be astute and sharp and sophisticated, I found them strange and sad and kind of stupid. They hurt me because I had decided that I was her.

'I don't think that's true, sir,' I said.

'What did you say?' he asked.

'I don't think that's true at all.'

'What?'

'That "Daddy" is just writing about the men in her life and overblowing what she went through by invoking the Holocaust to describe them.'

'Well, what's the poem about then?'

I hesitated.

'I think it's meant to be funny.'

'Are you being silly?'

'No. I listened to a recording of her reading it aloud over the weekend and it's just. It made me realise it's different to what I thought at first. It's kind of making fun of itself, the poem. It's sort of aware of what kind of poem it is and it's, like ... the poem knows it's a poem that brings up the Holocaust. And that's funny somehow?'

'Stop now. You're embarrassing yourself.'

'Okay.'

'Your behaviour is inappropriate. Totally inappropriate.'

'Why?'

'Stop talking and get out of my class now.' He was shouting in the loudest voice I had ever heard.

I said nothing and quickly gathered up my things without even zipping my pencil case up. As I was walking out the door, my unzipped pencil case slipped out of my grasp and gel pens, erasers, pencils, stickers, highlighters and general debris fell onto the floor like a waterfall. Patrick and Alec led the boys in laughing at me and soon the girls were giggling too as I knelt on the floor to pick everything up. I tried not to cry but I had always been weak like this – an easy crier. Tears came into my eyes and I ran out of the door as fast as I could. I sat on the floor in the hallway outside the classroom, listening to hear what everyone was saying. I felt displaced. I didn't know where to go, I didn't want anyone to see me, I'd never been sent out of class before. It made me think of what Ikanyu had said about being in primary six and being made to stand out in the hallway for some minor misdemeanour. The headmaster of his school patrolled the corridors with his ti nah looking for boys who had been sent out. If he saw you, he beat you with it and if he didn't see you that day, well, you'd spent the whole time worried that he would, which was almost as bad. No one was going to beat me but I still felt pretty worried and sad. The bell rang out and I watched as the class flowed out of the classroom chatting happily as if I didn't even exist. After all of them left, Mr Bishop came out and saw me straight away.

'Come back inside,' he said.

I walked back into the classroom slowly.

He began walking not just towards me but at me. It was a kind of aggressive dance of sorts. I backed away from him until there was nowhere to back away to. I was up against the wall and he was close.

'You are full of *sprezzatura*.'

'What?'

'You act like you don't care but you do.'

'Sorry,' I said and I began crying again.

'Stop crying!' he spat in my face. 'You are *sprezzatura*. You're losing your chance of becoming a writer.'

He took a handkerchief out of his pocket and gave it to me.

I cried into his handkerchief. When I had stopped, I gave it back to him.

'Keep it,' he said.

'No,' I said.

'Keep it,' he said.

'No,' I said.

But he looked so angry that I put it in the pocket of my school dress and zipped it up. I was so afraid someone would see it and so ashamed of crying. It burned a hole into my dress just sitting there. I had always thought I was so smart and strong and knew how to do anything and now I realised just how wrong I was. I had no idea how to get out of this.

Mr Bishop looked at my face like he could see the puny little brain behind it. He looked at my breasts like they were low-hanging fruit. I had seen this look before in the men that passed me on the street, were friends of my family, were teachers at school. Men who had begun looking at me like I was on the precipice of womanhood and only needed a small shove before I fell into that irrevocability. Men in cars that slowed down to scream at me 'nice legs' and oh, so so many others. The look was knowing and it confused me at the time because I was not just innocent of the world of men but completely idiotic about it. I knew nothing but my own doubt in myself, my thoughts, my abilities, my understanding, me. There was nothing to make me un-doubt myself and there was everything and everyone around me to tell me that I was the most unreliable narrator of my own story.

Well-meaning adults always told girls like me that looks didn't matter, but what they never understood was that it wasn't *my* looks that worried me but the looks that men gave me. They gave me looks like they were gifts they knew I never wanted in the first place and I didn't have the receipt to return them. I had to hide them all somewhere somehow as if they were mine. These looks were like a visual touching but a very cunning kind of touching because who ever lost their job or standing or family over a few stray looks?

Ma had taught me how to stamp hard on a man's shoe and knee him in the balls if he ever grabbed me from behind. In our role plays, Ma was the man holding me and I would twist out of her grasp and run while Ma yelled, 'Faster, faster, faster!' But what if no one grabbed you or did anything to you really? How did you run away then?

And it would all become so obvious to the adult version of that frightened girl in the classroom, but she was still much too far away to save herself. And there was no one else. There was no one there to march up to that school and make empty threats. No one to write a long angry letter. No one to tell her they were full of rage. It was just her. There really wasn't anyone at all. And she didn't want or need some great sympathy orchestra to play their song for her. But she needed someone somewhere to understand. So, the Girl said nothing. She sucked her tears back into her sockets and said nothing. She just stood there and thought to herself that she couldn't believe she had thought she could be a writer. She knew now that her words would never mean anything to anyone. Not compared to a teacher as tall as Ted Hughes and as cruel as a rumour.

After that, the rest of the school year was like the long crash after a sickly-sweet sugar rush. Someone told someone about what Mr Bishop had been doing in his classes, I never knew who, and he went on sick leave for the rest of the year. There was a sense among the students, many of whom had loved him, that a student had given Mr Bishop the sickness that now meant he could no longer teach. And there was a vague resentment that hovered amongst the school body that was held against the individual body that had made it happen to him. It all gave me this feeling of guilt for what I saw as my own sickness and how I had infected him with it. And all along I missed him, all the things he had taught me that had expanded my view of the world. All the new words I knew now and everything they meant to me and all the books he had given me. I shoved them all in the bottom drawer of my wardrobe along with the handkerchief and left them there.

I studied for my final exams but where the firecrackers going off inside my brain had made me feel something once, they gave me no pleasure now. It was the first time that the love affair I had with English and school and straight As and being a good, clever girl who was going to do good and clever things had been destructive to me. It chastened me and it took away all the special powers I had that Ikanyu and Ma and Ah Ma had given me. Ikanyu had led me to believe I was brilliant and could do anything in Australia if I worked for it, Ma had steamed and fried fresh fish for me every day so my brain would grow, Ah Ma had watched and guarded me from everything like a personal bodyguard and disciplined me with her bamboo stick. And they had all told me I was stupid at spelling or bad at maths or too slow at something so I would get smarter and stronger and better – so I would be good enough. The house that nurtured me had fallen like it was made of playing cards and I didn't know what to do with myself any more.

Eleven

It was early morning when I woke up from a deep sleep with fractured dreams that scared me. I looked up and saw the velvety drapes of the four-poster bed and the deep blue of the walls of my room at the residency. Most of my dreams involved me running from someone who wanted to kill or kidnap or rape me and I always felt so relieved when I woke up and saw that no one was pursuing me, that I was okay and had nothing to worry about. I was a weak person who was always running in this life.

I got back in bed and when I woke up again it was breakfast time. I dressed myself and washed my face and then went downstairs to see everyone for the first time since Edinburgh. Maeve, Clementine and Otto were at the breakfast table, drinking coffee out of a huge communal plunger and reading on their phones. Someone's toast was burning. I sat at the big dining table with them also on my phone. I saw the date and realised with a jolt that it was my birthday. Being sick and bedridden had made me lose track of time. I began dealing with the admin that inevitably comes with a birthday: replying to and liking birthday posts from family and friends on Facebook and texting people thank-you notes for their well wishes on my phone. I found birthdays a little embarrassing and a little tedious. All of this sugary attention in the form of these small repetitions. The same grammatical construction at the same time from the same people every year and the same responses, obliging me to do the same on their birthdays. It felt less like time was passing in clean linear movement and more like it was going in concentric circles that got smaller and smaller each year as if I was a vulture flying loops over the carcass of my own life.

Penelope appeared with a huge vase of white orchids. The almost life-size vase was all open neck and long thin waist and Brazilian-butt-lift hips. The effect was intended to be 'classy' but it just came across gauche and slightly orientalist.

'Special delivery for you,' she said.

I was embarrassed but I tried to smile and Penelope smiled back at me. I sensed that we were both trying extra hard with each other to accelerate our relationship over the Edinburgh stuff till it was a tiny speck in the past. She put the orchids down next to me and I hid my face behind the flowers.

'It's my birthday,' I said.

I was reluctant to share this with yet more people who would then have to fulfil some social contract that said they had to make much of this fact but I didn't know how else to explain the delivery.

'Happy birthday,' Otto said.

'You didn't say anything!' Maeve said. 'Happy birthday.'

'Happy birthday!' Penelope said.

'Who are they from?' Maeve asked.

'I don't know,' I said.

'Don't tell me you have a secret admirer,' Penelope said.

'How old did you turn?' asked Clementine.

'Twenty-three.'

'Twenty-three and already doing residencies halfway around the world!' she said. 'I must seem completely geriatric to you.'

The other artists smiled benignly at this. I said nothing. I was surprised because I had thought of our trip to Edinburgh and her care of me when I was sick as genuine. But then again, this seemed to be the structure of our relationship. In public, Clementine humiliated me and in private, she doted on me. I hated it when girls hate-complimented each other. I knew that now it was my turn to tell Clementine how great she was in some other way but I could be stubborn when I felt that I was made to play a role and in my stubbornness, I refused to do it. And I didn't want to lie. I wanted to save myself from that.

I grew up feeling like telling a lie was the worst way you could sin against another person. It was the sin from which all the other sins sprung because it was in the dark that the devil walked around tempting people and it was only by being in the light that you could be saved. If my Ah Ma didn't like someone she didn't smile. If she was angry, she beat me. When she was really upset, she prayed loudly to God, telling him that though no one on this earth understood what had happened to her, he did and asking for the wicked to be blown away as chaff. There was a certain innocence to a person who lived like this. I wanted to be innocent. *The Ang Moh will smile in your face while twisting the knife in your back*, Ma had said of her work colleagues. *It's a very artificial culture*, Ikanyu would say. *To them, everything is always fan-tas-tic!*

I knew that Clementine oscillated between liking me and then seeing me as some kind of threat but to what I never fully understood. Sometimes, being with other artists felt like being in a reality TV show. It would feel like a mix of *Big Brother* and *Survivor* and possibly *The Bachelor* but without the bachelor, the prize money or the fame. Instead of fighting over the usual spoils of reality TV stardom, artists fought each other for a prize that was completely invisible and unknowable. That didn't mean that the prize didn't exist but it did make it unclear how to compete or why you were competing given that no one knew what exactly they were competing for.

It felt very much like there were hidden cameras on us at all times and we had all been given roles that we were compelled to play to win some invisible trophy. At first, we jostled each other, trying to get the best roles, but after so many weeks, these roles calcified and we stuck to them.

'I should probably put some water into the vase,' I said as a way of changing the topic.

'Don't overwater, though,' Maeve said. 'That's the mistake people always make.'

'Really?'

'Yeah. And cut the stems at an angle. Also, a teaspoon of sugar can be good for them.'

'Thanks, Maeve. You're an amazing gardener.'

'I'm British, you can't say anything nice to me,' she said. 'It'll make me go all weird.'

'Okay,' I said. 'Thanks, Maeve, you're a terrible person,' I said.

'That's more like it,' she said, 'you absolute loser.'

I laughed and then got up and went to the kitchen for a jug of water which I poured into the mouth of the enormous vase. I lugged it upstairs and lay down on my bed to think. No one had told me to expect a gift of any sort and there wasn't any card. My family weren't the sort for these kinds of gestures. That morning, Ikanyu had texted simply 'Happy birthday' and Ma had written, '23. Getting old ah.' Ah Ma, of course, didn't have a phone and wouldn't have known it was my birthday if she did. Which was fair to me because I never knew when Ah Ma's birthday was – none of us did. We had just arbitrarily picked a date in November and estimated her age. Ikanyu said she had been born too poor for a birth certificate and they didn't celebrate birthdays in those days. This made me think of Ah Ma's strange freedom – she had no sense of time, no day that her life began, no clear sense of age – and it made me believe she would be a kind of never-ending person – because how could a person who had never really began ever end?

But the orchids reminded me, irrationally, of Ah Ma. And how much she loved the orchids in our backyard, how her love had been too much and they never flowered. They were never in expensive vases like this – they sat in their black plastic planters, green-leaved and barren. I wished I could give them to her.

I checked my emails habitually. Emails were like crack to me. An email came up from Leon – I supposed he wanted to make sure I was still at the residency and hadn't played hooky again. I opened it. It said: 'Did you get my flowers? I heard it was your birthday' and I felt disgust and confusion – flowers were for people who actually knew and liked each other, like married couples on their anniversary or teenagers on a Valentine's Day date or something like that. The sentimentality of the whole thing surprised and even touched me. Then it made me feel sick again. I pulled some of the white petals off the stems and crushed them in my fingers until they became slick and sticky. I hated the orchids and the stupid vase they came in. Was the vase racist? Could a specific breed of flower and type of vase be racist? I hated that I would also wonder about that. And what I hated most was that I couldn't say anything about it to anyone because I still needed his help. I deleted the email and lay down in my bed and had a nap.

I had already learned this all the way back in high school but everyday I was learning this even more: all the years of straight As and teachers thinking I was special and all the scholarships and prizes and grants and shortlists and long lists and dean's lists could be so easily poisoned by the people who controlled them and, by extension, controlled me. Or rather, maybe the whole thing had just been poison from the start.

I thought about all the things that I hadn't realised would happen to me the moment I left high school. I would apply for a local scholarship to cover my university fees but then I would go to the award ceremony and the nice man on the board who had spoken kindly and given me soft-ball questions in the interview would touch my waist, grab it like it belonged to him and ask me why I was so skinny. Red-faced, he would tell me there was still more money in the fund and wink and I would sink and sink inside.

Then I would finish my degree and submit my short story to a prize for young writers. And one of the judges of the prize would tell me he should mentor me and then tell me I should sleep with him. Then a bunch of local magazines would publish my poems and one of the editors would send me an email late at night telling me I was ungrateful for all he had done to spotlight me and make me what I was.

Then I would meet Leon. And so many more of 'them' that I haven't yet met. The promise they had said I had was a promise they had broken.

And I knew now that in spite of all the accolades and honours and grades and achievements they would shower on me, what they secretly wanted when the ceremony ended was for me to 'flatten out underneath [their] feet like Mrs Willard's kitchen mat'. And put all together, all of these experiences had made me go from being Samson who ate honey from the comb and killed bears with his bare hands to Samson with his hair all shorn off. They made me understand that I didn't have any special powers, or any powers at all.

I lay in bed thinking all of these things over and then I felt fatigue and a desire for sleep to overtake me. I hoped it would take away the weakness the illness had cast all over my body and make me strong again.

I woke up from my stupor to a small, polite knock at the door. Looking out the window, I could tell that it was dusk.

'Come in,' I said, not wanting to get up.

There was a struggle with the old doorknob and then Penelope appeared in my room wearing her arts administrator's look of exhausted enthusiasm. I jumped out of bed straight away, suddenly aware of the amount of mess in my room – clothes were strewn all over the floor and random bits of soft plastic wrappers

I hadn't binned and even an unused pad – they were all on display. I started trying to tidy up as if I could reverse the impression of myself I had already made.

'I'm fine. Really, don't worry,' she said.

'Okay.'

I stopped cleaning and stood up straight, curious about why she was here.

'How's everything going?' she asked.

'Great,' I said.

She looked at the mess and the seemingly human-shaped imprint I had left on the bed from my days of lying down.

'You've been sick, have you?'

'I'm okay now.'

She hesitated.

'Residencies are weird things.'

'Okay.'

'So, just don't worry, okay?'

'Okay.'

'We're nearly at the end now, anyway. Have you liked it?'

The answer was not really but I told her I had liked it and was very grateful to her and to everyone who had brought me over here.

'I've been meaning to ask you – there's a photographer coming to the convent to take pictures of some of the artists. The photographs would run alongside an article in a Scottish arts magazine about the convent and the scholarship programme for Commonwealth artists. Would you mind if they took some pictures of you?'

I had been in a lot of photographs for different organisations in my lifetime. The first time had been for my primary school when I was still in prep. The photographer had taken me, Matthew and Ralph out of class for it. Matthew was a little boy with brown skin whose mother was from Fiji. Ralph was an Italian boy with waves of blond hair and white-bread skin. I was me. We were taken to the library and told to read some books together. I was the only one who could read, so I picked a picture book and read aloud, pointing at the words. The photograph of us reading was blown up and put up on a billboard at the school gate with the school logo and the enrolment dates for the following year. Posing altogether like that, we represented the achievement of world peace.

In high school, a cameraman came in to film a short video for the National Assessment Program. They asked me to put my hand up and ask my maths teacher whether he could help me with a question on a test I wasn't sure about. I did it. Then they asked my maths teacher to tell me that he wasn't able to assist me with the test. And he told me sternly, *no, I can't help you with anything like that*. We had to do take after take because my voice was too quiet. I felt very embarrassed the whole time because, of course, I knew that teachers weren't allowed to help you with tests and having to ask the dumb question over and over again and be told over and over again what I already knew made me feel terrible, like I was a cheat or something. I knew, of course, that the video was scripted, that we were playing characters in a sense and not ourselves. But it was always the unreal things in my life that made me feel bad about myself, not the real things.

In university, they had taken me out of a lecture theatre one day with two other students I didn't know. We were told to walk around the grounds, pretending to talk to each other and smile. The photograph was used in the university brochure under a heading about welcoming international students to Melbourne, though all of us were local students.

So, I was unsurprised when Penelope asked me if I would get my picture taken. I was a professional at pretending to smile.

'Sure.'

'Great. Well, he's actually downstairs now. I have to go down and meet him. Will you be ready soon?'

'Of course.'

I got dressed in a big blue man's shirt and some white painter's pants and went downstairs. A month or living with other artists had made me adopt their dress code. Their tasteful, paint-splattered, I-don't-care clothes. They all dressed that way when they were in the studio – everyone except Clementine, who never got paint on herself and who always looked like she was trying to look like someone else.

The photographer was from the local newspaper. He had a great silver piece of foil in the shape of a circle, a light and a camera with him. After he had set up in the gallery, he asked me to hold a pen and a notepad in my hand and to sit on one of the great velvet couches.

'Look like you're dreaming of what you're going to write next.'

This man had watched too many movies. I looked out the window and saw the sky. I thought about how I had started feeling too sad and sore and tired and weak to write anything at all.

I thought about how little I knew about Plath still and how I didn't know what a postcolonial novel even was. I thought about how when I was younger, I could walk around in the wide-open space of my mind, enjoying that it was all mine, the way a person enjoyed their country property or large backyard. And how now, the whole space felt much smaller, claustrophobic, with a smog I couldn't see anything through. I thought about how—

'Come on then, give us a smile.'

'I don't smile when I'm writing.'

'No? Well, what's the point of being a writer then?' He laughed and shook his head.

I didn't know what the point of being a writer was so I said nothing. I tried to smile.. I tried to look like the idea in his head he had of what a writer was, a person that had dreams that fell into their lap which they could collect and use. I smiled as hard as I could. I brought my lips up so, so high and then just as I thought I was getting the hang of it, I felt myself crumpling up my face like it was a bad draft. I was crying.

'Ah. I think we've got enough to go on, thanks,' he said.

'Sorry,' I said. 'I can do it if you give me another go.'

'No, the stills look great,' he said.

He started packing up. I could tell he was lying to make me feel better and this made me cry all the more. I was still crying when he was gone.

That night I lay up in my bed doing nothing. I wasn't crying any more but I was still feeling sad. I had started to feel sad all the time here. Even when I was happy it felt like the happiness was a film covering my sadness but if you peeled it back a little you could easily see all the sadness underneath it. I wasn't sure why I felt that way. I just did.

And I felt sad that I felt sad because Ikanyu had told me he had never been sad even when he had nothing. And I who had everything should be as happy as him. He said sadness was what happened when you had it too good. Which was why sadness was a gweilo emotion. Something they soaked their fragile lives in. I didn't want to be a person who felt things and was incapacitated by the intensity of her feelings but I just was. This made me sad too.

Ikanyu didn't seem as happy as he said he was. Sometimes he came home from work in his blue and orange workman's clothes and kicked furniture or slammed it with his fists. He had a bad temper and was very moralistic, which made people sometimes dislike him. He told me it got to a point when a colleague had taken him by the throat and held him up to the wall in the lunch room. He never told Ma this. That's the thing about being an only child, everyone tells you their secrets because in some ways you don't count. I asked him why that had happened and he waved his hand and said it didn't matter.

Ma said that I should always be happy because I had God with me. But I didn't know if God existed and if he did, he had left me a long, long time ago. She also said I should be happy because Jesus was happy. I felt he was a pretty melancholy sort myself, what with the weeping blood and the constant predictions of his own death, but I didn't say this.

My Ah Ma never seemed happy. She was always angry at the world and she never spoke, she yelled and raged. That's what I loved about her. She made me feel like the oceans inside of me were normal. Like feeling sad or angry was a way of dignifying the bad things that had happened to you.

I loved Sylvia Plath because she always seemed sad and everyone loved her anyway, they even idealised her sadness as if it was a special type of happiness. Of course, this was an idealisation of her illness and her suicide. A reading of a writer that had nothing to do with her writings.

I didn't want to die exactly because death sounded so gruesome and strange but I did wish I could disappear into nothing. This is why books helped, I read one and my body dissolved into its pages and I had a kind of reprieve from being alive. It was the same with people. Sometimes you could disappear into their thoughts or feelings or charisma and feel yourself fading away. And sleep, too, floating away into the unconscious. That was something I loved to do. But I was struggling to sleep at night more and more in those days. I napped a lot in the day and perhaps that was part of the problem but it was agony to lie awake at night, waiting for the reprieve that never seemed to come. Instead of waiting that night, I decided to go down to the basement of the convent and do my laundry. I washed my clothes and then sat in front of the washing machine, watching them go around and around, hypnotising me with their obedience to the rotations of the machine. It was cool and dark down then. It smelled of sweet fabric softener and stale wet clothes. When the washing was done, I hung the clothes up on the makeshift line that had been set up for us. As I was completing my task, I saw a figure ducking under my clothes and appearing from behind a bedsheet. The figure was Clementine. I didn't know what face to place on the front of my head. A smile would be a lie. Anything less would be too honest. So I tried look deep into one of my T-shirts as if it held the meaning of life instead.

'I just wanted to say I'm sorry about this morning. I was just really tired.'

She looked like it. Her bleached hair was tending towards yellow more than it was white and her eyes were cracked blue marbles. I felt like a louse looking at her all messed up like that.

'It's totally fine,' I said automatically.

'Are we okay?'

'Of course.'

'Sure?'

'Sure.'

'Thank you.'

'No problem, don't worry about it.'

I never knew what to say in these instances. *It's fine* was untrue because if everything was fine there would be no conversation occurring. *I forgive you* was sanctimonious. It sounded like you thought you were Jesus praying for the Roman soldiers jeering you while splayed out on the cross. I only knew that I started to feel at some point like I was an air hostess, and the plane was going down, and I still needed to keep pushing out snacks and drinks and smiling my cracked-lipstick smile and saying it was all going to be okay.

'Also, I think I've finished the painting. I don't need you to sit for me any more.'

'Are you sure?'

'Yeah.'

I was surprised at how disappointed I was by this. As much as I disliked Clementine when she was with the others and was angry at her sometimes, when we were alone the hardness in her voice dissolved and she was funny and clever and sometimes kind and she had become my friend. My good friend. My bad friend. My only friend. We hugged and then she left and I was alone in the dark with myself. I was starting to think that only the people who hurt me knew how to make me feel at home.

Twelve

I checked my emails in the morning and saw that Penelope had sent out an email to say that everyone would be sharing their work in progress that night to celebrate the end of our time together. It was the last day of the residency and I really had nothing to show for it and here I was at my desk thinking about writing instead of actually writing. There was a time when I never thought much about what I was doing, when my typing was so constant and loud and obnoxious that the person I shared an office with couldn't stand me typing while I was in the same room as her. I think that this was back when I still thought that writing was a way of self-aggrandising. I thought it could make me human or at least humanlike in the face of my own dehumanisation. That I could make a person have empathy for me.

I used to have this line I saved and brought out for grant applications and writers festivals – that having been Jane Eyre, Anna Karenina and Esther Greenwood all my life, my writing was an opportunity for the reader to have to be me. Never mind that novels were not me and that there were so many novelists before me who had done this. It was all so embarrassing to me now, my naivety, my adolescent posturing in the mirror of my own self-image.

Now I knew it was the opposite – the novel was a powerless form. Powerless to effect real social change or even have any living consequences in my puny little life. It couldn't protect me from anything. But as I thought more about it, I decided that there was nothing deforming about this powerless form – it was appropriate to my own powerlessness. I thought I might be able to revel in it.

I used to worry about the ridiculousness of my English major, the self-indulgence of what I was doing, the failure of literature and, by extension, myself, to really *do* anything. But now I saw that it all made sense, that powerless form – it fit me perfectly.

I got up from my desk and went for a walk in the woods that surrounded the residency. I saw a squirrel for the first time in my life and I snapped a photo of it. I felt something when I saw it but then the feeling turned to ash and I felt nothing at all. I looked at the beauty of those lonely woods and thought about how I was supposed to have been happy here. I was supposed to have experienced the artist residency as a mythical place, filled with greenery and natural light and common goals. It was supposed to be the fulfilment of the fantasy I had been using to get me through most of my childhood and adolescence. That one day I would be with other interesting and clever people who would understand me and everything would be okay. But I hadn't experienced the fantasy of the artist residency at all. I had heard how good it was to have your meals seen to, to not have to work, to leave your family in a vacuum-sealed bag in some other country and to be able to dedicate yourself fully to your work, but I didn't feel it. I thought with shame that maybe it was because I lived with my family and they did everything for me anyway so that the privilege of being here didn't mean anything to me, this adult-sized child. Ma cooked for me, Ah Ma washed, hung and ironed my clothes, Ikanyu mopped the floor. They all complained about how messy and dirty I was and how much they were doing for me but then they did it anyway. Ikanyu even washed my bloodstained underwear for me on the first day of every period. *Shame-shame*, as Ah Ma would sing to me if I was ever naked as a child. Shame-shame.

In their vast and various collective minds, my family's job was to do everything for me so I could be freed up to be brilliant and clever and hardworking. But then that was how it was being a second-generation immigrant kid – everything was done for you to compensate that in other ways, there was nothing your family could do for you.

All this to say that there was a kind of emptiness to the artificiality of the artist residency for me. It was bizarre the idea of having your sheets changed without someone chastising you for being a maggot in a bag of rice, a soggy person who made their bedroom look like salted vegetables, a lump of wet mud that couldn't even stick on the wall and worst of all, *a girl that didn't even eat the biscuit around her neck.*

The girl with the biscuit around her neck was Ma's favourite story. She would tell it to me all the time. A mother goes away on a long journey. Before she leaves, she makes a biscuit in the shape of a circle and hangs it around her daughter's neck so that she has something to eat while the mother is gone. After a very long time, the mother comes home from her journey. But the girl, she still has half the biscuit hanging around her neck. The little girl has been too lazy to turn the biscuit around so she can eat it. She has only eaten what is directly in front of her.

Every time Ma told me this story, I wanted to know if the girl had actually been saving the biscuit in case the mother didn't come back when she said she would. I wanted to ask why the mother had left the girl with a biscuit around her neck instead of putting them on a plate in front of her. I wanted to know what kind of mother would leave her daughter by herself with nothing but a biscuit and where she went on the long journey. But I already knew the answer. I'd heard the story that many times.

The work in progress night was in the portrait gallery. Everyone was seated on various couches and chairs. It was strange to be surrounded by so many faces of important-looking men and women looking down at us from the paintings which were piled high to the domed wooden ceiling in their heavy frames. Ordinarily, I loved portraits because I loved seeing the warm open light of a human face on a canvas. But I didn't see any life behind the eyes of these paintings. The moonlight was shining through the skylights and refracted through the crystal-cut chandeliers, but apart from that it was dark as an abyss. Penelope was fiddling with a projector which filled the room with a blue light as she tried to get it to connect to her computer. Jack was squatting beside her trying to make it work and Otto was calling out suggestions about things they could try in his usual sensible manner. Clementine was talking to Maeve who was showing her something on her phone. Matisse the greyhound was there and I began playing with her the way I had seen people who said they loved dogs played with them. I knew that loving dogs like loving babies was a prerequisite of normal human existence. I noticed, for instance, that the general rule with strangers was that you weren't supposed to approach them in case they were, well – strange. A serial killer in the guise of an ordinary person or worse. But that it was okay to approach a woman walking a dog or a man with a pram because for some reason having either one made you safe. The stakes around dogs and babies seemed rather high so anytime I was around either species, I felt myself to be on display and performing the role of a nice, normal human person. I scratched her ears and rubbed her sides down. She shook herself violently and then sneezed. I had read somewhere that when dogs shake themselves, they are re-setting after a small trauma. I tried not to take this personally because that wasn't what a dog-loving person would do. Instead I said *aww* and smiled stupidly into the dog's face, trying to like it, wondering why it was here where it could probably get at the valuable artworks or piss on the heritage-protected walls.

I thought about the time I'd seen Ah Ma hold a baby. Whose was it? Probably some family friend's. She sat on the couch and rocked it too hard. She sang a crude song to it: *Sayang, Sayang, Sayang.* Then she looked up and laughed because that's what those words were – a little funny, a little bit embarrassing. I wondered if she'd rocked me like that when I was young. There were photos of her holding me as a baby and looking at me like she loved me. Frozen in the attitude of loving me.

Then the projector began to work, it began to play a video with Jack in it. It was hard to work out what was happening. I was still learning the difference between a video meant to be a movie with three acts and a narrative structure, and the kind of videos that were shown at art galleries. Jack was speaking about one thing but the subtitles were telling us something different entirely. The dissonance between the two things wasn't cute – it wasn't like he was talking about love and the subtitles were about sex as if it was a romantic comedy. The dissonance was odd and unsettling where it sounded like he was talking us through his shopping list and the subtitles said things about being and time and other foreboding things. Something had been done to the camera so you could only see bits of Jack and other parts of him were obscured. I started holding on to Matisse as a life raft so that I would not float off into this alternative universe and never come back.

'Any questions?' Penelope asked us when the screen faded to black.

'What kind of film did you use?' Clementine asked. 'Is it 35mm or medium-format film?'

'Actually, I just used my phone camera but I taped all sorts of things over the camera to "muffle" the visual. I taped dirt and sticks and bugs and things over the lens. I feel like visual clarity is a false view of the world. I prefer opacity to clarity as a more accurate way of representing what the eye sees.'

'Is that why the subtitles don't match the words?' Clementine asked.

'It's a comment on the uselessness of speech,' Jack explained.

'This is really quite lovely,' Otto said.

'Thank you, Jack. That was really opening,' Penelope said.

She might have meant eye-opening but she said opening which I liked better, as if we were all opening our hearts like unused envelopes to receive Jack's message.

'Clementine, would you like to go next?'

'Sure. Could I have the lights on?'

Penelope ran to turn the lights on and we blinked like moles coming out of our burrows as we got used to it. Then Clementine unveiled the painting, ripping the canvas sheet she had placed over it right off.

The painting was of a girl who had my face, hair and body. I had never felt so beautiful and destructive in my life. I looked cold and I had the smile of some omniscient person. In the painting I was lying down in the sand by the water like I was waiting to be painted. I wore a pink dress and my black hair dripped down and pooled over my breasts. My body was idealised, and my black eyes were sparkling with knowledge and the oily sheen of the paint. I could see that in the world of the painting I was about to speak – my pink lips were slightly open. My skin was not its usual colour – it was a high-vis yellow and the light fell on my face in blue and white patches. There was a smooth evening sky above me the colour of a warm summer's day that had just turned cool.

'There's another painting underneath that one, isn't there?'

'Yes,' Clementine said.

We stared into Clementine's artworks and I could indeed see glimpses of another artwork.

There was another painting underneath the painting. Underneath Clementine's depiction of me was a ghostly, barely present portrait of Plath, copied from one of the many famous photographs of her sitting with bleached blonde hair and a white bikini on the beach. She looked sexy and vulnerable and weirdly Australian.

'How did you make this?' I asked.

'I started by painting Plath and then once that was perfect, I painted right over it, I painted you right over it. Just as I felt like you, metaphorically speaking, paint over her,' she said, while looking at me.

'You painted her?' Jack asked, pointing incredulously at me.

'I painted her,' Clementine confirmed and I could see how surprised the others were given all they had known existed between us was a kind of barely suppressed animosity. Then I turned back to the painting and watched as the ghostly impression of Plath faded in and out of the painting. If I looked at it from certain angles all I could see was the superimposed painting of myself. I saw that the colours in Clementine's depiction of me did not just erase her depiction of Plath but rather that one hinged on the other. That the painting of me could only exist because it's base was a painting of Plath.

'What materials have you used, Clementine?' Maeve asked.

'I like using cheap materials as well as expensive artist oil paints. So, I use nail varnish as glue, as a kind of paint. It's a way of rethinking the traditional feminine idea of the "makeover". So, I've given the first painting, the one of Plath, a "makeover" in a different sense of the word than what you might expect. It's a violent makeover – one that erases Plath and makes her into something else.'

The painting was almost perfect. It divined a part of me that I hardly understood myself. And its vivid colours – alien green and sickly yellow and pageant-queen pink – moved me. The only part of it I didn't think made sense was the way it portrayed me as a person with a monstrous beauty and strange powers. I had never thought of myself as beautiful or in possession of magic powers. I supposed that in some ways I had power, plain and simple. I had an education, a so-called career, a mind that worked even when my body refused to comply. I saw how Clementine saw me here, as all the things she worried she was not (but was): beautiful, smart, young, gifted. But why should that make me monstrous to her? She was not monstrous to me, not even on her worst day. She was everything the light touched and more.

I set the monstrousness of myself aside for a moment. I thought for the first time, really thought, about how I saw Plath. Was it possible that when it was your life's work to become some- one you loved, to draw near to them, to know them really, you could be erasing them entirely? You could be painting yourself over the image of them you had in your head? I thought about what the painting had shown me – that I did have powers and I did sometimes abuse them, just as Clementine did, just as Ah Ma had, just as everyone did to the people they loved. I was in love with Plath and had always thought that knowledge and love were the same thing, but love could really be a way of unknow- ing a person, of othering them, of doing, in short, to Plath what Clementine had done to me.

'Thank you, Clementine,' I said, genuinely moved by what we had done together.

Penelope asked me to show my work next. I emailed the part of *Pillar of Salt* that I had been working on and she put it on the projector for everyone to read. I sat there and waited for everyone to read what I had written. I sat there still as a cat on a post. I de- spised people who became nervous and fragile when their work was being seen by others and prided myself on my thick skin, but the truth was that my skin was baking-paper thin. My skin was so thin that it was basically transparent – you could see through whatever face I put onto the front of my head and feel exactly how I felt about any situation if you wanted to. This was one of those times. I felt embarrassed and scared and also unsure of what would come next. There was so much silence, all of it difficult to interpret with any kind of acuity. I could make up what I thought people were thinking of it but that was no use, what I really wanted to know was what they actually thought. I wanted to know if my instincts about it had been right or if I should have followed the siren bleeding its hypervigilant sound in my mind that told me to STOP any time I wrote anything at all. I reached out for the dog, but she had abandoned me to Penelope's lap.

Pillar of Salt

Ma, she had this story of a nun slapping a girl across the face on the school stage because she had begun to show. The girl in the blue pinafore dress became an object lesson. And when the thin reed of her spine began to break and they took her off the stage, Ma said it was because they didn't want the other girls to see her cry (as if tears ever absolved anyone). There was a silence in the hall as they waited for God to intervene, but he did not.

Ma told me the nuns could be kind. *They taught us how to swim in their after hours; they taught us about periods, they gave us soft pads and taught us how to wash away the deep stain till it was faint. They turned our pinafores inside out to take away our embarrassment.*

Gua Ma had sent her to the convent school instead of Chinese school as an experiment. She had cared little for education and she couldn't read her children's school reports, good or bad. She preferred her five daughters to help at home and her four sons to work. If she found one of her children crying over the ink cake and brush she told them they could drop out anytime they wanted. But she thought Ma was – not gifted or clever or special – *they didn't say things like that in those days* – something else.

Ma told me how she thought the stone gods her mother gave food and drink offerings to were useless.

They didn't even eat or drink what was put out in front of them by the big hungry family. When she said this, her mother beat her for it but also watched her.

The missionaries did their door-knocking every Saturday, talking Jesus Christ this and Our Lord that and we hold a Sunday School at the Gospel Hall on Sunday mornings if you want your children to come. But Ma never saw them and they never saw Ma. When Gua Maheard the missionaries coming, she made Ma run and hide in the drain at the back of the house. It was her big sister's job to make sure Ma was lying down in the drain with the cold dark and the rats where even Jesus couldn't find her.

Ma went to convent school in a tapioca starched shirt and bright blue pinafore and shining white socks. But she didn't like to study, preferring to play hooky with her brothers – catching crickets and twisting their antennae until they got dizzy and fought each other, keeping the best fighters in a matchbox in their pockets, making lanterns, roughhousing, taking the ferry to Penang.

In her last year, the government introduced the five-year plan. And for the first time in the longest time, all of their classes were to be taught in Malay not English. And also, also, passing Malay would become a prerequisite. *And all the Chinese and Indians at my school they were getting extra tuition in Bahasa like mad. And if they couldn't get tuition they were dropping out.* And I

had to ask Ma every time at this point in the story: Why
didn't you drop out? And she would say, *Because Ma
is smart, she remembers things easily.* And it made me
laugh because of the way that Australian schools were
always saying they didn't just want us to regurgitate
facts like those overseas students who don't actually know
anything, just how to vomit out their perfect facts. But
Ma and Ikanyu, they thought what made you smart was
having a perfect memory. They said I had a perfect memory, I remembered everything, so I knew everything.

Ma passed her O levels and then she studied for her
A levels. But Ma dropped out because she felt like the
other students were too stupid for her to be around any
longer. *There were a lot of high school drop-outs at that
time just hanging about with nothing to do.* She saw an
ad in the newspaper:

NURSE TRAINEESHIPS AVAILABLE
SERVE YOUR COUNTRY
SEE GREAT BRITAIN AND THE WORLD

And her mother took the ferry with her to Penang
and she didn't like her children to be far from her and
she held the air ticket over the green-blue water and said
*never mind the money mai kee beo kin if you change your
mind I can just tiah tiah* (this was the sound of the
ticket being torn up) *and you come home and no one will
say anything.* But Ma didn't go home because what did

Malaysia really have for her and she had English and the world.

Ikanyu was the only person she knew in all of England, they had played backgammon together at the Gospel Hall Church in Butterworth. *The missionaries opened it up on Friday nights for games and they would always invite us to church on Sundays at the end but we never went.* And he met her at the airport and they took the bus to the Old Church Hospital Nursing Quarters in Romford and then he left her there because it was late and there were no visitors allowed after ten and no gentlemen visitors allowed at all and one pint of cow's milk every morning and the canteen is downstairs and linen and laundry is provided and check in and check out every time you leave at reception or the caretaker will speak to you.

There were two weeks of PTS, *patient training something, I don't remember what the S stood for and then it was work work work for nothing hardly any pay we were the cheap foreign labour then like the Indians are now. You worked from seven to one and then you collapsed into your bed and lay there for a few hours and then got up and up again from five to nine thirty the split shift it was called they gave us Malaysian girls the busiest times because none of the English girls wanted to work them. And while we worked the matron and the personal care assistant smoked and drank tea in the lunchroom and yelled at us to do the next thing.*

We lifted the heaviest stroke patients with our bare arms and somehow put them into the hot bath every morning and we cleaned them (nowadays in hospitals they only clean you every second day you know) then we carried them back to their beds sat them up and made them breakfast and fed them. And the ratio was not like how it is here – it was 2:40, two of us skinny seventeen-year-old Malaysian girls and forty big English patients and the English they were supposed to help us but they just sat in the lunchroom and smoked and talked while we broke our backs and watched them. And one day I just ... I just had enough and I opened the door to the lunchroom and said I need your help and it was mouths open wide eyes how-dare-you faces but they said nothing and the Ang Moh woman she helped but she was fussing I can't be doing this and my back hurts when I do that and the next day I realised I'd been told on. And the matron came with her big arms and pink lipstick and blue eyeshadow and white powder face.

The matron called me Ooh-Ooh *(that's how she said my name).*

But ~~behind her back~~ I called her Cleopatra (that's how I said her name).

And she said she said Ooh-Ooh go into the pan room and clean all of the bed pans till your face shines in their reflection I'll check them later then pack this dirty staff linen not this one that one then take the patients with the biggest wounds and wash out the pus and dried blood and dirt and think think before you take a wipe out of its packet do you really need to use that injection do you dear, Thatcher's at the helm now and she's cut our supplies and fold the lines of the bed down the middle exactly with envelope corners and no not good enough do it again and again and again and again and then this then that I can't remember what else but it went on and on and on one thing after another and by one o'clock I was crying and I called my mum and told her I'm buying an air ticket and she said, if you don't like it come home. I will wait for you at the airport.

But I didn't want to just run home crying. I wanted something more. I went to the education building and I found my tutor and I told her everything and she took me back to the hospital and she went into the lunchroom and shut the door. And when she came out she said it's all okay now you don't have to go home take today off and come back tomorrow. And at seven the next morning I clocked in and started washing the bed pans again and the matron said Ooh-Ooh Ooh-ooh Ooh-Ooh she followed me into the pan room and I turned around and she said, she said: don't worry darling Ooh-Ooh, make yourself a cup of tea and a piece of toast in the lunchroom before you start.

'Wow,' Penelope said.

'It's so fitting that you're sharing this because, of course, it starts in a convent school and where we are now used to be an old convent,' said Maeve.

'And there are so many memories here, so many layers of memory-making,' Jack said.

'And it's as if the spirit of their memory is compelling her in some way. And I wondered ...' Maeve began.

'Are you going to send this out?' Clementine asked.

'I don't know.'

'I think it would do really well. We need more diverse voices now. It's really important.'

'Yes.'

'And I feel like people are really coming together now and rallying behind these kinds of books, supporting, championing them.'

I nodded politely because, I'd started to realise, she didn't need my verbal encouragement to keep going.

'I don't know as much about the publishing industry but in the art world, I know diversity is kind of like hot now, like it's the new trend. Which I really stand behind and agree with completely. It's great.'

The strangest and most banal thing about this interaction was that I could sense that Clementine's apology from the day before had been entirely sincere. This was her way of meaning well even if I had the queasy feeling that I was disappearing from the conversation entirely. I sensed the way this night would go, as surely as a train pulls into a station.

'Would you like to share your work next?' Penelope asked Otto.

I felt the moment was passing us by like litter floating on the wind, bouncing along the footpath. And I wondered how

I could intercept it. For the first time in a long time, I felt the need to intercept it.

'Can I respond to Clementine's feedback first?' I heard my-self saying and then the voice from inside of me kept speaking, not waiting for anyone else to respond. 'First of all, you cut me off. Secondly, did you notice that all the questions you directed to the other artists were about craft and everything you said just then was about so-called "diversity"? And the work that I am doing, it is not a "trend", it is not "hot", it is not even anything as sentimental or pure as the word "important" implies. It is not something to be "supported". It is something else entirely, something varied and strange and wide-ranging that is entirely about itself and not about you. For once, it is not about you.'

Clementine had been frozen all this time in the attitude of a person fearing that a full-blown accusation of racism may jump out from behind a shadow like a bogeyman.

'I was just trying to be helpful,' she said. 'I just don't know what to do or what I can say any more. Everything I say is wrong. And your accusations are a kind of violence to me and my—' She started to cry.

Maeve began patting her on the back like a baby that needed to be burped. Otto walked over with a box of tissues and Jack began stroking Matisse in a neutral manner. Penelope looked constipated with confusion and ideas of what to do that would not come. Finally, she said: 'Should we take a drink or toilet break?'

Everyone knew that the work in progress night was over but out of politeness the other artists made movements towards taking the break Penelope had suggested. As for me, I walked in a daze to my bedroom, massaged my aching back with my knuckles and closed my eyes. I was hoping for the oblivion of sleep. I waited for hours, until it was the early hours of the morning and obvious that I wouldn't sleep.

So I got up. I was only wearing my batik nightdress that Ma had bought for me at the Pasar Malam with a jacket over it. I crept downstairs and left through the front door. It was dark out and I didn't know where I was going. There was no moon, no stars, no nothing, just the big black eye of the night. I walked down the driveway and it was still a long way to the street. Then I saw a figure sitting to the side, on the grass that bordered the driveway. It was a person hugging their body in the cold. The person stood up and began walking towards me. My eyes refocused in the dark and I saw that it was Clementine. For some reason, this made sense to me. I still loved her, a painful, choked-up kind of love. And I wanted her to love me, too, but I wasn't sure if she could ever know me enough to love me. She looked shy and small-faced when she saw me. She wasn't wearing any of her usual crazy clothes – she was wearing a quilted nightgown like a grandma and that touched me.

'I couldn't sleep,' I said.

'Me neither.' She seemed pleased that I was speaking to her.

'I wanted to go for a walk to clear my head,' I said.

'Let's go,' she said.

Without discussing where we were going, we began walking up the driveway and onto the empty street outside. There were no cars and there was only a little light.

238 / JESSICA ZHAN MEI YU

'Why couldn't you sleep?' I asked her.

She shrugged. 'You know.'

'Yeah.'

'Why couldn't *you* sleep?' she said.

'You know,' I said, and we laughed.

'You know, I'm sorry I was such an arsehole to you.'

'I know.'

'I think I had too much to drink before the whole sharing night thing. I was so nervous, I just thought I needed to have something before we started. Dutch courage and all that. But I know I can be an idiot when I'm drunk.'

'Oh.'

'But I get really lonely at night for some reason. Even if I have people around me. The nights were the hardest after my dad left. Sometimes, just night-time feels so lonely to me.'

'I'm so sorry, Clementine. I thought you said he was around.'

'I know I made it seem that way. It's because the opposite was true. All the stories I tell about him – they're like my way of feeling closer to him, but he never told me any of that. They're all stories from my mum and relatives and stuff. He left when I was really little, like two or three.'

'Oh. I'm so sorry.'

'But he, like, never told us why. My mum tried to work it out with him or at least get a reason off him, but he didn't have one.'

'I didn't know that.'

'No – so I just never got any ... I hate this word, it's so American. But I never got any closure. Whatever that means.'

'So, is he a gyno?'

'He is. He really has lived this illustrious life but it just didn't happen with us there. I don't know where he lives, for example. Mum thought he left for another woman, which I think was a self-soothing story ... It's easier to think someone else made him leave than to admit he just lost interest in us.'

'Yeah.'

'He's rich and he did support us financially. He "provided".' She made sarcastic air quotes with her fingers.

'I got to go to all these posh schools with all these girls who loved boasting about their dads – what they did and how much they earned or who they knew. And I would always be, like, why is everyone's dad around but mine. So, when I get into any fraught social situation boasting about my dad is a defence mechanism.'

'That sucks,' I said feebly because I didn't know what to say. Ikanyu had always been around. What would I know of a father who wasn't?

After that we walked up and down the street together not saying much.

'Do you ever feel like you just want to disappear?' I asked her.

'How do you mean?'

'Like just go poof into thin air. Go from being something to nothing.'

'Yeah.'

'Really?'

'Yeah. When it all just gets too much and you want to run into traffic or something.'

'You don't think I'm weird for that?'

'No. I totally get it. It's a desire for self-annihilation and sometimes it feels just so real. More real than your actual life.'

'It's when the pain gets too much for me. My body just hurts and hurts and there's no end to the hurting.'

'God, that sounds awful.'

'It is.'

'No, I totally get why you would feel that way. But, I know it can be so stupid when people say this, but from my own experience anyway, which is just so different, it passes.'

'How?'

'Just by itself. If you can just wait for it to pass it passes by itself. You don't do anything.'

'You don't do anything, no.'

'And it passes. I promise.'

We hugged and she put her arms over my sore, inflamed back, making it worse but better at the same time. We started walking back to the convent together.

'Can you see someone there?' Clementine asked.

'Where?'

'There.'

I squinted. It was a man walking slowly. He seemed to be approaching us. Clementine grabbed my cold hand and squeezed it so hard it hurt. She didn't seem to be able to say anything more. Then in the darkness, I saw it, a large silver kitchen knife.

I felt Clementine's nails dig into my skin. She was shaking. I had never seen her cowed before. I was surprised that she was scared. She never seemed vulnerable. Then I realised that while

Clementine was comfortable theorising about violence, she had never actually encountered it.

Before I had ever seen a knife pointed at a person, I had seen them in my mind. My dad had told me that when he was in the navy, someone had come up behind him as he was walking home one night and put a knife to his neck and told him he was going to kill him. He had turned up the volume on his usual voice and his face had hardened into a sphinx-like look. He spoke in riddles. *Don't you know who I am? Does my hair look very long to you?* He explained the riddles to me when I was little. I had to have very short hair in the navy and policemen at the time also had to have very short hair. The man was frightened and ran away.

There was a lot of knife crime in Malaysia in those days, Ma would tell me. She said she had been getting into her car after doing the marketing (which is what she called going to the wet market). She had gone to close the door of the car when a man emerged and held it open. He was holding a knife under his shirt. *Sister, sister*, the man had begged. *Do you have any money?* He sounded more desperate then threatening. She had given him twenty ringgit and driven away.

The first time Ma had seen someone use a knife in that way, it was her mother. A thief shot his hand through a hole in the wall of their house and felt around to steal something. Ma remembered how her mother took out the big meat cleaver and chopped down at his arm. He drew his hand back and disappeared into the dark.

I had seen knives like that before. Not often but a few times. Once just sticking out of a girl's backpack on the bus. Another time I had been at an eighteenth birthday party in high school and a boy I didn't know had answered the door and the person at the door had stuck a knife straight into his stomach, pulled it out again as if it were reusable and left.

So, when I saw a knife pointed at me now, I felt strangely relaxed. So many things scared me, embarrassing social situations, my parents' anger, being a failure, but not death. It was something I was probably too okay with but being comfortable with death made me calm in these kinds of situations. Before he could speak, I screamed like a demon into his face. He was startled, I saw the tiny red cracks in his eyes as they bulged. Taking advantage of his shock, I grabbed Clementine's hand and pulled her along as I ran. He didn't pursue us but we ran all the way back to the convent anyway. When we got to the front lawn, we collapsed onto the grass and buried our faces into its cool green scent.

'You're so weird. Thinking of a thing like that,' she said.

I knew I was weird. 'Quirky', as men who were attracted to me called it. 'Idiosyncratic', as a person trying to be polite would say. 'Strange', as someone who was repulsed by me might think. But I called it weird because that was all it was. And I considered it a special power in moments like this. Because I could repulse people with the force of my personality to the point where it saved me.

'I am,' I said.

We went inside and fell asleep together on Clementine's bed. She held me and I held her back.

Thirteen

I woke up with a terrible pain that seemed prompted by the way I had slept the night before. I regretted it but I didn't want to. Clementine was already up and about. She was clean and made up and zipping up her suitcase.

'I have the early train,' she said.

'Oh,' I said.

I got up and we embraced for a long time and she told me to stay in touch. I told her I would but I knew I was never going to see her again. We would start off by keeping in touch then fade out together. She left and I stumbled back to my room to pack my things.

I knew Clementine was sorry for hurting me at times but I also knew she would never see her mis-seeing of me, her wilful blindness because this blindness was part of what made her such a beautiful and charismatic person. Her bright light, her warmth and openness was not really her at all, but the carefully constructed house on a hill she lived in. And being porous to the pain of those outside this house would destroy the beautiful architecture of her life because it would be an admission. People called Clementine's way of seeing blindness but blindness was not the sin of the blind man or of his parents. It wasn't blindness but its opposite: a form of clarity, a hard certainty that could not admit the soft, painful uncertainty of another person's life. She wanted at times to deconstruct the foundations of her life, to love me well, but she didn't really know how to. And that hurt sometimes. But I wasn't sure how to tell her that at the time. I never got any 'closure' from her, but I forgave her anyway. Not because her dad was a drop-kick but because I loved her. She was the kind of friend you would always remember with both anger and love. I knew that.

I mustered the energy to get up and pack my things into my suitcase. There were a lot of videos on YouTube that showed the best methods for packing a bag but I preferred to use the method I had decided as a kid and always stuck to – to shove everything into the bag then zip it closed while sitting on it. The orchids on my window had died long ago. I had changed their water every day but watched them dry up and turn black and brittle. I asked Maeve what she thought had happened and she said I had probably overwatered them. I preferred to believe it was their placement near the huge heater in my room that had killed them. I went downstairs and said goodbye to Penelope and the remaining artists and we all promised to keep in contact which we all knew was untrue.

I took the train to London by myself where I was to stay at the clubhouse for a few days while I attended the postcolonial conference. Leon had sent me an email inviting me to an exhibition opening that night, making much of the 'opportunity' and telling me how it would benefit me and my 'career'. What benefit could actually come out of a 'career' in the arts? I hadn't replied to him because I hadn't really known what to say and I was getting sick of simulating enthusiasm about everything. I really hoped I would be able to avoid seeing him while I was in London. Blessing was supposed to be doing the same but he was still in Johannesburg. Jack had left earlier that day for Dublin where he would be working on his own exhibition of screen works with a gallery there. The programme was still structured along the lines of its original founders' aims – to bring artists from the Commonwealth over to the UK and forge lasting collaborations between the different countries. It was the last sliver of my time abroad and I wasn't sure I'd had a huge epiphany about my life or anything like that at all. I was still the same person who rather than growing upwards found myself moving slantways, downwards, backwards, forwards through life. And going abroad hadn't really been the disappearing act I had hoped it would be. It just made everything that was invisible to me feel strangely real.

I sat on the train and logged into the Wi-Fi using the passcode taped to my table. I checked my emails, hoping for a dopamine rush. There were a lot of email notifications but as I went through them I saw that each one was simply a new email from a mailing list of some sort – a clothing brand telling me that it was having a sale or a magazine I didn't realise I was subscribed to. These mass emails were becoming more and more personal in tone, now all of them started with my name and told me how much they cared for me, which was why I should buy their new product or read their recently published article. It was a lonely time to be alive.

When I had finally accepted that there was nothing to read in my inbox, I started trying to write the paper I was supposed to present at the postcolonial conference, feeling slightly panicked at how little time I had left to work on it. After an hour or so, I had some idea of what I wanted to say. I looked out the window; past my reflection I could see hills and the clean new green of England.

At the clubhouse, I worked on my conference paper from my bed. When Leon texted and asked if I had arrived, I deleted him from my phone. I realised I could do that now. I was leaving so soon anyway. By the end of the evening, I was sort of happy with what I had written. I had pressed hard into the bruise of confusion I felt around Plath and recognition/misrecognition and enjoyed the exquisite pain of it. Then my back hurt me with a grotesque, gravelly pain and I knew I had to stop revising it and lie down.

The postcolonial conference had pens with the name of the conference printed on them sitting in a bowl. The pens impressed me – they were the kind with four colours and, on top of that, if you took the cap off the top and turned them over, the pen became a highlighter. I took a greedy handful of them. I could never resist free things. I also picked up my name tag and my programme. I opened up the timetable for the conference and started circling the panels and presentations I wanted to attend. They had interesting, sometimes witty names and I wished I'd called my paper something more exciting than, 'The Post-critical, the Postcolonial and Plath'. Alliteration was so embarrassing. My panel wasn't till after lunch on the second day of the conference. I felt I had plenty of time to watch other people speak and model my presentation style off them. There were so many people there in the frumpy yet formal dress code that academics adopted on these kinds of occasions. I was wearing a pair of white slacks I had bought on sale. It was supposed to be one half of a girl-boss suit, but I had thought it would be too expensive to buy the blazer as well. So, I had tried pairing the pants with a silky shirt I had found in an op shop. The pants were slightly too big, and they kept slipping down the slippery fabric of the shirt. Before I had left the club-house that morning I had thought I looked smart and polished but now I was worried I looked like a tourist at a resort in India or a female CEO from a TV series. I wandered around the floor of the hotel that had been reserved for the conference, trying to appear purposeful. From my supervisor's comments about how strange she felt as a white woman in postcolonial studies, I had expected to see a 'diverse' group of people at this conference. But that wasn't the case. It was about as 'diverse' as a slice of white bread. White in the middle and brown on the edges.

The first presentation I wandered into was titled, 'You're White, You Can Do Anything!' and it was by a graduate student. I supposed that he was attractive by the standards of academia. The talk was as provocative as its title. It was a play on the invisible backpack of white privilege – where he laid out all of the things inside the backpack he carried as a white man and made them visible. He was aflame with the subject, but it just made me feel tired and heavy. So instead of sitting there feeling sapped by it I let my mind drift to Ah Ma. I thought about what she would say if I told her how tired I was. She would tell me I had gone out too much and should have stayed home with her. She would tell me I had nothing to be tired about, she was the one on her hands and knees all day cleaning up after me. She would tell me to lie in bed and rest first then she would give me some chicken essence. The chicken essence would make me strong again.

The questions after the talk were difficult to sit through. They were questions framed as statements and self-important pontifications on this or that. I wondered how many years I could do this for. Could I grin and bear this until I had gainful employment in my area of study? If I did receive this kind of employment then I would need to be the one to organise these conferences, to host guests from other universities and cities and to listen to more of these kinds of talks and to give many of them myself. I wasn't sure if I could do it any more, not even for Ikanyu or myself. I thought about Ah Ma until the question time was over and then I got up and stretched my stiff back and rubbed it.

That night there were drinks in the hotel's ballroom. While we waited at the bar to claim our free drinks, a man with naïvely combed-back hair introduced himself to me.

'I'm James. I'm from the University of Savannah.'

'Oh. Nice to meet you. I'm from Australia.'

'All the way from Australia. How long is that?'

'About twenty-three hours.'

'A whole day.'

'Yeah. A whole day.'

I looked at his name tag and it said that he was a professor.

'How are you already a professor?'

'Oh. I think that's a cultural difference. What Brits and Australians call lecturers we call assistant professor.'

'That's still pretty good, isn't it?'

'Yeah. Well, I was lucky to get this job.'

'Why?'

'I'm,' he paused, 'I'm a white man in postcolonial studies.'

'Oh.'

He laughed and I laughed too but we were laughing at opposite things.

'You know what I mean.'

'I know what you mean.'

His eyes moved towards me and I thought sadly that I could have sex with this man if I wanted to. He was attractive in a broad-shouldered and decent but sort of racist Southern guy way. But I never moved from A to B on these kinds of things. 'A' being transgressive desire and 'B' being the fulfilment of that desire. I wondered if that made me repressed or just ordinary. To fill the silence he showed me photos of his kids and wife playing by the hotel pool. The pool was a small, kidney-shaped hole of blue. The kids were splotches of colour and his wife was lying on a deckchair sunning herself in the grey weather.

'They're so cute,' I said.

'I know. It's nice they can make a bit of a holiday out of this.'

I was at the front of the queue, so I handed over my little plastic blue coin and received a glass of beer. I drank the bitter, gold drink and found that I enjoyed it a little. James also received his glass of beer.

'We should exchange emails,' he said.

'Okay.'

I sent him a blank email from my phone so he had my email address.

'Thanks,' he said.

Then he moved on and I thought, I guess we just 'networked', whatever that means. I wandered around until I was stopped by a woman with red lipstick and dark hair.

'I really like your shirt,' she said.

'Thank you.'

'Where's it from?'

'An op-shop.'

'What is that?'

'Oh. A charity shop. Is that what they call it here? Op shop stands for opportunity shop.'

She laughed.

'The charity shops where I live do *not* have shirts like that in them.'

'Where do you live?'

'I teach at a university in a pretty rural part of England.'

'Oh.'

'English pastoral and all that.'

'It must be really beautiful.'

'It is. It's quite isolated, though, and I'm away from my family and friends. But the students are interesting. I don't want to idealise it because they can be tough and sometimes a bit unprepared. But they also really don't let you get away with anything. They're really no bullshit. I've had to change my pedagogical style a lot.'

'Do you feel like it's hard in terms of ...?'

She patted her face.

'Yeah. Sometimes it's like they literally cannot see you. And the thing with being a professor is they really don't expect you to be an Indian woman. They expect you to be a white man. That's the face of knowledge that students at any university in the UK know and trust. So I have to put my formal face on and be a little bit distant initially. I need to earn their respect in a way another person wouldn't. Which is awkward given my research is all about dismantling power structures.

'I know what you mean,' I said.

'My name's Ruby.'

'Nice to meet you. When's your panel?'

'Tomorrow. In the red room.'

'I'll come and see you,' I said, opening up my schedule and looking for her session. 'What's your paper about?'

'The Said archive at Columbia.'

'Wow. I love him.'

'Of course you do. I actually met him years ago, before he passed. Edward was really so lovely and gentle.'

It was strange that theorists were real people who you could meet. When I said I had loved Said, I had meant his theories and his writing. I hadn't remembered that behind the words that I had read again and again there was a person that could be loved. As I was still working out how to explain this to her, Ruby waved over and then hugged a woman with brutal, thick high heels.

'This is Layla,' she said to me.

'Hi,' she said.

'Layla's very drunk,' Ruby said.

Layla pretended to be deeply offended while swaying slightly on her heels.

'This is literally the only perk of academia. This and spending every weekend marking and answering emails till you die,' Layla said.

'And being separated from your spouse who is also an academic in another country because you're just grateful to have a job,' said Ruby.

'Which leaves you more time to mark and answer emails,' Layla added.

'And being an adjunct for ten years before you might have enough "publications" and "experience" to get a normal job,' said Ruby.

'But at least you're British. As for me, I'm from a country where the president has just changed the rules to say that he can be in power till 2050.'

'Where?' I said.

'Egypt.'

'I'm trying to immigrate here but funnily enough no university wants to sponsor me.'

'Oh.'

'But I'll get there somehow. We always do.'

Ruby asked Layla if she was going to one of the big academic conferences in America for literary studies.

'I am. Luckily. I think it was hard to get your paper accepted this year because it's going to be in New York for the first time in a while,' Layla said.

'I remember I went to a conference in Hawaii once and no one showed up to any of the panels because of how great the location was. I wonder if that will happen with this one,' Ruby said.

'Homi Bhabha's speaking.'

'Wow,' I said.

'I really like this conference,' Ruby said. 'I come every year. It's really cute and friendly. That one's a bit overwhelming in some ways. There's just so many people.'

'I thought this one was meant to be really good,' I said.

'No, it is. But it's just smaller, which is nice.'

I began to think that I had come to the wrong conference. Why couldn't I ever get things like this right?

'I'm going to get a drink,' Ruby said. 'But before that I should get your email address. Let me know if you publish something interesting, okay?'

'Okay,' I said and I meant it.

We exchanged emails with each other. I thought Layla would move on once Ruby left the conversation but she stayed and asked me what my paper was on.

'Sylvia Plath.'

'Seriously, another Plath scholar? More ink spilled on this white woman *in perpetua*?'

I smiled and nodded.

'What's your paper on?'

'Urban planning during the colonial era in America as a kind of speculative fiction. Of course, the urban planning of cities is a colonial project so conceiving of these plans and drawings as a kind of fictional future for a place ... it makes sense to me.'

'That's really cool,' I said and I meant it.

The lights dimmed and then there was the scream of a sound system coming to life. A man was tapping the mic up the front on a little stage.

'I'm going to need another drink to get through this,' Layla whispered. 'Let's stay in touch, though. Get my number off Ruby.'

'Okay,' I said and she disappeared into the darkness.

'It's time to announce the Patrick Norland award for the best graduate paper. The award goes to William Powell for 'You're White, You Can Do Anything!''

I saw William emerge from the crowd of sweaty bodies in the room. He was surprised and a little embarrassed as he ran to accept the cheque and certificate being handed to him.

After this, the man introduced the keynote speaker for the conference, a tiny, old woman with loose-fitting clothes on. She walked to the front and spoke about ecology and postcolonialism. Suddenly feeling tired, I crept towards the door and left for the clubhouse.

I woke up feeling faded from staying up later than I usually did. But I was excited to present my paper at the conference that morning and to listen to Ruby and Layla's papers. Perhaps the conference wasn't as bad as I had initially thought.

I turned on my phone and there was a text from Ma. It said Ah Ma had had a heart attack and was in hospital. I sat very still. I felt nothing so that I could do everything. I texted Ma saying I would be there as soon as possible and booked a flight that night from Edinburgh airport. Then I emailed the organisers of the conference to let them know I wouldn't be able to do my panel any more. I decided that I wouldn't cry or anything as useless as that, I would take an Uber from the train station to the airport and board the plane back to Melbourne. And after the airport then what? I didn't want either of my parents to have to leave Ah Ma's bedside to get me.

On the plane, I looked out the window at the patchwork quilt of the UK beneath me and wondered why I hadn't called Ah Ma the whole time I was away. I had thought often about her but I knew that if I had called then the conversation would have gone:

'Eh?'

'It's Girl.'

'What?'

'I'm in ...' Ah Ma didn't know where England was let alone Scotland. It was hard to know what to say. 'Chiat hong,' I would say. *Eating air. On holiday.*

'Nothing.'

'Okay. Okay.' And Ah Ma would have hung up.

No, if I wanted to reach out and touch her then it was better to use the long fingers of memory than the false teeth of speech.

In my mind, she was using small knives and white vinegar to scrape the dark, calloused skin off her hands. Taking away the years of hard labour till her hands were red. She was screaming at me to come inside the house. She was waiting outside the school grounds for me where she stood for the next six years to walk me home. She was refusing to visit her best friend in the nursing home because she thought weakness was shameful. She was playing Tetris in her bed while I watched. She was ironing my clothes with a mathematical precision. She was talking and smiling out the window. She was feeding me fish balls from her bowl. I fell asleep and dreamed of nothing.

I woke up to the plane tossing and turning like an insomniac. There was a turbulence announcement and I saw the little red light indicating that seatbelts should be put on flash above me. An older woman fell over on her way to her seat from the lavatory and an air hostess helped her up. The plane was shaking as if it might fall apart and a collective sense of fear filled the plane. The man next to me started muttering as if he was praying to his god and all over the plane I heard them, these muffled tiny prayers people were saying under their breath. I hadn't prayed for years, not since Sunday School when I was made to. As a child, I had always liked the stories of the Old Testament, people's eyes being gouged out and swords going through the fat stomachs of kings and coming out the other side. But I had never cared much for prayer. It had always felt so fruitless, giving these monologues to a silent God who never seemed to speak or intervene or do anything. But I had been taught by my parents to believe that he listened and that he loved me. I found myself praying the only prayer I remembered. It was a prayer of the desert fathers, but I had been reminded of it when I read a variation on it in *Anna Karenina* and then another time in *Franny and Zooey*. *Lord, have mercy on me a sinner. Lord, have mercy on me a sinner. Lord, have mercy on me a sinner. Lord, have mercy on me a sinner. Lord, have mercy on me a sinner.* As I was praying, I knew that I didn't want the plane to fall into the sea and I didn't want to disappear into a pile of debris at the bottom of the ocean. I wanted to be with Ah Ma. I closed my eyes and kept saying it and somehow, I fell dead asleep in the heart of the storm. When I woke up, the plane had landed and I was in Melbourne again.

When I got to the hospital, Ah Ma was lying there with oxygen tubes in her nose. She was pale and small and when I asked her if her heart was *tia*, she said *only a little*. She didn't look like it meant anything. But then, she had never worn sickness like a garment in her life entire. It seemed impossible that she should die. I had this vision of Ah Ma outliving, outstripping us all, of Ah Ma being there, by my sickbed when I, not Ah Ma, died in her old age.

'Girl,' Ah Ma said, her eyes fluorescent.

'She's been asking for you, asking when you're coming home,' Ma said.

'She never asks for us, you know. Only you,' Ikanyu said.

'Does she know what we're going to do?' the doctor asked.

'They are going to put a tube inside your leg and check your heart to see what is wrong,' Ma told Ah Ma.

'Okay, okay.'

'Are you going to tell her about the second part?' I asked Ma.

I had heard the doctor mention the possibility of surgery, should they find anything, to Ma.

'No.'

As they began to wheel her away, I followed along, running alongside the bed.

'Cuat?' Ah Ma asked suddenly, sitting up. 'Cuat?'

Cuat. Literally, cut, that blunt Hokkien word for surgery. It rhymed with guat, hot, the Hokkien word for cremation.

'Cuat,' I said. 'If there is anything wrong, they will cuat.'

'Cuat.' Ah Ma began coughing and holding her chest. 'Sim tia.' Heart pain.

The nurses and doctors set her down again.

'Ah Ma, wa tan hor lou!' I yelled as the bed was wheeled into a room I couldn't enter. A room dark as an absence.

'Mein tan. Mein tan. Mein pontang sekolah.' No need to wait. No need to wait. No need to skip school.

Me and Ikanyu sat in the patient lounge and waited. Ikanyu had bought an orange and poppy seed muffin and coffee from a nearby petrol station. We spoke about globalism and free trade and Ikanyu knew everything there was to know about it, as he always did about everything. It was good to hear him speak. The door opened and a man, helpless and baby-faced in soft blue scrubs, came into the room. He sat down in the chair opposite me and adjacent to Ikanyu. He looked mostly at me; the staff kept speaking to me as if the only reason why I would come would be to interpret for my parents. But there was nothing to interpret between them.

'Hi. Hi. Okay. We've done the angiogram. There's a blockage in her heart.'

He took a pen out of his pocket and began drawing on the paper bag the muffin had come in. He drew a heart and shaded a black place where the blockage was supposed to be.

'She might have had this for months, years, it's impossible for me to know. I don't know how she's stayed alive. She should have died, really. But here the heart has opened up two new channels, and it's been pumping blood through them. We've also found that her kidneys are failing.'

I imagined the debris in the heart, hard and ugly. Calcium, waste deposits, fat, bits of stone and cement weighing it down. I thought about the heart's new valves, undoing itself to remake itself.

'We've stopped. We haven't operated. I don't think we're doing anyone a service if we operate and she doesn't make it through. At least now she can spend time with family.' He looked at Ikanyu.

'It's okay. It's all right. You've done everything you can,' Ikanyu said, soothing the doctor like he was a fussing baby.

I wanted to ask Ikanyu what would happen. I didn't know what the doctor meant by what he said. Did he mean Ah Ma would live because of the new valves in her heart or did he mean she would die because of the blockage? But I knew that this was the one thing Ikanyu didn't know. I thought with joy about the way Ah Ma had made life continue living for her, how she had made her future dance for her even when her heart was full of stones. I knew then and there that Ah Ma would still be with us for the next four, five, even six years. Until I was ready to let her go.

The new room was big with a large glass window that looked down at the life going on without us outside. Inside, Ah Ma was encircled by so many tubes from her legs, her nose, and there were so many colourful wires attached to patches all over her chest. They were going to heal her. Each wire was a pathway that led to a different way to heal her. Ma came in with a big bag of bananas, a Hershey's chocolate bar, a can of Sunkist and a bottle of apple and pear juice. Ah Ma sat up and ate a banana and a piece of chocolate. She was getting better, stronger. Perhaps she would be stronger than she had been before. Ninety years old and still lifting her feet to the bathroom sink to wash them like a ballerina at the barre. Now, I would see her at ninety-one, ninety-two, hell, one hundred, even, washing her feet at the sink. She was eating, she was tasting life and it had not forgotten her. It was here.

'What did the doctor say?' Ma asked.

'I wish I'd recorded him. Because I don't know.'

I tried to explain it as best I could and at the end of it I could see how Ma's mind, a whirring machine with every part in place, running smoothly, could understand it better than I could.

'So there's a blockage in one place and then the new arteries, the magic arteries open up, and she saves herself,' I said.

I was laughing, I was so proud of Ah Ma.

We stood by her bed and watched the free television channels on the TV that looked down on us. There was a seemingly endless infomercial on the benefits of turmeric powder. Two women with bright hair and thin smiles and a man wearing a velvet blazer that I could tell he thought a lot of were presenting the powder. They were mixing it into banana smoothies, into chocolate milkshakes, into hyperactive curries. Everything was a dull, thick, yellow colour. Ah Ma started laughing and laughing and pointing at the TV. We laughed too. A nurse came to take Ah Ma's blood pressure and when she was done, Ah Ma sat up and said: 'Okay, Okay.'

She said it with the voice of two hands clapped together to indicate an ending. She was ready to leave the hospital now that the test was done. She tried to get out of bed and they pushed her back down.

That night, I couldn't sleep. I kept waking up to this vision of Ah Ma with her mouth open in sadness or in pain, I couldn't tell. Then there was an image of Ah Ma curled up and naked, with soft white hairs all along her back like a wounded animal. My dreams had turned to this. I was so afraid for Ah Ma. What if she wanted something in the middle of the night and she couldn't tell the nurses about it? What if they didn't understand her? What if she woke up and felt lonely? I didn't want her to be alone. Some years ago, Ah Ma had been in hospital for a broken leg and when she had needed to go to the toilet, she had pressed the button to call the nurse over. The nurse hadn't come so she had jumped out of her high-up hospital bed. They had tied her to the bed after that. They said she couldn't understand English, but it was really they who couldn't understand Chinese. What if they couldn't understand her tonight? And what if they tied her up now? I imagined walking into the hospital with all its lights off. No, I shouldn't go.

The next morning, I woke up to a text message from Ma saying Ah Ma was worried about me, wondering when I was coming to see her. She also sent a photo of Ah Ma sitting up in bed, eating a banana. *The nurses didn't want her to sit up yet, but I took control of the situation*, Ma texted. She was making a recovery that only those who loved her could see. She had always risen from the dead like that. *They laugh at us when we call for Lazarus to leave his tomb but here he is, unharmed and smelling sweetly of myrrh and aloes, dressed in linen strips*, I thought. I loitered around the house, tired, and eventually sat myself in front of the TV in my pyjamas to watch an episode of *Seinfeld*. What was it that Ah Ma had called *Seinfeld*? Siao Lang Hee. Crazy People Show.

When I got to the hospital, Ah Ma was lying down with an oxygen mask over her face. Her skin looked paler than before. She was trying to get up again. Ikanyu set her back down.

Ah Ma tried to get up again. Ikanyu pushed her down.

'Wa ai pung,' *I want to put it down*, the Hokkien words for going to the toilet.

Ikanyu explained that she couldn't get up. She needed to lie down.

'Tam.' *Wet*, she said.

'Boh tam.'

'Chow bee.' *Bad smell*, she said.

'Boh chow bee.'

It was true, there was a catheter connected to her, hanging on the bed. I waited to see the tubes turn ochre. But they didn't. This might have been a sign, but I was not sure if I believed in signs then.

I went back to the hospital at dinnertime that night. Ah Ma was sleeping but she woke up when she heard our voices.

'I made her some mi sua soup,' Ma said. 'Go and get it.'

I went to the patient lounge where Ikanyu was eating fried rice and retrieved the soup.

'I'll eat later,' Ah Ma said.

'Have a bit now,' Ma told her.

'Okay,' Ah Ma said.

Then it took her over. I had heard of demon possessions, evil or impure spirits that filled the soul as if it was an empty bottle. But this was different. It was a body possessed by pain, pure pain, white and furious. The pain was taking the body away as if it was the body that belonged to the pain not the pain that belonged to the body. Ah Ma's pupils were always sad black centres circled by a computer-blue pigment. Now her eyes rolled back in her head again and again. Now she closed her eyes tightly like the skin was a bag and the drawstring had been tightened. She was thrashing around on the bed as if she might be thrown off it. She scratched wildly at her skin and scratched hard at her hair. There were colourful wires attached to every part of her chest and arms and she was tearing them off with a frightening articulateness. She felt each wire and ripped it off her, she threw the oxygen tubes in her nostrils off the bed, she took one hand to the plastic hospital tag circling her wrist and broke free of it. She pushed their officious hands off her and waved them away. She was like Samson breaking his cords.

And Ma, who had always reasoned with her and saved her when she was half-dead, who had brought her from the grave time and time again, now she was telling her, 'Okay, okay, tia? Tia ah? Jai jai jai. Okay okay okay.' And every time she said okay, she was letting her go, even helping her rip off the patches and cords.

She was a nurse who had always felt she had to fight to maintain the sacredness of life, to the point of controlling, manipulating, persuading, resurrecting the body. Now she seemed suddenly convinced of the sacredness of death, its rightful claim over the body. She was crying as she did it because she could not make it right for Ah Ma. She lay on top of her and hugged her. I felt Ah Ma's hands gripping my hands like she wanted to hurt them. And the pain it went on and on while the nurses tried to find the doctor, told them to wait for him – he was coming, he was busy, he was somewhere on the other side of the ward, he was here he was there – but he was not in front of them. The nurses were afraid to give Ah Ma morphine without the doctor's permission, they were afraid of the family, of what we might do to them in our grief, they were afraid of death itself. They were young nurses, with squirrel eyes and bird voices. They didn't know anything about it and their lack of knowledge made them afraid. Ah Ma was throttling herself, gripping the thin skin around her throat, beating her chest as if it was her enemy. I took her hands and she tried to use my hands to beat herself. She used my knuckles like they were a grater she could shred her skin with. But Ah Ma pushed me off her. Her eyes opened suddenly, and they were still. She looked at me. *Girl, Girl, Girl, Girl.* She called me. I held her with ungentle hands. The nurse came in, the doctor had been found and he had given his permission. The bandages on her arms were undone and the nurse injected the liquid that would render Ah Ma barely conscious. *Tia, tia, tia. Gin tia,* Ah Ma was saying. Then slowly her breathing was turned down. She was here and not here, and underneath her not-hereness was the oldest pain. *Har?* she cried out now and then, as if asking what it was that was happening to her. Then the morphine made her quiet. She breathed and did not open her eyes any more. Ma told me to go home. She said Ah Ma's breaths were still strong and they might last for days. I should sleep and then if Ah Ma was still there, I could take the next watch over from her and Ikanyu. I went home. I fell asleep at ten.

At half past one in the morning I had a phone call from Ma. She said nothing when I picked up. The silence on the line was what she had to say. I went to the hospital. Ah Ma's body was beautiful. Though I knew she was dead, she looked so happy that she might have been alive. Her skin had a smooth sheen as if it had been sanded down. She was shining. Her hair was neat, parted to the side; it was as if she had been to the movies, not to the last great fight. She did not look like a shell; she looked full like the moon. She had left me without saying goodbye. But then she had never said goodbye, only kee, *go*.

We sat around the bed with Styrofoam cups of water and slow faces. It was 1:45 a.m. There was a story, and they were telling it, from when Ikanyu was a boy and Ah Ma had taken him to Penang. The island was only a ferry ride away, but it was special for them to go there. On the street was an Indian and a bird in a cage filled with scraps of paper. Ah Ma paid one ring-git to the Indian and the bird bent down to pick up two scraps of paper. The woman read aloud the first one, 'You will travel all over the world,' she said to Ikanyu. The second one, 'Your life has been wrong but your old age will be right,' she said to Ah Ma. Ikanyu nearly cried with anger. How cynical to sell lies that looked like dreams to them, he had thought. And yet they had all come true.

We left the hospital. It was raining out and the wet tarmac shone so brightly in the face of the streetlamps that it had no colour. In the car, I sat in the driver's seat and watched a ray of dust float across my eyeline. It was the part of the morning that looks like night, way before the light time has come. That night was the night that I was reborn. The person who had raised me had been raised up. I put the key in the ignition. I had to raise myself now.

Acknowledgments

Thank you so much to my agent, Ellen Levine. My book has been in such safe hands with you. I'd also like to thank Audrey Crooks for her support as well as the rest of the team at Trident Media.

Thank you to Brandon Taylor for understanding and believing in my book. It really meant a lot to me and helped me keep believing in it, too. Thank you to Allison Miriam Smith for your enthusiasm and expertise in shepherding this book out into the world. Thank you also to Cassidy Kuhle and the whole team at Unnamed Press. Thank you to Zack Rosebrugh for your brilliant artwork and Jaya Nicely for your thoughtful design of the US cover. I love it so, so much.

Thank you to my PhD supervisors and first readers, Maria Tumarkin and Amanda Johnson. I learned so much during that time and afterwards. Maria, thank you for how much you pushed my ideas, challenged my ethics and listened to my voice. Amanda, thank you for supporting and encouraging me since I was an undergraduate student. Thank you to the whole creative writing department at the University of Melbourne.

Thank you to early readers: Ellen Cregan and Jon Tihja. I so appreciated your input and encouragement.

Thank you to Kee How of the *Penang Hokkien* podcast for checking the spelling and grammar of any Hokkien and Malay words.

Thank you to the following scholars whose work informed Girl's ideas in this novel (in no particular order):

Jane Badia, Renee Curry, Tim Kendall, Hiromi Yoshida, Sianne Ngai, Rita Felski, Lisa Ruddick, Linda Martín Alcoff, Trinh Minh-ha, Barbara Christian, Viet Thanh Nguyen, Anne Anlin Cheng, bell hooks, Ghassan Hage, Yen Le Espiritu, Susan Sontag, Edward Said, Daniel Harris, Frantz Fanon and Rey Chow.

Thank you to Faber and Faber and the Plath estate for allowing me to quote from *The Bell Jar* and the Journals of Sylvia Plath. Thank you for trusting me with this book. Thank you also to Sylvia Plath for her blazing, beautiful writing.

Thank you to my family for all of the home cooked meals and love. Mum and dad, this book is for you. Koh Koh, Debbie, Matty, Timmy this book is also yours (as are any Switch games I've clocked).

Thank you to Lachy for being my heart. You have been the best decision of my entire life.